By John Bragg

The Broom of God

Exit 8

Exit 8

Exit 8

A Novel

John Bragg

Backroad Press / Rockport, Maine

Backroad Press

Rockland, Maine
© Backroad Press
All Rights Reserved. Published 2019

John Bragg is the author of
The Broom of God, A Novel of Patagonia

Website: jkbragg.com
Email: john@jkbragg.com

Bragg, John K

Exit 8

ISBN: 978-0-9964529-3-9

1. Vermont—Fiction.. 2. Farm life–Fiction.

3 Highway development–Fiction

Cover Artwork:
"Strafford Farm Road" by Barbra Bragg, 1989

Romaine Tenney 1900 - 1964

I was deeply moved when I read the story of Romaine Tenney in Yankee Magazine. But this is not his story, that is for others to write.

This is a work of my imagination, but I hope that in some small way, it might be accepted as a tribute to his memory.

Vermont Governor
Joseph B. Johnson
1957 Inaugural Address

"Highway improvement continues to be at the very core of Vermont's future development . . . Progress rides on wheels today. Hopes for our Vermont future are closely tied to the use of the automobile, the truck, the bus and other highway transport."

Merriam Webster's Dictionary

eminent domain \'e-mi-nant\ \dŌ-'mān, d-\ n (1783):
a right of a government to take private property for
public use by virtue of the superior dominion of the
sovereign power over all lands within its jurisdiction

September 12, 1964

A HOT, AIRLESS NIGHT. Roland Tuttle stands in the middle of his farmyard; he holds his arms out to his sides and turns slowly, but it is as if he is standing still and the farm's buildings—house, barn, coop, spring house—orbit about him, as if the world revolves around him. He looks up, sees stars, heat-blurred, indistinct, circling above him.

He walks to the edge of Mountain Road, looks at them there, lined up, waiting. The machines. They are pale silver-gray in starlight, but he knows that in daylight they are yellow, and that in the days to come their great black wheels will turn and their metal tracks will churn and grind.

There is the iron smell of rust, the sweet, rotten smell of diesel.

He turns back to face the way the machines face. The big farmhouse stands there, mute, windows dark save one where the yellow light of a single kerosene lamp flickers.

Fireflies like sparks drift in the dark. Stripes of cloud drift across the star-filled sky.

He stands, stranded between two worlds.

It is a night that simmers with possibility, with questions to be asked, with choices to be made. He can hear his cows snuffling in their sleep. A great horned owl calls in the forest. Coyotes yap somewhere in the distance; dogs in the village answer.

He looks at his farm, his life's work.

He ducks under the feedlot fence, stands among the cows, feels them press in against him, and breathes in their grassy, milky smell, their breathy warmth. He feels himself one of them, these gentle creatures.

Again, he stands in the middle of the dooryard, suspended. Then, decision made, he walks slowly back to the house.

A dry wind with no promise of rain. Distant thunder all around, flashes of heat lightning, rumbling and flickering on the horizon like some distant war front.

Twelve Months Earlier

September

COME AFTERNOON, THE DARK SHADOW of the mountain creeps down the hillside, washes over the Tuttle Farm, and falls across the village. There is an early frost one night, sparkling in morning sun, lingering, come mid-day, only in the shade on the north side of things. The days are bright with high clouds in the afternoon. Corn is harvested. Oats lie cut in the fields. A temporary office trailer appears one morning parked on the village ballfield, and orange pick-up trucks with a US government seal are seen coming and going. A single-engine airplane flies back and forth above the west side of the river.

≈

BOWKER'S GENERAL STORE OCCUPIES a white clapboard building next to the Wethersfield, Vermont Town Hall. At least, it was white at one time, but now, as Roland Tuttle looks at it, it is faded gray with only a few flecks of the original paint remaining. Roland hears a loud car horn and realizes he's standing in the middle of the Connecticut Post Road. He steps to the side; the car swerves around him. The driver shouts something, but the words are lost in the growling of the car's engine. Roland watches it go, wonders why someone would be so angry on such a fine day.

Roland climbs the steps to the front porch that runs the width of the building and stands facing the door into the store. The back wall of the porch is covered in metal signs and posters: Old Navy Smoking Tobacco, B&B Poultry Feed, a flyer for the Village Players production of "Our Town," a poster for the Community Dance coming in October. Roland remembers how his brothers, James and Daniel, snuck down here so many years ago and stole the sign for Pousin's Tweddle Chicks because their sister Eliza had said how pretty it was, that sign, with its big yellow chick on a bright blue background.

Wood-slat rocking chairs and straight-backed cane-seated chairs are spread out on both sides of the door. Otis Bowker himself is sitting in a rocker in front of a wide metal sign advertising Crimson Pouch Tobacco. Otis is a big hulk of a man, too big for the chair he's sitting in. He's wearing overalls rolled up at the ankles and black work boots, but no shirt covering his bulging, hairy shoulders. Soaking up a bit of the warm September sun.

—Roland Tuttle, hisself, Otis says, then, Jaysus, Roland, how the hell you get so old?

—Didn't die, that's how, Roland says.

—That'll do it, Otis says.

Herman Bowker, Otis's older brother steps out of the store. He runs the place. No one is exactly sure what Otis does, other than sit on the front porch with his meaty forearms resting on the arms of his chair, or come winter inside in the back of the store near the pot-bellied stove. Herman is wearing a cardigan sweater, white shirt and tie, covered by a long white storekeeper's apron. Same clothes he wears every day. Roland often wonders if Herman wears that outfit at home, assuming he has a home other than the store, and imagines him in a house somewhere, wearing that apron. The opposite of his bulky brother, Herman is thin, wears spectacles.

—And how's Roland Tuttle today? Herman Bowker says.

Same thing he says every time Roland comes to the store.

—Needing some red beans, that's how he is, Roland says. And a can or two of tomatoes.

—Well, come on in.

The store itself is a long, narrow space with dark wood walls and shadowed corners. A glass-fronted counter runs the length of the left wall, high wood shelves behind it stocked with canned goods, bottles of cooking oil, vinegar, boxes of flour, cereal. The opposite wall is covered with more shelves, in front of which stand bins and barrels of bulk foodstuffs. Herman goes to one, takes out a silver metal scoop.

—How much you need?

—A pound'll do me.

Herman fills a small brown paper bag, puts it on the scale, adds a little more, nods, and carries the bag over to the counter next to an ornate black gold-trimmed cash register that's been there since Roland can remember. Herman takes down two cans of Hunt's Tomatoes from the shelves behind the counter.

Roland stands there, makes no move to reach into a pocket. Bowker gives a small sigh.

—On your account, I guess, Herman Bowker says. I'm fixing to close out all the accounts I've been keeping. Need you to pay up sometime soon.

He hands Roland the bag.

—Don't got it with me, Roland says. Next time I'm down.

The screen door creaks open, then closes with a bang. Roland looks around to see Hamilton Ames, the town lawyer.

—Roland, good to see you, Ames says. Can I buy you a pop?

—I wouldn't mind a Moxie, Roland says.

Back on the front porch, Roland sits in a straight-backed

chair near Otis. Ames takes himself a seat, but Herman, arms crossed, stands next to the door, like, as he's working he shouldn't be sitting, like there's a rule somewhere says he can't sit.

Bob Garfield, Town Moderator, appears out of nowhere, and soon there's a regular gab-fest going on. Roland sits, quiet. He always did like the taste of Moxie, always wondered how something could be both sweet and bitter at the same time.

—You coming to the meeting? Garfield says to Roland.

—I suppose.

—It's important. They took seven houses down in Wethersfield Bow, Garfield says.

—Half of Wilkerson's hayfield, Herman Bowker says.

Roland knows what they're talking about, decides not to listen, looks away. Across the road there's a couple of small houses. He looks past them, past cleared fields, to where the land begins to rise, gently at first, then steeper, forested, up toward the mountain. His farm is somewhere off to the left through the trees.

—They can take anything they want, Otis says.

Everyone turns to look at him. Otis Bowker, a quiet man, doesn't say much, but when he does, folks tend to listen.

—Imminent domain they call it, he says.

Otis Bowker doesn't so much speak as make pronouncements.

—Eminent Domain, Hamilton Ames says. Not imminent.

—What's the difference? says Otis.

HOW LONG HAS HE BEEN STANDING at the barn workbench? Roland Tuttle isn't sure.

In front of him is the haywagon harness that needs fixing, the scythe that wants sharpening, the axe that needs a new handle, but he can't seem to focus. This tendency to wander off in his thoughts, to have trouble with the simplest task, is new. There is a distant noise, the faint rumbling and growling of engines, that he can't stop straining to hear, and that effort, that attention paid to something far off, takes his attention away from the thing that's right in front of him. He senses rustling behind him, turns to see one of the barn cats, the tabby, sprawled along a cross-beam watching him.

He returns to work on the harness. He needs the wagon to get in the last of his hay. One of the traces on the right-hand side, where he hitches his older horse, Sam, has worn almost through. He holds the strap up to the light. It's still good solid leather, must be a quarter-inch thick, except in that worn spot. He needs a piece to patch it, the awl, some thread. There's a line of big tin cans, the kind his mother used to buy molasses in, on a rough wood shelf above the work bench. He pulls one down.

Nope, it's filled with rusty hand-cut nails.

He takes down another, finds pieces of leather he'd salvaged, spools of heavy waxed thread, and a Speedy Stitcher hand-awl that must be more than fifty years old, the wood grip worn smooth by generations of Tuttle hands. He threads the awl and starts to work, but hears tires crunch on the gravel driveway. He puts the harness down, walks outside to see a brown Windsor County Sheriff's car shudder to a stop, and Sheriff Homer T. Wiggins lever himself out of the front seat. The sheriff stops, hitches up his pants, and looks around the farmyard judging, it seems to Roland, what he sees and finding it in some deep-set way, wanting.

Roland looks past the sheriff to the haze-covered horizon where a dust cloud has lingered all summer. There's something in the air that he has never seen before, like he is looking at the world through a dirt-streaked window. The barn, his house, the sheriff's car, everything is coated in dust.

—Roland.

—Sheriff.

—How long I known you, Roland?

—Longer'n I can remember.

—Fifty years, Wiggins says.

—There you go, Roland says.

—Think you might start calling me Homer?

—Don't feel right, Roland says. Too late to change.

—How're things? Wiggins says, after a long pause.

These kinds of questions, the casual inquiries, the offhand way they're delivered, puzzle Roland, leave him unsure what to say. Is an answer required? Apparently not, for Sheriff Wiggins talks on without waiting for a reply.

—Still hanging on, I see. Things are looking a little peaked around here, Roland.

—Car ain't looking so good neither, Roland says.

—Can't keep the damn thing clean, Wiggins says. Wash it one night, it's coated in dust the next day. Finally gave up.

A black dog comes out of the barn, creeps toward Wiggins, stops a few feet away, stares at the sheriff, lips curled back from his teeth.

—Don't think Sam here likes you.

—Wasn't the yellow one named Sam?

—Yep, Roland says.

—You're keeping up are you? Wiggins pauses, then says, I stopped by to make sure you come to the meeting at the town hall tonight. Been talking about it for weeks. Things are changing around here, you know that.

—Don't hold much with meetings. Too much talk. Got work to do. Don't have time for all that gab. Besides from which, I don't give much of a damn about the road and all those changes you keep goin' on about.

—Like I told you last week, this is important, Wiggins says.

The sky that, in September, should be a deep, clear blue with the cold air of autumn on its way, is instead thick and filled with dust and haze. Roland can smell it, taste it, feel it in his throat when he breathes.

—You listening to me? Wiggins says. Lotta changes coming. I'm retiring. I'm done with sheriffing. Going to take the missus someplace warm.

Wiggins has been sheriff for as long as Roland can remember. He'd arrested his brothers when they were caught stealing beer from the local store. He'd found Roland when, as a boy of twelve, he got lost up on Mount Ascutney. He'd come to the house, siren whining, when Roland's mother had taken ill.

—Yep. Retiring.

This idea strikes Roland as impossible.

Wiggins looks straight at him.

—You should think about doin' the same.

SHERIFF WIGGINS DRIVES AWAY, leaving Roland Tuttle gazing south across his lower meadow. It is September of 1963, and if he bothered to mark the year, he would realize that it was his 63rd year on this earth. Beyond the empty meadow, long since overgrown, he can see the broad curve of the Connecticut River as it flows south past Bellows Falls and the growing town of Brattleboro, to go on to the five colleges of western Massachusetts and the towns of Amherst and Northampton, past the city of Hartford, Connecticut, the insurance capital of America, and finally all the way to Long Island Sound and the teeming metropolis of New York. But all that is beyond his ken or concern—though born as a child of the 20th century, Roland lives more as a man of the 19th.

He lists the chores he has still to do. It is early afternoon and he is behind. The cows—his herd is down to twenty—are in the back pasture. They can take care of themselves until it's time to milk. Roland will hear their bells clanking as they wander down the hill toward home to stand patiently at the pasture gate waiting to be let into the barn. He adds that gate to the list. The hinges are almost rusted through. Soon it will fall to the ground, the cows will wander off and he'll lose a whole day rounding them up. He walks to the barn and steps into the cool, dark interior and is carried off into memory by the odors of hay, manure, horse sweat, and the smell of ancient barn wood.

Some of his earliest memories are this barn, playing in the straw with wooden toys his oldest brother, Marvin, made for him—haywagon, rough-carved horses, cows, a plow, a cart—while his father fed and milked the cows, and the smell of warm, sweet milk filled the air. Marvin was the clever one, good with his hands, doing repairs and work around the farm by the time he was ten. He was always busy, Marvin was, making things of wood, furniture even, fixing the harnesses and farm implements when their father would look at the problem with a puzzled expression on his face.

Roland finishes stitching the harness, looks at his work. Not sewed up as clean and straight as he used to do, but it'll hold.

Everything around him is old: the wagon purchased from Paine Wagon Makers by his grandfather, the single plow that belonged to his great-grandfather, the shovels, the rakes, the barn itself. He spends a good part of his days keeping these tools and implements working. Can't afford new ones, but it's more than that. Repairing these things is, for Roland, deeply satisfying, and though he wouldn't explain it that way, is a way of honoring the past, his ancestors. Surrounded by these things, each of which trigger memory, he feels at times—alone as he is—that he's living in the past and the present at the same time. Not only the past, but the many pasts of the generations of Tuttles that have lived and worked this farm before him.

THE SIXTH CHILD IN THE FAMILY, ROLAND was born years after his parents had thought they were done bringing children into the world. His mother, Abitha, was thirty-two years old when Roland was born. She was, after two days of difficult labor, too sick and still mourning the two babies she had lost, too scared of losing him to love him right away, to care for him the way a mother should.

Roland as a young child had thought his oldest sister, Margaret, was his mother.

Things were good on the farm when Roland came along, as good as they could be on a rocky hill farm in northern New England. The older boys, James, Daniel and Marvin, worked with their father, Albert, in the fields and barns—plowing, sowing, reaping, milking—and the girls, Margaret and Eliza, worked with Gramma Ida May and their mother, Abitha, in the kitchen—churning, cooking, washing, cleaning, mending—and young Roland was left to himself to play in the dirt and wander the woods behind the barn, creating for himself a magical world of Indians and creatures and adventure.

Five generations of Tuttles have lived and worked on that rocky terrace between the river and the steep wooded flanks of Mount Ascutney. Mountain Farm, they called it, but it came to be known—and would always be so—in the village and the towns across the river in New Hampshire as the Tuttle Farm.

ROLAND FINISHES HIS AFTERNOON CHORES. Milks. Mucks out the barn. Puts down fresh straw for the cows. Carries the milk cans out to the spring house to cool. Walking back to the dooryard, he hears a buzzing, like the biggest horsefly ever was, stops, looks up, and sees a single-engine airplane flying overhead. He watches as it disappears behind the tall pines south of the farm. The sound fades to just a distant, irritating whine then changes, gets louder, and soon he sees the plane heading back north, flying low over the river.

He steps up onto the porch, looks back at the sky, empty the way it should be, then turns back to the house, opens the door and goes into the kitchen. The linoleum that had seemed new and modern when his mother had it put down over the old wide-pine floor is cracked and worn, coated with dirt. The sun passes behind the mountain's ridge; the kitchen dims. Roland lights a kerosene lamp.

Place doesn't look so worn in the yellow light.

He sits at the battered Formica table, thinks about dinner. He's got the red beans, but they need soaking for hours before he can boil them up. There's plenty of potatoes, the tins of tomatoes, a few onions, the last of the chicken he butchered a few days ago.

Should be a meal in there somewhere.

SHERIFF WIGGINS HAD OFFERED him a ride but Roland likes to walk, so after supper he strolls down Mountain Road as evening comes across the sky, and the summit of the mountain hovers behind him in the dusty haze. He turns north and walks up the Post Road—folks mostly call it Route 5 now—toward the village. Cars are parked up and down both sides of the road. The Wethersfield Village Town Hall is brick with white window trim and a steeply pitched slate roof. Roland hesitates, his hand on the doorknob. Finally he turns it and walks into the entrance hall, a space running the entire width of the building, planked in pine wainscoting, dark with age. Two doors lead into the meeting hall. One on the far left of the space, the other right. He can hear the hubbub of voices through the closed doors.

Josepha Collins, the oldest man in town, once told Roland that back in colonial times, when the town hall was built, women weren't allowed to vote at town meeting and they had to enter by the left-hand door and sit on the left side of the meeting hall. Even after women could participate the practice continued, women entered on the left, men the right.

Most folks don't worry about that anymore, but the elders of the town, you can still see them, couples arriving together then splitting apart and entering separately.

There is a long line of black-and-white photos pinned up next to each other across most of the wall between the two doors. A man steps out of the meeting hall, sees Roland staring at the photo display, walks over, and stands next to him. A man Roland has not seen before.

A man from away.

—Aerial photography is interesting, is it not? The man says. You can see the world in a whole different way.

The man is dressed casual, but there's something about him, the way he stands, slouching a little, his clothes—khaki pants, plaid shirt, work boots—that seems, to Roland, off, like these are not the clothes he usually wears, like this is not where he belongs.

Roland stares at the photographs until he realizes he's looking at the river valley from above. He recognizes the big bend in the Connecticut River where it turns back on itself at Wethersfield Bow, traces with his finger the river up to the small cluster of houses that is the village, the buildings tiny dark squares. Roland sees the wide fields of the Wilson place—almost white in the photos—that run along the banks of the river.

—Needed a break, the man says. You country folk sure do like to talk. A pause. Then, Coburn, he says. John Coburn. Sticks out his hand.

Roland is transfixed by the photo display. He looks at what must be his farm, small irregular shapes of cleared land bordered by the dark forests of the mountain. It's small. It's been his entire world for his entire life, and it's so small.

—You must be Roland Tuttle, Coburn says.

Must I? Roland thinks. I suppose so.

—The meeting's about to start up again, Coburn says. Time to get in there.

His face, tanned, clean-shaven, is nice enough at first glance. His expression might pass for a smile were it not for the cold, gray eyes. He turns, holds the door open.

—You coming? Coburn says.

Roland doesn't move. The man shakes his head, closes the door behind him.

Roland has never seen the world like this, laid out flat,

marked and measured. He doesn't much like the idea that people were up there looking down on him.

Something about it ain't right.

He stops at the door to the meeting hall—the voices are louder now—then turns around, goes out the front door, and walks back up the hill toward the farm. Never did have much use for meetings. Besides, if it's important, they'll have another meeting, and probably another after that.

It is almost dark. The rim of the mountain shimmers with the last pale light from the west, and the crickets in the woods and fields start their endless chirping. It has been another warm, dry day, but the air is cooling fast. It's full-on night by the time Roland walks up his drive, his mind still unsettled by the aerial photographs and the smug superiority of the man from away. He'd said his name, but Roland wasn't listening. What was it? Colton? There's Coltons living up in Windsor, good folks, but Roland is sure that man is not one of them.

Coburn . . . that's it, and remembering the name brings back the uneasy sense that the man was somehow, though not because of anything in particular he'd done or said, up to no good.

The big two-story farmhouse looms in front of him, blank, dark until the moon emerges from drifting clouds and the house is there, spread out before him. The silver light slants across the face bringing out the details—the quartered columns, the pediments, the diamond-leaded windows, the ornate gingerbread trim—stretching out the shapes into strange distorted patterns of light and shadow.

Attached to the big house is a simpler building: the ell, a low-roofed cape, the original house, built more than one hundred and fifty years ago. Roland lives in the ell, in the kitchen and pantry on the first floor and the bedroom above. There's a weak yellow light in his kitchen window, but Roland is not ready to go inside, not yet. He stands, washed by cricket-sound, and remembers being outside in the dark like this when he was maybe nine or ten, feeling then the same strange sense of detachment he feels now.

As a boy, standing in the dark looking at the big house all lit up, the windows clean and the light streaming out across the front porch making diamond-shaped patterns on the grass, he'd seen the family moving about in the dining room, heard their voices but not their words, and had felt himself separate, alone, the dark around him, and had wondered when they would notice that he wasn't inside waiting like the rest of them for dinner to be on the table, wondered, as he often did, if they would miss him if he just up and disappeared. Walked away. Headed on down the road and never came back.

Roland, the boy, felt his feet were rooted in place, like he couldn't move, but at the same time felt that if he didn't move soon, didn't go in to the rest of the family, he would never be able to, and he would never get back to the center of things. He would always be on the outside, looking in.

EVERY NIGHT THE TUTTLE FAMILY, all nine of them, sat down for dinner, the table always set the same. Everyone had his or her seat. There weren't name cards and Roland doesn't remember anyone ever saying anything, but every meal they all sat in their same places—Marvin, the oldest, at their father's right, then James, then Daniel. Roland, across from Daniel, sat next to his mother, Abitha, on her right, then Eliza, then Margaret, then Gramma Ida May next to her son, their father.

Most dinners were the same, nothing to remember, but one time, when Roland was six, he thought he would switch seats with his grandmother and sit next to his father.

"You sit where you always sit," snapped Gramma Ida.

"But, Ida—" his mother said.

"Don't go changing things don't need changing."

"I think it would be acceptable to let the boy sit next to his father," Abitha said.

The children, all six of them, looked back and forth from their grandmother to their mother.

Outside the house—the barn, the fields, the farm—Roland's father, Albert, was the boss, no question, but the house, the kitchen, seemed to Roland a battleground between two strong women. Ida May Tuttle had been running the household for a long time before Abitha arrived to marry her son, and Ida May being as strong-willed as she was, intended to keep on doing it, and doing it the way she always had even as her physical strength diminished.

"Depends who's doing the accepting," Gramma Ida said.

Roland got up from the seat he'd taken, walked along the table, stood next to his mother. "It's okay, Ma," he said. "I like sittin' next to you."

Abitha looked at the boy standing next to her, reached up and messed his dark hair. Patted the seat of the chair. "And I like having you next to me," she said.

"I'm thinking we need to get the house painted soon," his father said, changing the subject.

"Don't waste your money on this place," Gramma Ida said.

"It's a fine house. Shows what all the family's hard work has accomplished."

"More like showing off," Gramma Ida said. "Your grandfather and your father"—she fixed Albert with a fierce look—"the pair of them, were fools to build this place. Not sure who was worse. Lucius should have known better, he was the adult, but my Roland . . ."

Gramma Ida looked down the table at young Roland. "Man you was named after, Boy."

She always called young Roland "Boy."

Everyone at that table knew how she felt about Abitha naming baby Roland after his grandfather, with that first Roland, Ida May's husband, just days in his grave.

"Well, my Roland just egged on his father, kept making the place bigger, added all this Gothic Revival business, the front porch. Wool prices was high. They thought it would last forever. Should've known better. Pshaw! Didn't need such a fancy place, such a big place. Didn't need it then. Still don't." Gramma Ida looked across the table. "You're the oldest, Marvin. What do you think?"

By rights, the farm would someday pass to Marvin, him being the first-born male. That's the way it had always been, and that's the way the family assumed it would be, disregarding the fact that Marvin had no real aptitude or love for farming. By the time he'd turned fifteen, he'd made it plain that the dirt, the constant worry about the weather, looking at the sky wondering if it was ever going to rain, or cursing the clouds not knowing if it would ever stop, wasn't for him.

They ignored him, figuring the boy would come to his senses.

"I'm not going to be a farmer," Marvin said. "Why ask me?"

ALONE IN THE DARK, Roland is still staring at the house when his old dog, Sam, brings him back to the present with a bark. The dog, one of the countless mongrel beasts that Roland has adopted during his life, wags his tail so hard it's more like the tail is wagging him. Roland sits down on the porch steps, arm around the dog's neck, and watches the night.

He thinks about the meeting, probably still going on, the arguing, the back and forth with nothing ever decided, like every other town meeting he's been to, and thinks about those photos and wonders how that man Coburn come to know his name.

The last of the summer's fireflies flit back and forth across the open dooryard, blinking in and out, the crickets in the woods seem to move closer, the clouds drifting off the summit of the mountain send faint shadows marching across the open fields, heading east.

—Time to go in, old boy, he says. Ruffles the dog's ears.

The yellow light from the kerosene lamp glows on the kitchen walls. To his right, a steep set of stairs climbs up to the bedroom; next to those stairs, a door, handcrafted of cherry, leads into the rest of the house. It has been twenty-five years since that door opened, since he set foot in the big house. If he thought about it, which he didn't much, he would realize that it was the last time his sister Margaret had visited.

That summer Roland had been alone on the farm for five years, doing it all himself with just the occasional hired hand. Margaret and her husband, William, had stopped on their way to a vacation on Cape Cod—'a second honeymoon' she'd called it.

Margaret opened up the big house, the dining room, the upstairs bedrooms, dusting, cleaning, opening the windows,

airing the place out, while William stood, impatient, out in
the yard, smoking. She cleaned and polished the big oak
dining table, took down the family's china, wiped it clean
of dust, and proceeded to set the table just the way Abitha,
their mother, had done when the family was together living
in the big house.

Roland stood by, watching.

As a young man, Roland didn't know what to think about
Margaret. She'd cared for him when he was little, and he
wasn't sure how he felt about that. She acted, sometimes,
like that gave her sway over him, but it was more than that.
She looked nice, wore a pretty dress, city shoes, hair done
up and all. William drove a fancy car. Who was she, to
him? This city woman? And, who was he to her? After all
these years? Why would she bother with all that cleaning?
He couldn't escape the feeling that Margaret was somehow
disappointed in him, that her cleaning and polishing and
arranging was a criticism.

LATER, HE TAKES A SINGLE GLANCE at the door to the big
house. Everything the family once owned is still in there,
the furniture, the photos, the dining room table with nine
places set for dinner by Margaret during that visit twenty-five
years ago—a dinner that will never come.

"What're you doing?" Roland had said when he walked
in on her.

"Just putting it the way Momma liked it," she'd said. "Looks
nice, don't you think?"

What Roland thought, but didn't say at the time, was that
it was downright strange.

And now, at night, when he lies in bed trying to sleep, he thinks about that table, all set up like folks were gonna sit down for dinner, folks that was gone and weren't coming back, and he thinks about all that stuff over there, the furniture, the knick-knacks, the clothes still in the closets. It isn't just the table and the family's things that is bothersome. He hears noises, probably critters moving in, but if he thinks about it too much it starts to sound like chairs being pulled back, scraping on the wood floor, china clinking together, and quiet, whispery voices.

October

*T*HE WORK CONTINUES IN THE SOUTH, the distant noise echoing off the mountain. The faint smell of diesel fumes drifts on the morning air. A lone coyote bolts out of the underbrush, crosses Mountain Road heading north, and disappears up into the forest. The river flows thick and green from early autumn rains; bare fields are covered in brown stubble. The bear that dens high on the mountain is seen gorging on the last of the wild berries. The nights are longer than the days. A government pickup truck driving too fast on the Post Road hits Widow Johnson's dog, Penny. The truck doesn't stop. The dog dies by the side of the road.

~

*H*IGH ON THE MOUNTAIN, the trees are tinged with red and yellow. The colors will flow down the mountainside until the huge maples that his great-grandfather planted around the house erupt in an explosion of color. Squirrels race up and down their trunks, stocking their nests. The songbirds are gone. It's been a good year. The hayfield waits for the last cut. Waves, like water, ripple across its golden surface in the morning breeze.

A HARD FREEZE HITS the night of October 12th, the first of the season. If Roland planted flowers or vegetables the way his mother used to, they would have been killed, turned into ugly rotting pulp, but he doesn't, and it isn't a problem.

What it is, is a warning. Winter is coming, coming fast, and there is work to do.

The barnyard is deep in shadow as Roland walks in first light—the sun has yet to clear the hills across the river in New Hampshire—to let the cows out to pasture. They are restless, impatient, as if they know that soon they will be inside or in the small feedlot next to the barn for months. Their breath steams and billows in the cold morning air.

He cut his corn yesterday; it stands now in stooks lined up in rows, waiting to be loaded and brought in. Wood waits to be split, potatoes to be lifted. Everything, all of it, waits for him to get to it, but he stands by the barn and watches the swaying rumps of his little herd as the cows amble up to pasture. The sun crests the New Hampshire hills and sends a slash of golden light across the farmyard, lighting up the worn siding of the barn as if it's on fire.

He enters the dark interior of the barn, takes the scythe down from its pegs on the wall, sights along the edge, nods with satisfaction. He passes through the farmyard gate, noticing, as he has every day for the last two weeks, that it wants repairing, and walks up the hill toward his hayfield.

Sometimes this farm can seem a heavy weight, but as he looks out east where the sun hangs above the hills of New Hampshire, he knows it is also a comfort in its way. Here, he is needed; here he is part of something; here he belongs. He stands amid the hay with the scythe held up, the curved blade glinting in the sun. The day calls to him in a way he hasn't felt since he was a young boy, calls to him to be up on the mountain breathing the sharp fresh piney air, not this air filled with drifting clouds of dust and the chaff of mowed hay and corn.

—Roland!

A shout rouses him from his thoughts. It's one of the Wilson boys, walking up the road. He can never tell them apart. Might be Bill, might be Eddie.

The Wilson farm is his nearest neighbor to the north on the Post Road in Wethersfield. Roland went to school with the boys' father, Macklin, who's been laid up for a couple of years, and the two work the farm together. Eddie has a wife and three kids, but Bill is still single.

The Wilson place, they call it Riverview Farm, is down on the flats close to the river, rich in deep, river valley soil. The two boys. Roland still thinks of them as boys, but they're not. They're grown men—strong, stocky, sandy-haired men—faces burnished red by the sun. Men who have worked hard, modernized, bought more land, and built the finest dairy in the county.

Roland lays down the scythe and walks down to the dooryard.

—Hey, old man, you still using a scythe? You're a picture with that thing, I'll tell ya. Thought you were the grim reaper himself come to take old Roland Tuttle away.

—Not yet, anyway.

—Me and Eddie are all caught up. Thought you might need some help getting your grains in.

Roland thinks to say no, he doesn't need any help, but thinks again. Why not? Never hurt a man to take a little help from his neighbors.

—Reckon I could use a little.

—We'll bring the tractor around tomorrow morning, get this hay cut and in before you know it.

—No need for a tractor. Can't stand the noise. I'll get the

cuttin' done, but my corn is still out in stooks. Extra hands getting that in would be a benefit.

THE NEXT MORNING, THE WILSONS come rattling up the road, Eddie driving the tractor, Bill standing behind him on the transfer case.

—Brought it anyway, Roland says.

—Eddie's too damn lazy to walk, Bill says.

Roland has his team hitched, the haywagon ready to go.

—You sure this thing's safe? Eddie says before he and Bill jump on the back.

Roland flicks the reins and the wagon creaks and groans up the hill. The dog, Sam, follows along, sniffing and peeing and hoping one of the horses decides to take a crap so he can grab a little snack on the way. The Wilson brothers talk and joke with each other, but Roland can only hear a bit of what they say.

The sun is well up when they reach the cornfield.

—Gonna be a hot one for October! Eddie shouts over his shoulder.

The corn stooks are lined up like pylons a bit more than the wagon width apart. Bill works the left side, Eddie the right. They take each stook, bundle it up, and toss it up onto the wagon while Roland sits high on the driving bench and eases the wagon up the row. The corn piles up, the two men have to toss it higher each row, but it's a funny thing, the harder they have to work the younger they seem to Roland, the more energy they have. Soon they're laughing and throwing bits of stalk at each other.

They stop when they're about half done with the field and sit, all three in a row, their legs dangling off the back of the wagon. The sun hovers above the hills to the south. The dust cloud from the roadwork sits on the horizon, backlit in lurid shades of orange and yellow. The dog lies down in the shade of the haywagon.

Roland takes out a jug, three tin cups, pours a drink for each of them.

—Holy moly, Eddie says. Switchel. I ain't had switchel since I was a kid. Didn't think anybody knew how to make it anymore.

—Tain't hard, Roland says. I'm not likely to forget. We always drank it.

—You use molasses or honey? Bill says.

—Molasses. Don't cost as much.

—This brings back good memories, Bill says. Working with horses and all.

—How's your Pa? Roland says.

—Holding on, Bill says.

—Going batty is what he is, says Eddie. Claims he sees ghosts in the old house.

—Probably does, Roland says.

Eddie takes a long pull of switchel, smacks his lips.

—Damn, that's good, he says. Reminds me of when Pa was better.

Roland watches the two drinking their switchel, leaning back against the stacked-up corn. It brings back good memories for him, too. He's been at this alone for so long he's forgotten what it was like working with a couple of good men, how fast things get done, how there's pleasure in sharing a jug of refreshment, and he remembers working the farm with his brothers, James and Daniel.

He had thought, then, that it would always be that way.

THE TUTTLE KIDS GREW UP FAST. Farm kids did. Marvin had a job and lived in Windsor and sent a little money back every week. James and Daniel did the farm work with Roland tagging along until one day—a warm day in October—Daniel had looked over and said, "Holy Cow, Roland how much you grow this summer?"

Roland was fourteen, Daniel six years older.

"I dunno. Seem the same to me."

"I don't know Roland, I think you been holding out on us," James said. "You're near as tall as Danny here." He looked over at Daniel, winked. "We'll have to start getting more work out of you."

That was fine with Roland. Working with his brothers was all he wanted to do. When he was busy, working hard, he didn't have time to think, to wonder how come people get old, die all of a sudden, how come things change.

They were in the upper hayfield, Roland driving the wagon, James and Daniel forking the hay up like it was a contest—everything with the two of them was some kind of competition—hay flying this way and that, raising up a cloud of dust and bits of straw that filtered the sun and had them working in a pale cloud.

Finally Daniel stopped, bent over, breathing hard.

"Got you again, hotshot!" James raised his arms in triumph. "You may be the best ballplayer in town, but I can out-work ya any time. What do you think, Roland? Enough for the day?"

Roland looked at the sun still high in the sky, the fields hot and bright.

Roland drove the wagon slowly down to the barn, James and Daniel clinging to the slat-walled sides. They pulled the wagon into the shade of the barn, wiped down the horses.

"Last one to the pond mucks out!" Daniel shouted.

His brothers took off. Roland put the horses in their stalls, gave each of them a handful of oats. He crossed Mountain Road and ran down the slope toward the pond. He could hear James and Daniel splashing and shouting at each other. He dropped his overalls to the ground, pulled off his shirt, stumbled down the bank and launched himself into the water.

This was the best part of the day, what made the hot, dusty work of haying worth it. No matter how warm the summer, the water in the pond was always cold and clear.

"Spring fed," James had announced after he claimed to have dived down to the bottom of the pond and seen where the water flowed out of a crack in the bedrock. Nobody believed he'd been down that deep, but to Roland, James could do about anything, and he had no reason to doubt him.

Roland floated on his back in his own world and watched white clouds drift lazily across a piercing blue sky. He felt the water hold him up. He heard voices. Lifted his head.

"Ma's calling," James said, then pushed his head under.

Roland came up sputtering and coughing.

Daniel grabbed James and pulled him under, and then they were all three splashing and rough-housing, ignoring the distant voice of their mother.

A closer voice. Eliza stood at the edge of the pond in her faded calico dress, her hair put up tight in a bun, her face red from working in the hot kitchen.

"Ma says you better get on up to the house, you want any supper."

"Come on in, sis," Daniel said. "The water's mighty fine."

Eliza used to be a tomboy, as rough and tumble as the three boys, but ever since Margaret went off and got married and

Eliza had turned sixteen, she started to change, act more girly, didn't join in their games.

Roland stood in the water, his toes touching the bottom. He could see she wanted to real bad, being so hot and sweaty. James and Daniel swam over to the pond's edge.

"We'll get out," James said. "We won't look. Promise."

Eliza stood there looking at the pond. The boys got out, and still dripping wet, struggled into their overalls. She pulled her dress up over her head like she didn't care whether they looked or not, let her hair loose, and knifed into the cool, silver water, barely causing a ripple. It was as if the water didn't even know she was there.

Of course they looked, James and Daniel. Roland tried not to, but he peeked and saw a flash of white skin, and then felt his face turn red. He turned away. If his brothers saw him blush, he'd never hear the end of it.

Eliza swam in smooth strokes to the center of the pond.

Their mother called again, louder this time, and the boys left Eliza there so she could get out and dress in peace, and headed up toward the house, carrying their shirts and work boots, barefoot, overalls sticking to their wet legs.

THE OCTOBER SKY ARCS high overhead. The three men on the wagon sit, quiet, lulled by the warm sun.

—What do you think of the road coming? Eddie says.

—What? says Roland. He'd almost dozed off.

—The road. What do you think?

—Seems like we got enough roads already, Roland says.

—This is different, Bill says, waving his arms. Gonna be a super-highway, wide, two different sides and all. They showed the plans at that meeting a couple of weeks back. You can drive real fast on it, don't have to stop for all the towns. Get where you're going.

—What if you're already there? Roland says.

—What? Bill says.

—Where you're going.

Bill looks at Roland, puzzlement on his face, like he has no idea what the old man is talking about. Eddie jumps down off the back of the wagon and walks around to the front. He stands stroking one of the horses.

—Couple-a good nags you got here, Eddie says. They got names?

—'Course they do. That there's Sam, the other's Joe.

—Isn't the dog Sam? Eddie says.

—Yep. Not likely to get 'em confused.

Eddie laughs, shakes his head.

—Roland Tuttle, he says. You are one son of a gun.

—Let's get back to work, Roland says.

The day moves forward slowly, the sun hot and the air still. The wagon creaks as Roland drives it forward one wagon-length at a time, and the stooks of corn crackle as the Wilsons toss them into the wagon. They come to a small clump of trees, right there in the middle of the cornfield.

—What're these trees doin' here? Eddie says.

—Trying to grow, Roland says. Not doing a very good job of it, I'll tell you that. Never seem to get any bigger.

—Why don't you cut 'em down?

Roland sits high on the driving bench and looks at the spinney of maples and poplars. It's maybe ten feet across, the leaves on the trees bright red and orange.

—Pa mowed around them, Roland says. His pa mowed around them, and maybe his pa too, for all I know.

Bill stands next to the wagon, looks up at him.

—County Fair starts in two days, Bill says. You going? We're showing our Guernseys. Gonna win a blue ribbon, I'll bet. Won last year and the year before.

Roland doesn't answer at first, looks away, lost in thought.

—Not likely, he says at last.

—You could ride with us, Eddie says. We'll be driving there and back every day.

OVER THE NEXT TWO DAYS Roland rises early, sees to the cows, then works the rest of the day cutting and harvesting his hay. The Wilsons are busy getting ready to show their prize cattle at the fair, and Roland misses their help, their company. The third day, he finishes milking, watches his cows meander their way to the upper pasture, then walks to the house and sits on the front porch in the warm morning sun.

These early autumn days—the throbbing of crickets, the sun lower in the south yet still hot on his face, the river fog not burning off until mid-morning—bring to him a certain kind of melancholy, a yearning for things he can't define, and a lassitude that leaves him sitting on the front porch, face to the sun, until well past noon. Later, come November, when the approaching winter is evident everywhere—in the bare trees, the frozen ground, the dark, short days—he will regret a single wasted day, wood not brought in, threshing not done, and berate himself for that indulgence, that laziness. But, on this day in the second week of October, he cannot rouse himself, and so he sits.

A Ford pick-up truck pulls over at the bottom of Roland's drive, honks. Bill Wilson leans out of the window.

—Hey, old man! You comin'? We'll be back by milking time.

Roland feels the warmth of the sun in his aching bones and tells himself it is fine to rest, it would be fine to take a break. Other people do, why not him? But, at the same time, the feeling of something coming his way can't be escaped. It isn't only winter—the cold, the snows, the endless feeding of the wood stove, the isolation—that looms. No, it is something more. It is the feeling of some thing encroaching, moving slowly toward him that he can't shake.

—You boys go on.

Eddie guns the engine and the truck bolts, leaving a cloud of yellow dust swirling in the angling sun. Roland watches them drive off. In a way, he's surprised the fair still goes on, hadn't thought about it in years, kind of surprised, as well, that men like the Wilsons would take a whole day off from more important things.

ROLAND'S DAY PASSES in a series of small tasks: cleaning the milking parlor, washing out the cans, sweeping out the haymow. As he works, Roland wonders what the fair's like these days, what Eddie and Bill get up to, and for a moment wishes that he'd gone with them, and wonders why he said no without even considering the possibility of saying yes.

He feels the beginnings of hunger.

Roland stands at the kitchen table, tries to remember what is in the larder. There's leftover oatmeal from this morning's breakfast crusting in the pot, and last night's bean soup. He can make johnny cakes, dip them in the soup. That would be a dinner like many others. Nobody calls it that anymore; it's lunch now, this mid-day meal. He remembers how the family used to sit down to dinner, done with morning chores, hungry for the meal. There had been cooked lamb, just-baked bread, slabs of fresh-churned butter, potatoes, boiled vegetables, and tall glasses of milk, cold and fresh from the spring house.

The day has started to cool. He lights a fire and sits in the rocking chair next to the stove, figures he'll sit for a bit, let his meal settle, then get back to work. The chair creaks as he rocks slowly back and forth.

It was in this chair that Roland's grandmother, Mrs. Ida May Tuttle, had spent much of the last years of her life. She would sit and rock and supervise the family's doings in the kitchen, telling his mother how to do things Abitha had been doing fine for years. Ida May had difficulty standing and walking, but she could talk: oh, how she could talk. When she wasn't bossing Abitha and Margaret and Eliza around, she would tell her stories to anyone who would listen.

"You know what Ascutney means, Boy?" Ida May Tuttle said. Roland—seven years old, soon to be eight—had been on his way out to the barn, but her words pulled him back.

"No ma'am."

"It means three peaks."

Roland was silent.

"Don't you want to know why?"

"Yes'm."

"Come closer. Sit. You know about the Indian Wars, Boy?"

"Yes'm."

"Well," she said. "Three Abenaki braves raided the settlement at Fort Dummer, slaughtered Major William Smith's entire family, and as they were running off he cursed them, shouted that if they ever stopped running they would turn to stone. What do you think the settlers did?"

"Chased 'em?"

"Of course they did! Chased them across the river, up through the woods, right up onto the side of the mountain. And those Indian savages? They ran and they ran until day turned to night, and then they hid right up on the top of that mountain. And did they ever get up?"

She looked at him, sitting where he always did, at her feet. Her hand, all bent and twisted with rheumatism, felt like a claw on his skinny arm.

"No they did not."

"But, how—"

"And what did the settlers see the next morning when they looked up at the mountain?"

"Don't know."

"You don't know? Of course you do. Three summits where before there was only one."

Young Roland's eyes were wide. Ida May rocked back in her chair, pleased with herself.

Roland's mother, Abitha, had been standing in the doorway between the kitchen and the buttery, listening.

"Ida May Tuttle," she said. "You've got to stop filling the boy's head with nonsense."

"Tain't nonsense," Ida May said, then turned and winked at Roland.

FIVE YEARS YOUNGER than his nearest sibling, young Roland, coming along after such a gap, never felt a full part of the farm's workings. He had his chores: collecting eggs from the hen house, helping his mother in the garden. But especially in the fall, when his father and the three older boys were busy in the fields with the last cut of hay, the corn in stooks, shocks of grain—wheat, oats—standing in rows, and his mother and the girls busy in the kitchen putting up food for the winter, Roland as a small boy would be left on his own to slip away, to wander the woods that surrounded the farm.

Seemed like everyone, so busy, almost forgot he was there.

It was October when, days after hearing his gramma's story, he'd first stumbled on a narrow opening in the hedgerow near the far corner of the west meadow where thick forest came right down to the fence line. He ducked under the barb wire fence, squeezed through the bushes, and walked into the shadowed woods. He stopped, looked down. Paw prints covered a trail: deer, fox, coyote maybe, and bigger prints. The five rounded indents in the soft dirt could only be a cat. A big cat. Had to be the catamount. He looked around nervously. Remembered standing next to his father down by the store, hearing Robert Pierson say he'd found one of his sheep dead in the field, gutted, half-eaten. A mountain lion for sure, he'd said.

Nonsense, his father had said, just a couple of goddamn dogs.

Roland wanted to go further, to find those three Indian braves that had turned to stone, but he heard his mother calling him for dinner. It would have to wait.

TWO HUGE MAPLES GROW NEAR the south side of the house, not sugar maples, just big old gnarly trees that spread out, cover the sky. The shade is welcome in the summer, and in the fall they turn a deep, thick red and filter the afternoon light coming in through the kitchen windows, making the whole of the kitchen glow as though you're inside a red globe like the one on the top of Sheriff Wiggins's car.

Roland sits in the kitchen rocking chair. He thinks of his

grandmother. She'd been trying to tell him something with all those stories, something important, but he's never figured out exactly what.

The kitchen shimmers as the leaves of the maples outside the windows shiver in the cool breeze coming off the mountain, then turns dark when the sun passes behind the ridge. He hears the cows coming down from the pasture. It's already time to milk. He steps outside and sees the girls standing patiently at the gate. He opens the gate and watches as they file into the barn, the same as every day, content, it seems to him, in their life and their duties. Milking done, he watches them eat, faces deep in the feed trough.

He, in his way, loves those cows, their calm brown eyes, their smooth flanks, their smell.

HE HEARS THE TOOT of a horn. The Wilsons drive by, on their way back home. These last few days they've been at the fair, and Roland's been here thinking about them being at the fair. The fair. He hadn't thought about the damn thing in years, but now that he has, it comes back to him. The last time he went, he was seven years old. The family kept going for a few years, but not him . . . no, that time was the last.

THE WINDSOR COUNTY FAIR, held in the middle of October every year, was one of the highlights of the year for the Tuttle family, as it was for farm families throughout the county.

The boys—his mother called his three brothers the boys, while he was always Rollie—would sweep out the wagon the night before, clean the harness. They were strapping lads, those three—tall, heavy, broad-shouldered like their father.

His mother and sisters would bake all the day before, filling the cupboard in the pantry with pies and special breads.

Their life was isolated. There was little time to visit neighbors, too much work to do, and the fair was a chance for farm families from miles around to visit, to gossip, and exchange information about improving the quality of their crops. They brought their best livestock, produce, baked goods, and needlework to compete for blue ribbons. The midway, the rides, the carnival barkers, the games, all were a welcome reward for the summer's hard work.

The morning chores done, the cows out to pasture, his father would hitch the horses to the wagon, and the family would pile in, adults in front, his sisters next, the boys standing, all eagerly looking forward. Though Roland was as excited as the others, he would sit on the tail of the haywagon, dangling his legs out over the rutted dirt road, looking backwards. They would proceed down Mountain Road slowly, the wagon twisting and creaking, then turn right to head south on the Connecticut Post Road. Roland would watch the river reflect the slate-blue autumn sky as it wound its way south, imagining all the places it went, places where he was sure—though he had never seen them—exciting things were happening, and lives much more interesting than his own were being lived.

ROLAND HAD BEEN RIDING on the back of the wagon that last time, staring dreamily at the river like he always did, seven years old, small for his age, when, near the junction with the Perkinsville Road that would take them through the hills to North Springfield, the future came barreling up the road behind them. Roland heard it before he saw it, then there it was—a dark ominous shape trailing a billowing dust cloud. The black automobile was upon them then it roared past, leaving the Tuttle family coated in dirt.

His father cursed and shook his fist.

Marvin stared at the passing car, looking to Roland like he'd been struck by lightning. "Did you see that?" he shouted over his shoulder to Roland. "That was a Model T! A real Model T Ford for sure!"

Roland loved the fair, the dust rising around his feet as he wandered the pavilions looking at the prize animals displayed by other farms: the chanticleer rooster with its outrageous plumage, the ducks, the geese, the hogs with their bloated pink bellies, the prize cows—Jerseys, Guernseys, Randalls— and the mighty oxen.

Roland was sitting with his mother in the Baked Goods Tent. The judging of the pie contest had just finished and Abitha was disappointed. She had won only a red ribbon, not the blue.

"I don't know, Rollie, something's the matter with those judges," she said. "Can't see how they would judge Maisie Pierson's apple pies better than mine. Everybody knows she uses molasses to sweeten them, not good maple sugar. I think Orsen Tolliver's sweet on her. I think that's what it is. Nobody can say her pies taste better, nobody."

Roland knew his ma's pies were the best. Even Gramma Ida said so, and if anyone knew anything about pie it was Gramma Ida. He was trying to think of what to say to make his mother feel better when his father came into the tent.

"Where are the boys?" he said, his voice too loud.

"Albert Tuttle, have you been drinking?" Abitha said.

"No ma'am," his father said. He looked at Roland, winked, turned back to Abitha. "Where's James?"

"Off with his friends."

"Daniel?"

"The same."

"Come on, son," he said to Roland. "Need your help."

His mother held Roland's arm for a moment. "You look after your father," she said. "Keep him out of trouble."

Keep him out of trouble? What did she mean?

Roland at the age of seven had started to think about things—things like his father. He sometimes felt that his father forgot that he existed. Sometimes, when he lined up the family and doled out the chores, he wouldn't even call Roland's name, unless Roland's mother reminded him. And now the idea that his father needed his help was something that he couldn't quite grasp.

His father strode off through the crowds, Roland running to keep up. His father seemed to know everyone, tipping his hat to the women, greeting the men.

They passed the livestock building, came to where the Atkinson Farm had a set-up. The Atkinson place was outside Perkinsville in the Black River Valley. Roger Atkinson kept a breeding bull name of Thunder, and had brought him to the fair to show off. Time was, Atkinson used to load that bull into a specially-built wagon and take him round to the farms, but he had now adopted the new technique of artificial insemination, and there was a table with a big sign explaining the new service. Half the herds in the area were descended from that bull.

"Stay close," his father said as they walked up to the fence. The bull was standing in the middle of a circle of bare dirt, tied to a massive iron stake with a thick rope.

Roger Atkinson walked over. "So, Albert, we gonna freshen your girls this year?"

"Reckon so. What do you think Roland? Ain't that some animal?"

The bull snorted, pawed the ground, looked at them with yellow eyes. Roland thought that animal was the most fearsome thing he'd ever seen.

"Not sure about this new business, though," his father said.

"It's safer. You get better results," Atkinson said.

"So I been told," his father said. "But I'm gonna miss seeing that bull do his work, that's for sure."

The men laughed. Roland stared at the beast, unsure how he was helping.

On their way back to the Baked Goods Tent and his mother, they stopped at the intersection of the two busiest lanes of the midway. Booths with their games of skill and chance lined the lanes, the Ferris wheel turned against the sky, a merry-go-round played tinny music. There was a narrow alley that cut off at an angle behind a row of tents and stalls, crowded with men. Roland could hear loud voices, laughter.

"Rollie, you wait here," his father said. "Only be a minute." He disappeared down the lane, ducked into a tent.

Roland, buffeted by the teeming crowds, felt very small.

"Hey, Rollie," a man called to him. "C'mere."

Roland turned around to see who knew his name, then around again until he saw a tall, gaunt man with a beak-like nose wearing a red-and-white striped vest. How did the man know his name? The man gestured; Roland wandered over, stood staring at the booth. It was a bean bag toss, the prizes all lined up around the sides: stuffed bears, kewpie dolls, brightly colored wood spinning tops.

The man watched Roland stare at those spin tops.

"Want to win a prize?" he said. "Three tries for a nickel." Roland shuffled his feet.

"C'mon, kid." The man, more insistent. "Don't be chicken."

Roland looked down at his feet, didn't want to admit that he didn't have a single nickel. His father should have given him a nickel, if he was going to leave him here.

"What'sa matter? Cat got your tongue?"

The man seemed to grow taller, to lean out from the booth, to loom over him, and Roland turned and ran, pushing his way through the crowd that had stacked up behind him to watch the game, the man calling after him.

He ran to where the crowd thinned out and he could breathe again and looked around him and realized he had no idea where he was.

Where was he supposed to wait? His father had left him. Would he even notice that Roland wasn't there?

He stood, watched people rushing past. Families together, laughing. Kids eating cotton candy. He wished he had some cotton candy; that would be something, at least. He wandered, looking for the booth with the man with the striped vest until he realized that most of the men running the games wore the same vest, and then he knew he was lost, and he stopped and stood in the middle of an open square near the merry-go-round trying hard not to cry. People streamed by, bumping him, pushing him as if he wasn't even there.

Roland felt a hand on his shoulder. He jumped like he'd been stung, started to run.

"Rollie!" It was James. "Take it easy. You're like to jump out of your skin."

Daniel came up. "What're you doing Rollie?"

His brothers. Roland had never forgot how his brothers rescued him, took him around, bought him cotton candy, let him play that game.

When they returned to the Baked Goods Tent, his father was nowhere to be seen. His mother was furious, but at who, Roland couldn't tell. For the rest of that day, he never went far from the farm exhibits, the animals, the produce judging, the Baked Goods Tent. He couldn't forget the terror of being lost in that crowd, but what was worse was the realization that his father had left him there, had forgotten all about him.

THE NEXT YEAR, HE REFUSED TO GO. The family stood around, almost stunned. It was as if they, for the first time, realized that Roland at the age of eight had a will of his own.

"I'm not going either," Gramma Ida said. "Too old for all that foolishness."

Albert and Abitha both knew well the futility of trying to change Gramma Ida's mind. Roland's brothers and sisters were growing impatient, anxious to get to the fair.

"Go on," Gramma Ida said. "We'll watch out for each other, right, Boy?"

Roland found himself briefly torn between the terror of the fair, of the crowds, of all those big people pushing past him as if he wasn't there, and the glint in his grandmother's eye that said she had another story to tell.

THE OTHERS HAD LONG SINCE outgrown her attempts to terrify them with tales of bloodthirsty ghosts lurking in the dark New England forests, or stories of deceased family members haunting the house at night. They would laugh, say they had work to do, but Roland would be pulled in and sit wide-eyed as she spun her latest tale.

They were in the kitchen, Ida May in her chair.

"Boy," she beckoned to Roland after the family had left. "Come here, keep an old woman company. I ever tell you the one about Colonel John Buck?"

Ida May Tuttle loved ghost stories.

"Colonel John Buck"—she leaned forward—"served in the Revolutionary War. When he returned to his village, he became convinced that a young woman was a witch and was responsible for the misfortunes that had struck his family while he was gone, and sentenced her to death by hanging. That was his mistake. You got to burn a witch or they'll haunt you for sure. Everybody knows that. And as that unfortunate woman dangled on the end of the rope her last words were a terrible curse. She swore she would dance on his grave for all eternity.

"And, I tell you what, you go into that graveyard at night, oh yes, you'll see her dancing away. You get too close, she'll pull you right into that dance, and then you're lost for sure." She leaned back and cackled. "Lost forever."

"Are there ghosts in this house, Gramma?" Roland said.

"Oh, yes ..." she said. "Of course there are."

Roland looked over his shoulder, at the door to the main house, then back at Gramma Ida. She winked. Something about that wink, that scrunched up leer in the old woman's face, was to young Roland near as scary as all her ghost stories.

Satisfied that she had sufficiently terrified the young boy, Ida May went upstairs for her afternoon rest. "Behave yourself," she said to Roland.

It had been a year since Gramma Ida had told him the meaning of Ascutney, but he hadn't forgotten. He had waited and waited, and now—with everyone else at the fair for the day, and his grandmother upstairs in her room taking a nap—was, he realized, his chance to explore the mountain, to discover where that trail went, and to find those three rocks that were once Indian braves.

The trail wandered south, angling up across the lower slopes of the mountain until it reached a ridge that ran straight uphill alongside the Blow-me-Down Brook. Roland followed the narrow path as it dropped down into the gully, crossed the brook, climbed the other side, then contoured up across the steepening mountainside.

Quiet surrounded him.

He walked beneath pine and birch and larch, the leaves of the white-poled birches bright yellow against the dark green of pines and fir. He felt he was somehow getting away with something, as if unseen eyes followed him, and that any moment someone would call out, stop him from going further. He moved with exaggerated stealth, trying not to dislodge a single stone, snap a single twig.

He was a young Indian brave fleeing his pursuers.

The trail was steep, the trees smaller. A final switchback brought him to where a slender stream of water flowed out of a cleft in the mountainside across a broad, flat expanse of shale to drop some fifty feet and splash on shattered rocks below. His eyes grew wide with wonder that such a marvel existed this close to the farm. He was—he was sure he was—the first person ever to see this. There were crystals embedded in the rock.

Roland named the place Crystal Falls.

He scrambled up into the cleft to see where the water came from. He wormed his way along a narrow passage. Walls of layered shale rose on both sides to a thin slice of sky. He came to a place where the water flowed out of solid rock, and felt as if he must be deep underground within the mountain itself. The floor of the cave was littered with shards of shale, some shaped like arrowheads.

He pocketed one.

This would be his secret. Wouldn't tell no one. His brothers would only make fun, tell him it ain't nothing but a rock, a plain old piece of gray shale, but Roland, when he held it and felt its flat smooth surface and chipped edges, was certain other hands, hands deep in the past, had held it, had made it.

Ascutney was for the most part a forested mountain, not one of dramatic crags and plummeting cliffs, but here was different. Standing by the lip of the falls was, to the boy, like standing on the edge of the world.

The forest fell away beneath his feet to the valley below, where the river twisted and sparkled in the sun. Far to the south, he could see the dark brooding lump of Fall Mountain in New Hampshire. He knew there were farms and villages and somewhere Fort Dummer, but he couldn't see them and he imagined himself the only person in the world, and strangely, that felt okay.

Roland hadn't found the three summits, the three rocks, but he knew they were somewhere close by, those three Indians. Maybe, if he stood there long enough, he would turn into the fourth.

He wondered if anyone would miss him when they got back from the fair, notice that he was gone.

It would be lonely, but lonely was better than those crowds, better than being lost and forgotten. To be lonely when you were alone like this, was, at least yours, was something you could wrap around yourself like a warm jacket, something you could hold onto.

November

THE SUN RISES FURTHER TO THE SOUTH, stays low in
the southern sky, and passes behind the bulk of Mount
Ascutney earlier each day. Maple branches are bare; a few
brown leaves cling to oak trees. The barn swallows are gone.
Crows squabble over dropped bits of grain in the barnyard.
At night the sound of geese flying south clamors on the edges
of people's dreams. Nights are cold, the days gray and not
much warmer, and the ground is frozen hard, and the river
is fringed with ice. A convoy of trucks, some with trailers
carrying gigantic earth-moving equipment, is seen leaving
the village, heading south for the winter.

∾

ROLAND STOPS SPLITTING when he can barely see the
wood in the graying light, but keeps stacking firewood
until it's night-time dark. He's got two dry cords in the
woodshed attached to the kitchen, though they're not
going to stay dry if he doesn't patch that roof, and he's got
another two, not as dry but getting there, stacked outside
under sheets of metal roofing that he scavenged from the
old sugarhouse, and two more logs to cut and split. That
should get him through the winter, though if this last spell
is any indication, it's going to be a hell of a cold winter,
and it might not be enough.

Two or three days work, he figures.

He lights the kerosene lamps in the kitchen. There's still

embers in the cookstove, hot from the morning fire. He slides in a few small splinters of wood, blows on them. Little flames dance and dart around the dry kindling. He adds more wood, builds up the fire until he has that old Glenwood glowing and crackling. He takes off his barn-coat, hangs it on a peg near the door, pulls up his chair and sits by the open stove door warming himself. His hands throb. He takes off his boots, sticks his feet right up close to the fire and sighs. It feels good to be done with the day's work, to be sitting here thinking about supper.

He goes to the big pantry off the kitchen. His mother always called it the buttery and the old churn still stands in the corner. One wall is lined with shelves. He's got a basket of potatoes put up, bags of corn meal, oatmeal, jars of dried beans, a wheel of cheese he'd picked up from the Wilsons, and a few store-bought cans of tomatoes, peas, but most of the shelves are empty. The family used to make butter and cheese, can vegetables from the garden. The tin buckets and milk cans and cook vats line the other wall, all coated with the dust of time. He takes a pot with what's left of last night's potato soup, walks back into the kitchen, and puts it on the back burner to warm.

The wood in the stove crackles; Sam snores on his blanket in front of the stove; the house creaks and shifts as Roland waits for the soup to heat. He can't sit in this chair without it starting to move, even if he doesn't mean to move it, and so he sits and rocks gently back and forth and lets his mind drift. He has lived his entire life in this house, and his father lived his entire life in this house, and his father before him, going back and back, and to Roland, at times, it's as if all those lives lived in this house are still going on right alongside his.

A lot of that comes down to Gramma Ida.

Ida May Tuttle believed in the past, that it was alive as long as someone remembered, and believed it was her job to make sure that they did. Sometimes, when Roland first comes into the kitchen from the outside, or from the woodshed, and looks at that empty chair, he can see her as she was those last years of her life, in that chair, talking and talking—didn't matter if anyone was listening or not—and he thinks back to all those stories she told him.

"How old are you, Boy?" Gramma Ida said.

Roland had come in from the woodshed, his arms loaded, and was standing by the woodbox.

"Nine."

"Hmm . . . nine years. Nine long years."

"What?"

"Never you mind. I ever tell you about the first winter that Tuttles lived on this land?"

Roland shuffled his feet, turned to put down his load.

"You listening?"

"Yes'm."

"It was the end of October, eighteen hundred and thirteen, when Edmund Tuttle helped Susannah down from their wagon. Come all the way from Rutland, they did. He was a damn fool to get here that late in the year, I'll tell you that. Weren't nothing here but a pile of lumber and a half-cleared piece of raw land. How do you think she felt when she saw this place?"

"Happy?" Roland said.

Ida May laughed. "Lord, no, she was terrified. You know that woodshed you came out of?"

Of course he did, and he was about to say something smart, but she kept on, and Roland knew that when she was in one of these moods it was best to keep his mouth shut.

"Built it themselves, the two of 'em. The only reason you and me is here, is 'cause of how hard they worked, starting before light, not stopping until dark. They needed shelter and winter was coming."

He stood there, afraid to turn away, put down his load.

"It was a long dark winter in that shed." She was just getting started. "Living on a dirt floor and the snows piling up past their window and the wind whistling in the cracks of the back wall. Edmund up every day in the woods, bringing down logs, splitting firewood, trying to keep up with the fire that Susannah tended. It was all they could do to keep warm. That winter darn near killed them both. Killed their first baby, I'll tell you that."

"How do you know all this?" He dared to ask. His legs started to shake with the load, standing there like he was, arms full of firewood.

"Go on, put it down." She waved her hand.

He filled the woodbox. The door from the main house opened and his sister Margaret walked in, went to the sink, stood with her back to the two of them.

"Susannah told me. How do you think I know? I see her. Nobody else does, but I do."

Even at the age of nine, Roland knew that was impossible.

"Gramma, she's been dead for a hundred years."

"Don't you sass me, Boy. She still comes to visit, you know."

Margaret came up behind him. "You're a ninny if you believe that silliness," she said.

Ida May waited until Margaret left.

"Don't you listen to her," she said. "Some people got the gift, most don't."

Roland started to leave, but she called him back.

"Edmund comes too, you know. I see him. Those trees in the upper field? That's where he comes. You want to see him, you go there right before dark. Maybe you'll see him. Maybe not. Depends."

"On what?" Roland said.

He knew those trees, a little bunch of them. His father plowed around them, and something about the way they were gnarled and twisted had always seemed creepy to the young boy. There was a dark shadow at the center of the grove—even in the middle of the day—darker than it should be.

"Whether you're ready." Ida May rocked back in her chair with a pleased look on her face, like she'd accomplished some important task.

"WHAT ARE YOU DOING?" Roland was in Marvin's room, sitting on the edge of his bed while Marvin stuffed the last of his clothes into a grain sack.

"Packing. Got a job."

"But you've got a job here."

"Well . . . maybe you can take over for me. What do you think?"

Roland didn't think he could. He was only nine, and Marvin was the farm's fixer, had been ever since, at the age of ten, he had fixed the kitchen swing churn when no one else could figure it out.

Marvin, seventeen, was moving to Windsor, to a rented room at Mrs. Jameson's Boarding House and a job at the Windsor Machine Company. He'd spent the previous couple of summers working at the Amsden Sawmill, learning how to use the joiner, the planer, but ended up mostly repairing things; those machines were old, always breaking down one way or another. The Windsor Machine Company used to be the Robbins and Lawrence Armory. Made thousands of guns for the Union in the Civil War, but now the company made the Gridley Automatic Lathe that was used all over the country to make all kinds of things, and Marvin would be an apprentice working for Mr. George O. Gridley himself.

"But, you're leaving . . ."

The four boys couldn't have been more different. James and Daniel loved being out in the fields, working alongside their father, and Roland loved the animals. Soon as Roland could walk there was some beast, a dog or a cat, a chicken or a piglet, following him around. Roland started in milking with his father when his hands were barely big enough to squeeze a cow's teat.

And Marvin?

Marvin was a mechanic at heart, liked things, liked figuring out how they worked.

As Roland watched Marvin pack, the knowledge that his life—playing in the dirt of the dooryard, hiding in a dim corner of the barn, hanging around the cows out in the field, or off somewhere in the woods—might change, might not always be what it had been, that he would not always be nine, that the people in his life might go away crept up on him, but was quickly pushed away.

"You'll be back, right?"

"Now and then, don't you worry, and I'll be able to send some money to Ma. That'll help, don't you think?"

Marvin carried his sack of clothing down the stairs and out

onto the front porch, Roland on his heels. Old man Bowker was waiting in his freight wagon. He was heading to Windsor to pick up some goods for his store coming in on the Boston train, and he was going to give Marvin a ride.

The family, all of them except their father, watched him load that sack onto Bowker's wagon.

Marvin gave his mother a quick hug, waved at the rest of them, then climbed up next to Bowker on the wagon bench. Albert came out of the barn, stood in the doorway in the bright sun wiping his hands on a rag. He looked at Marvin, turned away, disappeared back into the shadows of the barn.

"I DON'T UNDERSTAND WHY you would oppose Margaret marrying this man," Roland heard his mother say.

When the weather got too cold and damp for Roland to spend his time hiding out in the woods or behind the piggery, he liked to be in the parlor, surrounded by the dark wood paneling, liked to look at the shelf with his mother's books, and liked to sit in the big easy-chair that she sat in come evening, when her work was done for the day, when she could finally rest. The chair smelled like his mother, and if he curled up tight and hunkered down, someone looking into the parlor, even if they were searching for him, would scarcely be able to see him.

The other reason he liked curling up in her big stuffed chair in the corner was because of the furnace system with its hot-air vents. If you sat in that chair by the floor vent and there were people talking in the kitchen, you could hear their voices through the vents like they were right next to you.

"I ain't against it," his father said. "Hell, I didn't think anyone would ever want to marry that girl, plain as she is."

"Albert! How can you say that about your own daughter? Margaret is not plain. You're blind, is what it is. You can't see how she's grown to be a good-looking woman."

Roland thought she was fine, Margaret. She was his big sister. He was eleven years old, soon to be twelve, and he still idolized her.

His parents were talking in the kitchen.

"I ain't opposed, like I said, but I ain't sure about the man she wants to marry. Besides, he's years younger than her. She'll get old. He'll tire of her."

"Are you tired of me?" she said.

"Course not."

"Well then . . . "

Roland pictured her putting her hand on his arm in that way she had.

"William Fairbanks is a fine man," she said. "He's got a good job. He'll provide for her."

"But why does she got to move all the way up to Saint J?"

"Oh, Albert," his mother said.

Roland knew she was fixin' to marry. She'd told him right off when it was official. She was so excited, she was. Told him all about William Fairbanks, how he'd courted her all that summer after they met at the county fair the fall before, how he would have a fine job working for his uncle's big company in St. Johnsbury, and how they would have a house of their own. But it had not hit him that she would be moving away. He hadn't thought about it, had assumed that they would both, her and William, move to the farm, or somewhere close by, but hearing his father say it that way made it real. She was going away.

Roland heard his father coughing in the kitchen.

"Sit down, Albert," his mother said. "Rest for a bit."
"Can't," he said. "Got work to do."

ROLAND IS STILL CARRYING FIREWOOD, same as he did as a
boy, stepping out into the cold shed, piling up an armload,
coming back in to fill the woodbox next to the stove. How
many times has he done this exact same thing? Laid the
splits of wood into the crook of his left arm with his right,
shouldered the plank door to the woodshed closed behind
him, placed the wood, one stick at a time, into the woodbox,
bent down, checked the stove. More times than anyone could
count, that's for sure.

Feeding that stove, like everything else on the farm, is
work that's never done.

He thinks to go back for another load, but stops at the
woodshed door, turns and looks back across the kitchen at
the door to the big house. It's a six-panel Bible door with the
rails and stiles forming the cross. His grandfather had that
door made special by Elmer Johnson, a joiner up in Windsor.
Roland doesn't think of it as a door. Doors are meant to open
and close, for people to go in and out. This one was shut years
ago, and hasn't opened since. It's become more like part of
the wall, most of the paint long since flaked off, the grain
of the wide, raised panels of cherry burnished gold by time.
Roland's mother talked often about how proud his grandfather
had been of that hand-crafted door, and it reminds Roland
of the grandfather he never met.

ROLAND'S GRANDFATHER DIED ON November 3, 1900, two
days before Abitha Tuttle gave birth to a healthy baby boy,
and it seemed almost pre-ordained to her that this latest male

Tuttle should be named after him. Indeed, as young Roland E. Tuttle grew, he seemed to almost everyone to resemble the elder Roland H. Tuttle more and more.

That was not the only time death visited the Tuttle farm in the dark, bleak month of November. Rachel Tuttle was stillborn November 15, 1895, and Marlene Tuttle, born in October of 1897, lived no more than three weeks before dying of the croup.

November's bare trees and gray skies, cold piercing rain, frozen ponds, and bitter winds came to be met with great dread at the Tuttle farmstead. And the year Roland turned twelve, along with its cold and damp, November brought still more heartbreak.

Albert Tuttle, Roland's father, was a commanding presence in the family's life. A big man, rooms seemed to get smaller when he entered. He ran the farm, and by extension, their lives, though, in many ways, it was the farm that ran all of them. He was one of those men who seemed to never be without a cigarette in his hand or dangling from the corner of his mouth, squinting through the smoke, and in the evenings, when the work of the day was done, a drink as well. He started coughing the summer of 1912, and by that fall Roland would see him out in the field, the horse and wagon stopped in the middle of a row of corn stooks, doubled over in pain.

He swore he was fine.

"You got to keep at it," he said to Roland one time. "That's what a man's got to do. You can't question it. It's the way things are."

Margaret was due to be married in December and Albert was determined to make it to the wedding of his oldest daughter. But it was not to be.

HIS FATHER WOULDN'T LET THEM take him to the hospital even after he collapsed out in the field one late October day and had to be helped up into the haywagon by James and Daniel, and carried into the house and laid down in his bed, Roland standing by, feeling useless.

"No hospital," Albert said. "Can't stand the smell. People get sick in hospitals, die. Nosir, I'll get better here at home."

Doc Ferguson came down from Windsor in his black one-horse buggy. He did the usual doctor things, listened to Albert's chest, took his temperature, then came down the stairs in the main house with a serious look, the whole family sitting around the drawing room. He took Abitha aside and they stood in the corner near the big clock leaning into each other, talking in quiet murmurs that seemed to flow together like it wasn't words they were saying at all but some kind of sad, melancholy chant.

Albert didn't get better. The family carried on. James and Daniel out in the fields doing what they'd been doing, working harder, taking longer without the guiding hand of their father. Roland wanted to be with them, but James said, "You'll get in the way, and besides, Ma needs your help in the house what with Margaret being distracted and all."

"You need your education," his mother said.

And so, Roland went to school, all the time thinking about home and his father lying alone in his bed staring out the window while his sons did his work, and how it must've ate at him, him being so proud, and when Roland came home from school he tended to his father.

He emptied the bedpan, washed him, changed his bedding, cleaned his soiled pajamas. No twelve-year-old boy should ever see his father that way. A father who had seemed to

Roland a god, a distant, sometimes uncaring god, but a god nonetheless. Indeed, when Roland sat next to his mother in church (his father never went, said it was all a bunch of malarkey) and Reverend Wilkins talked about God, the image that came to Roland's mind was his father standing out in the field, cigarette in the corner of his mouth, leaning on a scythe or a rake.

Albert Tuttle rarely rose from his bed. Doc Ferguson came more and more frequently. The house grew quiet, as if sounds were muffled by cotton, but through the quiet, the family heard the sounds of Albert's tortured coughing. Even the boys, when they came in from their work in the fields and barn, lowered their voices, stopped their pushing and teasing.

"How's he doin', Rollie?" James would ask, as if he couldn't walk up the stairs any time and see for himself. Roland would shake his head. How could he speak of what he knew, what the rest of them could still avoid knowing?

THANKSGIVING DINNER—the harvest had been good, the corn, the oats, the hay all in and stored, the potato crop bountiful, the carrots, turnips, onions all put down in the root cellar—but there seemed little to be thankful for. Albert Tuttle had not risen from his bed in more than a week.

The table was laden with food: roast pork, gravy, two cooked chickens, potatoes, onions and carrots stewed in a pot, mashed turnips, collard greens, tall glasses of thick fresh milk. Abitha had carried on in the kitchen as if the act of cooking could change the course of events, as if that man lying in bed upstairs, her husband, the father of her children, was not days from his death.

Roland knew. Hadn't he, Roland, watched his father shrink and shrivel before his eyes? Watched the man turn gray? Cough like to tear himself inside out? Seen the blood-spattered handkerchiefs?

They were all there around that table. Marvin down from Windsor. Ida May Tuttle sat stone-faced—her son upstairs on his deathbed—next to an empty chair and a place setting at the table's head, the plate loaded with food, served, at her insistence, like all the others.

"I hoped your father would make it down for dinner," Gramma Ida said.

No one else at the table thought that was going to happen.

"Rollie, why don't you take his plate up to him?" Abitha said.

"He ain't going to eat nothin'."

"Roland Tuttle!" Abitha said.

He did as he was told, took the plate, gathered up the knife and fork and napkin, and walked slowly, quietly up the stairs, feeling the eyes on him.

The birthing room, they called it. Dyin' room too, Ida May said one time. A small bedroom in the back of the house, a single bed beside a single window, a small bedside table, a kerosene lamp, floor and walls bare, no decoration save a framed devotional picture of Jesus Christ hung by Abitha in the center of the wall opposite the bed.

Roland found his father lying back on his pillows, eyes closed, face as gray as the November sky outside the window. He put the plate on the small table, didn't speak, sat down beside the bed and watched his father struggle for breath.

His father let out a wheezy, whistley breath like a long

drawn-out sigh. There was a pause. Would he breathe again? Then a short in-breath, like a startled gasp, as if the man himself was surprised he still lived, still breathed.

He opened his eyes.

"Roland?"

"Yessir."

"Where's . . ."

"Downstairs . . . it's Thanksgiving."

"Ah . . . yes . . ."

Quiet. Another gasp of a breath in, the long slow wheeze out. He tried to cough. Didn't have the strength. He turned toward Roland, moving in little jerks like he was fighting against some unseen force. He lifted his hand, made a weak fluttery gesture for Roland to lean close.

"You've been a good boy," he said.

Roland heard the wind outside, tree branches rattling against the window sash. He could hardly bear to look at his father lying there underneath a grayish sheet and a red and black checked blanket. His face was drawn in, emptied out, and his hair was thin and plastered against his scalp. His father gazed up at the ceiling seeing something Roland could not.

"Take care of your mother . . . the farm," he said in a weak, strangled voice. Roland could barely make out the words.

Another gust outside. The north wind moaned around the edge of the bedroom dormer.

"I'm sorry," his father said. He closed his eyes. "Sorry . . ."

A short gasp in, the long sigh of a breath out, then silence.

Roland waited, anticipating that next gasp, the next heroic intake of breath. Time passed. He didn't know what to do. He looked at the figure in the bed and realized that it was not his father anymore and wondered where his father had gone. The plate of food sat untouched on the little table, the gravy congealing into a mass too awful to look at.

He stumbled down the stairs.

"I told you he wasn't going to eat nothing!" he shouted as he ran through the dining room and out the door into the gray November afternoon, not stopping for a coat, not stopping for anything, up past the barn to the trail that led up onto the mountain, and he kept on running not caring where he was going, tears streaming down his face.

"I told her he wasn't going to eat nothing!" he shouted into the wind.

Crystal Falls. His place. Roland wasn't sure how he got there. It was like his feet kept moving, some force kept pulling him up the trail. He collapsed onto the shale next to the flowing water and listened to the murmuring current as it flowed over the rocks. He sat there as the sky darkened and clouds like watered ink raced off the summit of the mountain.

Why me? He thought about his father's last words. The man had barely seemed to know Roland was there half the time, yet he'd put this burden on him. Why not the rest of 'em?

Roland sat. Though he grew chilled and started to shiver, he couldn't summon the will to get up, to start down the hill. It was almost dark when he heard distant voices shouting his name. Soon, he saw flashlights bobbing up through the trees like fireflies on a summer evening.

A light shined in his eyes, dazzling him.

"Roland Tuttle, what the hell you doing up here, boy?" It was Homer Wiggins, first-year Deputy Sheriff of Windsor County. "Come on, let's get you home. Your poor mother's worried sick."

Roland was so cold and stiff he could barely stand.

Wiggins lifted him to his feet.

"Here, take my jacket." He put his sheriff's jacket with its badge and shoulder patches on Roland. "Maybe you'll be a sheriff someday."

"It's kinda heavy," Roland said.

"It is that, sometimes," Wiggins said. "It is that."

WHETHER IT IS EARLY DECEMBER or late October or the middle of November, Roland doesn't much care, doesn't put names to the months. He lives by the seasons, by the feel of the weather, by the changing of the trees, the habits of the birds, and winter, he can feel, is coming on early. The ground is frozen solid, the pond thick with ice, the sky a thick feathery ceiling of gray that seems to promise a blizzard though no snow comes. Night after night, the bitter cold drives the frost deep into the bare ground like an iron spike, and if it doesn't snow soon, his water line will freeze and he'll have to carry water from the spring house all winter.

He worries about wasting the hay, worries he'll need every bale to feed the cows if it's a long winter, but with this cold he knows he has no choice, so he lays a thick layer of hay on the ground above where the line is buried, figures he can always get some from the Wilsons if he runs low, and then turns to getting the last of his wood in before the snows come. He has a big pile of cordwood waiting to be stacked and covered, and one more log to cut to stove-length and split. An old hunk of oak he dragged down the winter before, it is hard to saw, so dense it might as well be ironwood. Seems like he has to sharpen the crosscut saw every other cut.

There has been a lot going on the last few days, orange pickup trucks with bright blue triangles painted on the door going back and forth on the Post Road and up and down Mountain Road. He'd see one parked beside the road and a couple of men in yellow hardhats out on the side of the road, measuring, talking back and forth. Why the hell they needed hardhats when there was nothing above them save the sky, he had no idea.

Roland is out by the woodshed, surrounded by split wood, sawdust, and scraps of bark when one of those orange trucks pulls into his driveway, parks right in the dooryard. A man gets out, kind of tall, though not as tall as Roland, wearing a pale blue windbreaker, khaki pants. Roland leans the splitting maul up against the woodpile, walks over to him, trying to remember where he's seen him.

—Mr. Tuttle?

—The same.

—Name's Coburn. John Coburn.

He sticks out his hand.

Roland wipes his hand on his dirty overalls. Man's hand is soft. Not a worker, then.

—Do you have time to talk a bit?

—Got work to do.

—I won't take too much of your time. We talked back in September. The Town Hall?

That was it. Roland didn't much care for the man then, still doesn't.

—I just wanted to stop by, re-introduce myself.

Roland waits for him to get to the point.

—I'm sure you've noticed all the activity in the area.

—Hard not to.

—Anyway, there'll be a couple of men coming through, surveyors. They need to take a few sightings and then they'll be out of your hair. Wanted to let you know.

—Well, now you have.

—Okay then. I'll be back around when the time comes. You take care now.

When the time comes . . . now what time might that be?

He watches the man drive off, stands looking at the place where the truck was parked then heads back to his woodpile. He wants to know what's going on, who all these men are, but he doesn't like to ask questions. You ask a question, you don't know what you're gonna get back. Might not like the answer. Might not want to know.

He returns to the woodpile. How many times has he done this? Raised the heavy splitting maul up high, arced it through the air, brought it down, letting the pull of the earth do the work, hitting the big block of wood in the one place where the grain will open up and the halves will peel apart like that's what they've been waiting to do the whole time the tree was growing.

Wood he knows. Mr. John Coburn he's not so sure about.

NOVEMBER WOODS IN a cold drizzle, tree trunks black, the gray sky lowering around him, Roland walks his woodlot, figures it's good to take a look around and check out the trees before snow covers the ground. He won't fell until winter, when the snow is deep and firm enough to carry the logging dray. The family's been cutting from these acres for generations. Roland himself came up here with his father when he was barely big enough to walk, standing at the front of the dray, his father holding him tight around the waist, his brothers, all three of them, standing on the crossbeams behind, holding onto the sides for dear life.

His great-great-grandfather, Edmund Tuttle, had started cutting here about a hundred and fifty years ago, and he and the Tuttle men that followed—Lucius, the first Roland, Albert—had felled only what they needed, culling the weakest, and the remaining trees—birch, oak, maple, chestnut— had flourished. Their crowns arc high above Roland's head. They form a leafy canopy in summer, but in the dark of November, the bare branches grasp at a sky the color of lead.

He walks among the tree columns, breathing hard from the climb up the hill, boots crunching the frozen leaves. He stops. Quiet—not the gentle peace of that shade-filled forest floor in summer, marked by the soft rustling of critters and insects—a hard frozen quiet, everything locked up before the coming of winter.

It's too quiet. Where's the dog?

Roland looks around, realizes Sam isn't with him. He never goes anywhere without that dog hard on his heels, but there's no sign of him. Roland walks back down the hill, comes out of the woods to the edge of the north pasture.

Still no dog.

Then halfway down the pasture he finds him, lying on his side, front paws scrabbling at the frozen ground trying to drag himself up the hill. Trying to follow like he'd always done. But the back legs aren't working.

—Hell, boy, what happened to you?

The dog looks at him with those big dog eyes and whimpers a little and drops his head and lies there, breathing hard, his side heaving with pain. Roland squats next to him, strokes his black fur then picks him up, staggers under the weight—Sam is not a small dog—and carries him toward the house. Clouds thicken and gather overhead as he struggles down the hill to the farm. He lays Sam down gently on the front porch, goes inside, comes out with a saucer of milk. Sam lifts his head, gives it a sniff, but drops his head back to the worn wood of the porch floor and lies there, quiet, patient.

—Hell, Roland says. Dammit all to hell.

Roland remembers there was a family down in the village one time had a dog, a small scruffy mutt, got stomped by a horse, its back legs paralyzed. They made a cart-like thing with two red wheels and strapped that poor animal to it and damned if that little dog didn't wheel himself around looking as pleased as all get out.

But this is Sam, a proud beast, a noble beast.

Roland sits next to him, puts his hand on the dog's head, light, gentle, pulls at his ears, strokes his neck, then leaves his hand there almost fluttering over the dog's brow and sits, and the sky turns and the cold rain comes and he sits next to that dog until it is dark and the cows in the barn start to complain about not being milked when they were supposed to be.

—You wait here, boy. Roland says to him. I gotta milk those cranky cows. You know that. I'll be back, take care of you, don't you worry.

Roland walks to the barn, thinking, the dog knows.

After milking, he returns to the house carrying a shovel, takes the farm's rifle down off the high shelf in the kitchen, checks to see that it's loaded—hasn't used the damn thing in years. Goes back out to the porch and heads out behind the barn. There's other dogs buried there, cats too. Figures he'll dig the grave then carry the poor thing, but hears scuffling behind him and looks back and sees Sam dragging himself along, pulling with his front legs and his strong back and not complaining or whining or nothing. Sam always was a brave dog.

He knows, Roland thinks again.

Roland's throat is thick and he can't hardly swallow and his eyes sting and he can barely breathe and that dog, that goddamn brave dog, just keeps coming.

The shovel won't even dent the frozen ground. Roland comes back from the woodpile with his axe and chops at the ground in a frenzy of anger and grief. It'll ruin the axe, but he doesn't care.

The gunshot isn't loud.

In the barn, a few cows look up then return to their feed, but as Roland fills in the shallow grave, it echoes in his mind like the loudest thunderclap that ever rolled down the slopes of the mountain when lightning struck its summit.

December

WORK HAS HALTED ON THE HIGHWAY. The village is quiet and peaceful. Coyotes are heard running through the streets in the night. The river flows, a narrow black channel between sheets of silver ice. The Christmas crèche is up on the town green next to the memorial for the town's war dead, but a windstorm blew down the manger and the hasty repairs have left the display a little crooked. Houses have small lights, like candles, in their windows. Icicles hang from snow-covered roofs. There are wild turkey tracks in the fresh snow.

∾

THE SNOW STOPPED SOMETIME during the night and all is white. Snow clings to the branches of the maples, clumps on top of the bushes in the overgrown meadow, coats the haywagon that is parked outside the barn. The arrival of snow brings relief from chores, from the piles of branches that need picking up near the barn, the broken plow parts Roland had meant to put away, the fields.

The sun clears the ridge of hills across the river; shadows of the maples and the oak reach across the undulating surface of the snow like veins in a working man's arm.

A car crunches to a stop on the snow-packed driveway.

—How're you doing, Roland? Sheriff Wiggins says.

—Just watchin' the morning.

Thin mare's tails of white drift across the painful blue sky.

Wiggins leans against the white panel of his car with its big, round Windsor County Sheriff emblem.

—Didn't see you at the meeting.

—At least we got some quiet, Roland says.

Wiggins shakes his head.

—They'll be back in the spring. Enjoy it while you can. I heard down at Town Hall they only got half the survey done before the first snow.

—That so?

—Guess we'll find out more when they get around to it. You got to start paying attention, Wiggins says.

—I'm payin' attention alright . . . see that sky, those clouds coming off the mountain? Gonna be more snow tonight, then turn wicked cold.

—Your house okay? You got enough of everything?

—Reckon I'll be fine.

Wiggins waits for something more, then turns and walks back around his car, climbs in slowly, shouts over his shoulder.

—You take care now, you hear?

He drives off, wheels spinning before they gain traction, the rear end of the car sashaying back and forth across the driveway. Roland watches the snow churned up by the car sparkle in the sun. A film of cloud turns the sun into a milky white ball.

Yep, more snow coming.

December has quieted the world, halted the wave of noise from the roadwork.

He'd thought, way back last spring, that the noise was in his head, but it got louder and louder until it was like a swarm of angry bees all around him. He remembered that sound, that angry, threatening sound like a distortion of the air itself from when his father had those hives up behind the spring house. But this morning, this pale, sharp, winter morning, the bees are gone. He breathes a deep sigh. What is harvested is in and what was left unfinished is now covered with snow. There will be a tree or two to fell, wood to cut, once the snow has set up, but for now, there is less to do. Roland finds this somehow disturbing. The rest is welcome enough, but the emptiness of the days leaves too much time for thought and too much time for memory.

It is strange to him, how these memories come without him choosing. Why is he thinking of bees on a cold December day with snow on the way?

Makes no sense.

A lot of his thoughts these days make no sense. It's quiet, there isn't much to do, but that doesn't mean the mind slows down. Seems like the opposite to Roland, the thoughts keep coming, especially it seems, thoughts he'd rather not have in his head.

The first Sam, Samuel J. Dog Roland had called him, was a pup from a litter of eight dropped by Silas Bowker's bitch, Minnie. Roland was five, had ridden in the wagon down to the store with his mother to pick up some staples—dried beans, molasses—and there, in a big basket off to the side of the store, was a pile of motley-looking pups not more than a few weeks old, squirming and mewling around their mother who lay on her side with, it seemed to the boy, a bored expression. He knelt down and one of the smaller pups, a patchy white and tan and brown thing, crawled out of the basket and sat at Roland's feet looking up at him.

There were more after that: a yellow hound of some sort, a big rangy long-haired beast, a shaggy cattle dog, a big black mastiff-like animal. It got so anyone in the village come on a stray, they'd bring it up to the Tuttle Farm, bring it to Roland. All of them named Sam, all of them devoted to Roland. But now, on this December day, with deep snow on the ground and more on the way, when Roland comes in from the cold and sits at the kitchen table and looks over at the woodstove, all he sees is an empty place next to the stove where Sam used to lie curled nose to tail. He feels the loss of the dog in ways he has not allowed himself to feel other losses.

IT HAD STARTED SNOWING before Thanksgiving the last year Roland's father was alive and almost never stopped. Roland came home from school one day to find James pacing in the kitchen, all the lamps turned up bright.

"Look, Rollie, look what Pa got from the store." James held up a magazine.

Roland looked at it. "Popular Mechanics." That his father, who as far as Roland knew never read anything, had bought a magazine, even if it was only five cents, left him with nothing to say.

"Look," James said again.

He held the magazine open, pointed. Roland struggled with the words, but when he saw the drawings all he could think was . . . he remembered. His father remembered that time they were at Lambert's General Store in Claremont, Roland looking at those snowshoes up on the wall, asking, pleading.

"We ain't got two dollars to spare," his father had said. Roland started to beg, his father turned angry and pulled him out of the store. Made him wait in the wagon out in the cold until he was done with his business.

"What do you think, Rollie?" James pointed at the magazine on the kitchen table. "Think we can do it? Make our own snowshoes?"

Roland looked at the drawings, the diagrams, how to bend the frame, weave the rawhide, fashion the straps to hold them to your feet.

"But . . ."

"Pa said we could, you'n me, long as we keep up our chores. We'll need some ash. That's the best for bending." James went on like he was talking to himself as much as to his younger brother. "We've got some old harness we can cut up for the webbing and straps. Got plenty of straps. Yep, reckon we can do this alright."

The next three evenings they stayed in the barn after milking, working by the light of a single kerosene lantern, fingers numb with the cold, their father standing to the side, watching, breath pluming in the frozen air.

Roland still remembered that day, a sharp day, bright with cold, when he first strapped them on and walked on top of the snow out into the woods, into the thick, muffled quiet, and looked at the bare trees, their snow-draped branches, the birches white against the white snow, and the pines a green so dark it was almost black in the different light there in those woods. He saw animal tracks in the fresh snow. All that life he'd never known about. He saw little holes in the snow and coming out of them the skittery tracks of mice, voles, and leading out from a thicket of pine the pock-marks of a fox and where they met, a smear of blood on the snow.

THE YEAR ROLAND'S FATHER died the November rains had continued on into December, the fields brown and sodden and the bare trees black and wet against the tumbling sky. It was dark in the morning when young Roland walked to school, dark when he walked home.

"I ain't going no more," he said to his mother one bleak, wet morning. "I'm done with school."

"You need your education," his mother said.

"Why?"

His mother gave him the look. He had disappointed her again.

"What are you going to do when you're all grown up if you don't get an education?"

"Don't know . . . farm here, I guess."

"Come here," she said.

She sat across from him at the kitchen table.

"This farm can only hold up one family." She reached out her hand to him. "Marvin is the oldest, but he's got himself a job in Windsor, not going to stay on the farm. James is next, it will pass to him when I'm gone."

Roland had never thought about what would happen, had assumed they'd be together, him and Daniel and James. He didn't take her hand.

"Margaret's going to be married soon, starting her own family. I don't know what Daniel and Eliza will do. I worry about your future, Rollie. I want you to go to school. Will you do that? For me?"

What could he say?

The stove in the schoolhouse was cranked up high against the damp, and the schoolroom was hot and stifling and smelled of old clothes and unwashed young bodies. Roland hated being cooped up in that room. He longed to be outside, running wild, exploring. Especially now, his father dead and buried, the rain coming down, the roads deep in mud, near impassable, and the family locked in with their loss. On his way home he would think of his father, wonder what he had done that day then remember that his father would never do anything again.

Trudging home from school in the rain. The snowshoes that James made from the magazine his father bought hang in the barn. If only it would snow.

ABITHA, ALREADY A SMALL WOMAN, seemed to shrink after her husband died, but at the same time grow somehow stronger. She took the weight of managing the farm on her narrow shoulders. She worked with the girls, Margaret and Eliza—though they would have Margaret for only a few weeks—cooking, cleaning, churning butter, making the big wheels of cheese they sold through the dairy co-op. She made sure Daniel and James worked the dairy proper, milked at the right times, fed the cows the right amount. She put Roland in charge of the chickens, letting the birds out in the morning, gathering the eggs, cleaning the coop, closing it at night.

This seemed to Roland a judgment, a criticism, and in his boyish way, he resented it. His older brothers got all puffed up, treated him like a child. He blamed the chickens and was less than careful in his duties and there came a night, not three weeks after Albert's passing, he forgot to close the coop. The family was jolted awake in the middle of the night by a pack of coyotes baying and yipping and barking as they came closer and closer, until they tore through the barnyard like a wild, terrible wind. Roland heard the rooster crow, heard the hens scream and squawk, heard the panicked birds crash against the walls of the coop, heard the coyotes growl and rip and tear.

The family scrambled into their clothes and charged down the stairs. Daniel grabbed a lantern, James the shotgun off the wall, but they were too late. They heard the retreating noise of the pack as they carried off their victims, the coyotes yipping and yapping as if they were laughing at the stupidity of humans.

Roland had never been able to erase the memory of standing in the coop next to his mother in her housecoat and rubber boots as she held up the lantern. There was blood everywhere, clumps of feathers, body parts. In a corner, covered with hay, they found the battered body of Goliath, their prize rooster. He was still alive, but grievously wounded, a wing half torn off, one leg chewed to shreds. He lay there, that rooster that had won a blue ribbon at the county fair, that had fought to save his hens, dying for sure.

"Oh, Rollie," his mother said.

In the morning they searched the farmyard, found more bloodied body parts, but also five birds, four layers and a banty rooster, hiding in the bushes and trees, alive and unharmed. Roland, without a word said, cleaned up the mess, collected the bits and pieces the coyotes had left behind, raked and swabbed out the coop. He left the remains of the dead birds at the edge of the forest for the wild animals to finish what they'd started.

"Rollie," his mother said. "When someone gives you a job to do, you got to do it. You don't always get to choose what job that is."

"Pa never did the chickens. Said it was women's work."

"Maybe not, but I'll tell you one thing, young man. Your father sure did love his eggs for breakfast."

In the family's fragile tight-rope existence, the loss of those birds, of the eggs, the meat they provided, could mean hunger that winter. Word got out about the chicken massacre, neighbors came by with a bird or two, and they rebuilt the flock, but it was a lesson Roland never forgot. Take care of your animals.

EVERY YEAR, AS DECEMBER trailed toward the longest night of the year, the Women's Committee of the Baptist church in Wethersfield took to the roads and visited the farms, reaching out to the families in their remote homes, bringing fruitcake that they had spent the first two weeks of the month baking. Roland's father had always made it a point to be scarce when they showed up. "Here come the church ladies," he'd say.

Two years after Albert's death, the weather had been clear and cold and the roads were rolled flat. Roland heard the squeak of the sled runners coming up Mountain Road. He looked out the window and watched the one-horse sled turn into the dooryard, plumes of snow swirling up into the air, sparkling in the thin winter sun. Two women, one of them the imposing Mrs. Wilhelmina Burr, head of the Women's Committee, the other a woman he didn't recognize, sat tall and rigid on the front bench of the sled swaddled in thick layers of proper black robes and scarves.

"Here come the church ladies," he said to himself.

It had been like that since his father died, everything Roland did, everything he saw, he would hear his father's voice, remember how his father did something, or wonder what his father would have thought of what had happened. At times, it seemed to the boy that he was closer to his father dead than he had been when he was alive. And so, like his father, he made himself scarce.

"I'll stoke up the furnace, Ma," he said.

He hated that dark basement, that beast of a furnace with its round metal arms spreading up and out to the underside of the floor like it was reaching up to pull the whole house down into its firebox. The family had burned coal in the past, and he hated the oily, sinister smell that still lingered, the taste of it on the back of his throat. Roland stoked up the fire with wood so the ladies could sit in the parlor and be warm and drink their tea. He climbed quietly back up the stairs, sat on the top landing, the door to the living room cracked open.

"We haven't seen you at our committee meetings lately, Abitha," Mrs. Burr said.

"I have been very busy since Albert died, as I'm sure you can understand."

There was a note of irritation in his mother's voice that surprised Roland, sitting there eavesdropping. She had always been a churchgoer.

"Well, dear," Mrs. Burr said, "it's when times are hard that we most need the support of our Lord. I know when my husband, Tucker, passed, the church was a true comfort."

To this, his mother said nothing.

"And how are you doing, dear?"

"I'm fine, Mrs. Burr," Roland heard Eliza say. She had a quiet, high voice. A voice suited to a younger girl. Roland hadn't realized Eliza was there with the ladies, and he felt a surge of sympathy for her, trapped with those old biddies. Biddies. That was another thing his father called them.

"Eliza, dear . . . would you be so kind as to go into the kitchen and make us some tea?" Mrs. Burr said.

"Go ahead, sweetheart," his mother said. "It's okay."

There was a silence, then a rustling of clothing, a squeaking of chair legs on the bare wood floor.

"We were talking about Eliza at our last committee meeting," the other woman said, almost in a whisper. It had a rough edge to it, this voice, a little gravelly, not clear and superior-sounding like Mrs. Burr.

"Oh?" his mother said.

"There is some concern of her being here, unmarried, with three young men," she continued.

"There are places, homes, for young women like her," Mrs. Burr said, trying to put as much understanding and Christian charity into her voice as she could, but to Roland's ear, failing.

"Is that so." Roland felt his mother stiffen, heard that steel that came into her voice. "Like her . . . exactly what do you mean by *like her*?"

"You know, dear . . ."

"No. I'm afraid I do not know."

"Well—"

"Now that I think of it," his mother interrupted, "I forgot. We're all out of tea."

Roland heard chairs being pushed back, the rustling of stiff clothes, and footsteps heading for the door.

"You can come out now, Rollie," his mother said. Three chairs had been pulled out from the wall, placed in a cozy circle. She started moving things around.

"The nerve," she said. "Can you imagine?" She grabbed a chair, pushed it back to the wall like she was mad at it. The legs of the chair grated across the hardwood floor. "The nerve . . ."

Abitha looked at Roland. "Remember one thing, Rollie. We Tuttles stick up for each other. That's what a family does."

Roland found Eliza in the kitchen standing by the window, watching the church ladies march out across the snow-packed yard, all huffed up, stomping their feet. They climbed onto the sled and perched on the driving bench like two big black crows.

Mrs. Burr snapped the whip and off they went.

"They was talking about you," Roland said.

"I know."

"Ain't right to talk about a person behind their back."

"Everyone does," Eliza said. "I hear them sometimes, when they think I'm not listening."

"Don't you pay them no mind," Roland said.

"They say I'm slow," she said. "I . . . it's just that sometimes . . ."

Eliza had grown into a beautiful young woman, tall, slender, delicate, with long golden hair. She was nineteen, but she had a child's simplicity that made her seem much younger. Roland had heard the talk, even heard his mother talking to a neighbor one time. What did they mean, slow? Eliza was quiet, for sure . . . peaceful. She had trouble with complicated tasks, had to be reminded about things, but worked hard alongside their mother in the kitchen.

"I think you're a fine gal," Roland said.

It'd been two years since their father had died and Roland still remembered how everyone in the family took it on their own, never talked about it, retreated into themselves, leaving him, the youngest, to deal with the tragedy alone. Everyone

except Eliza. She'd comforted him, told him everything was
going to be alright.

Weren't nothing wrong with her, far as he could see, except
what other people put on her.

CHRISTMAS WAS A SPECIAL TIME for the Tuttle family when
Roland was young, his father still alive, his grandmother well,
the farm prospering. Roland's father was a reluctant keeper
of Christmas, but Abitha loved Christmas with a delight and
excitement that was childish in its way.

"What's the big deal?" Roland said one day as Christmas
approached. He was ten, trying to be like his father.

His mother had looked at him as if wondering how she
could have such a heathen as a son, then shook her head
and smiled. They were in the kitchen. She sat him down at
the table.

"You like Santa Claus, don't you? When I was a little girl,
my father didn't allow Santa Claus to come to our house."

Roland squirmed in his chair. He couldn't remember his
mother ever talking about her family. No one talked about
her family. He'd asked Gramma Ida once why he didn't
have two grandmas like the kids he knew at school and she
shushed him and said, "We don't talk about that."

"She"—meaning his mother—"got a mother, don't she?"
Roland said.

"Don't you be fresh with me, Boy," Gramma Ida said. "You
want to know, you ask your mother. See where that gets you."

Now, here he was and his mother was talking about her
father.

"Why couldn't Santa Claus come to your house?"

"My father . . ." she looked away as she talked. "He had

certain beliefs. Christmas was for church, for praying, not for foolishness." She sighed, and Roland, even at ten, could see that she was sad. He didn't want her to be sad, he wanted her to be happy. He started to reach to her, but pulled his hand back, not sure what to do.

"But, I love foolishness at Christmas, don't you?" she said. "The candles and the tree. I love the tree, the way the trim sparkles, the way it smells when we first bring it into the house and the snow melts all over the floor." She looked at him. "It's okay to be a boy, Rollie. Don't grow up too fast. You love it too, don't you?"

Yes, he thought, he did, but what he loved most was seeing his mother happy and smiling.

ABITHA, MARGARET, AND ELIZA would start decorating the place long before the actual holiday. There were garlands and wreaths and candles in the windows. Closer to the day, his father would take the four boys up the hill to cut a tree, and they'd drag it down to the house through the snow and set it up in the sitting room, the ice and snow on the branches melting and dripping all over the floor. They'd dry the floor and put a white cloth sewn from bleached grain sacks around the base to make it look like snow, and decorate the tree with homemade ornaments, paper chains and cut-outs, strings of stale popcorn, and the few store-bought glass ornaments the family owned.

Those ornaments were his mother's special treat. Albert would hitch up the wagon, take Abitha all the way into Claremont to Lambert's General Store and buy her an ornament, a new one each year: a red ball one year, a silver and yellow pendant the next, a silver star, a green and gold elf, a red Santa Claus. Once the tree was decorated, there'd be hot cider, and they'd all sit around the parlor admiring their handiwork, and Gramma Ida would declare it to be the best one yet.

The big house was warm—the furnace stoked—and bright, lit with oil lamps and candles, the woodwork in the sitting room glowing golden brown in all that light.

THE LIGHT IS WHAT ROLAND remembers about Christmas, the house all lit up at night, and those glass ornaments, how his mother loved those glass ornaments. They're still here, somewhere, those decorations that the family had acquired over so many years, put away in boxes by his mother the last Christmas she was home, probably up in the attic.

No, he thinks, that ain't right.

Margaret pointed them out on the tree at her house the one time he'd gone up to St. Johnsbury for the holiday. Seemed a long way to go, but his mother was there, and Abitha had written to say how much she wanted him to come up for Christmas.

It was 1932. Abitha had been living with Margaret for two years. Roland rode the train from Windsor to St. Johnsbury, first time ever. Didn't much like it.

Margaret, William, their three kids, Abitha, and Roland sat in chairs in the living room. The tree was in the corner, shiny with Abitha's glass ornaments and store-bought tinsel and new red and green electric lights. William was proud of those electric lights.

"Those lights are the latest thing," he said. "I had them sent all the way up from Boston."

"This is the prettiest tree yet," Margaret said.

"You say that every year," Becky, Margaret's oldest, said.

"Well, it's true!" Margaret said. "Some of these ornaments are almost fifty years old. It means so much to me to have them."

She held up a silver and pale-blue ball with a round opening in one side, the ball cut away in receding layers of silver like you were looking into the wrong end of a telescope to a little scene in there all done in red and gold of the baby Jesus and the manger and the animals.

"Do you remember when you got this one, Momma?" Margaret said.

"Of course I do, dear," Abitha said. "It was the last one your father ever bought for me . . ."

"Do you remember, Roland? You must of been eleven. It was the Christmas before Pa died." Margaret got all misty. Christmas did that to her. Like she was remembering everything and missing it all.

They spent the days after Christmas in the sitting room, Roland getting restless, thinking about the farm, worrying that Jack, the hired man, wouldn't do things right, wouldn't milk proper, wouldn't feed the cows enough. There was a heater built right into the fireplace, and Roland kept feeling like he had to get up, get more wood, even though he knew the thing used kerosene. Margaret said she'd seen enough firewood growing up to last her a lifetime, and besides, it was dirty, bringing all that wood in, and she liked a clean house, she did.

When Roland looked at his mother, dwarfed as she was by the big stuffed chair by the heater, it was like he was seeing and hearing his grandmother, Ida May Tuttle, all over again.

"I think about all of them, you know," his mother said. "All those Tuttles. That first winter, when they almost didn't make it, and Susannah . . ." She drifted off, thinking, perhaps, about those two babies of her own that'd never had a chance to live.

She went on and on about Edmund and Susannah, folks dead and gone long before she was born. She'd tell the story of Edmund crossing the Green Mountains to find land on the Connecticut River, of the Indians standing by that road through the mountains.

She told these stories as if she was the one who crossed those mountains, cleared that land, but in all that talk, never a word about James or Eliza or Daniel. This bothered Roland. Why go on about ancestors from a hundred years ago and not your own kin? But then, Roland thought, watching his mother when she turned silent and drifted off, maybe it's easier to talk about things that are far away than things that are close.

"You know, there was six of them living in that kitchen building—can you imagine it?— before your Grandpa Tuttle, the first Roland, and his father, Lucius, built the big house."

"How did you come to know all this?" Margaret said.

"Your Great-Grandma Patience told Gramma Ida all this. Ida May told me, and I'm tellin' you. It's important," Abitha said to Margaret. "You need to pay attention. It's us women that keep the stories alive. A family's nothing without its history."

DECEMBER DAYS ARE SHORT, nights long. Roland walks to the barn in morning darkness, carrying a kerosene lantern, returns to the house in darkness. He walks to the barn in evening dark, the yellow circle of light caressing the snow, returns to the house in the dark. Christmas for Roland is like any other day. He does his chores, feeds the animals, keeps the kitchen fire going. Doesn't bother with decorations.

The snow from days before has been scoured hard, chalk-like, by the wind, so dry it squeaks underfoot. The sun's barely up when he walks out to the barn for the second time that morning. The weak winter light slants across the yard. The shadow of the oak down by the road stretches all the way to the barn, its black fingers reaching up the side like it's trying to pull the old building down.

Roland feeds the cows, puts hay and corn fodder in the bins, pours the hot water he's carried from the kitchen to thaw out their water trough.

It's snowing as he heads back toward the house and the wind picks up and tumbling squalls of snow blow across the fields, filling in behind fence posts, drifting up against the front of the house. His eyes crust over. It's hard to see. He looks straight up and can see a circle of pale blue sky, but the wind has kicked up a ground blizzard and a windblown wall of snow swirls around him, closing off the world. He can barely see the dark bulk of the big house through the blowing snow. He's squinting down toward the road when he sees something moving, a shadowed figure behind a white curtain, coming up toward him.

Who the hell is that, he thinks, out in this?

The shadow gets closer. It's a dog. A neighbor's? Lost in the blowing snow?

The dog is moving slow; as it gets closer he sees that it can barely walk. A gust of wind nearly knocks it over. It's medium sized, its fur plastered with snow and dirty lumps of ice. Roland can't tell what color it is. Frozen icicles of drool hang from its muzzle. The dog drags itself up to him, collapses at his feet and looks up, its eyes crusted with ice.

Roland carries the dog into the kitchen and lays it down on the floor next to the woodstove. He stokes up the fire, puts a saucer of milk to warm, and sits looking at the beast there on the floor lying in the middle of a spreading puddle of snowmelt.

—Where on earth did you come from? he says.

The dog doesn't move. Its eyes are closed. Its fur is wet and matted, clumps hanging off in places next to bare skin. Ribs showing. No collar. No sign a person ever cared for the beast. The stove hisses and crackles. Spots of yellow light from the air vents of the stove tremble on the dog's dark fur. Roland is soaked through from carrying the dog, starts to feel chilled. He sits in his chair and watches the dog, and wonders how this animal came to be here, came to find him, how the poor thing ended up out in a blizzard, alone, starving. He realizes at that moment how much he's missed Sam, missed having a dog, having somebody to talk to.

You talk to yourself, people start to think you're crazy, but talking to a dog? Well, that's okay.

And he feels again the pain of losing Sam, a dog that had been his daily companion for more than a decade, a pain he had walled himself off from until this mangy mutt staggered up the driveway into his life. Is it breathing? Is it even alive?

—Where did you come from? Roland says again.

The dog's ears prick at his voice. It raises its head, looks at him with dull red-rimmed eyes, then flops back down.

Roland kneels next to it. His knees creak and crack. He strokes the dog's wet head, scratches behind its ears. He goes back to the stove, takes some stale bread, mashes it up in the warm milk, and places it in front of the dog. A sniff. The dog laps at the milk—bright pink tongue, white milk drips on brown fur. The dog is too tired to move. Roland pulls it over closer to the stove, out of the puddle. It gives a low moan and falls asleep.

—Guess you're here to stay, he says. What'm I going to call you? I'm done with Sam. Can't do it. Too many memories. He was a great one, that Sam, but he was the last. Guess I'll have to think on it for a bit.

Roland Tuttle is a man who believes that the things that happen in this life are somehow connected, that one thing leads to another, and as he sits in the kitchen looking at this stray dog that appeared out of nowhere, he ponders and wonders. How did the dog know to come here? Who or what knew of his, Roland's, loneliness, sent this beast? How did this dog come up the road at that moment? If Roland hadn't been standing there looking that direction, at just that moment, the dog would have died in that blizzard for sure.

Over the next days and weeks Roland nurses the dog back to health, feeds it milk with bread, fries up salt pork, mixes it in, fries oat cakes. He doesn't have much, but what he has, he shares, and soon light returns to its eyes and flesh to its bones. The dog waits on the porch at first when Roland does his chores in the barn, but soon follows him everywhere, sits by him as he milks, drinks warm milk from a pan Roland fills straight from a cow's udder. They become inseparable. The dog sits by him as he rests in the evening, waits at the base of the steep stairs when Roland goes up to sleep, then one night climbs those stairs right behind him.

But, through this time together, Roland can't bring himself to give the dog a name, as if the act of naming something somehow puts a limit to it, marks a coming end.

January

SNOW IS PILED IN FRONT of the Town Hall. A record low temperature of thirty-six degrees below zero is recorded. The extreme cold has cracked the stone slab of the village's World War I Memorial. A notice has been posted for a special town meeting in February, and all are urged to attend. The new snowplow won't start; the diesel is too thick to flow. There is a chimney fire in the residence behind Bowker's General Store; the volunteer firemen put it out before too much damage is done. The building is coated in ice from the fire-hoses.

≈

THE YEAR TURNS, but Roland Tuttle takes no notice. Whether it is December 31 or January 1 the bitter cold and long nights are the same to him. He rises early, before dawn. He can see his breath in the frigid air of the bedroom. Pulls his coveralls over the long underwear, once white, now gray, he slept in. Puts his socks on. The heel's getting thin on the left. The dog follows him down the stairs, goes over to the stove, looks at it then crawls under the pile of old wool blankets, sticks her brown head out, looks at the stove again, looks at Roland.

—I know, says Roland. I'll get right to it.

It's still dark outside, but the kitchen windows shimmer with the snow-reflected light of the stars. The light gives the everyday objects of the kitchen a ghostly glow.

'Snowlight' his grandmother called it.

"Only time you can see the spirits," Gramma Ida said one

time, "is snowlight." She leaned closer. "But only if you don't look. Look at them, pffft"—she flicked her hand—"they're gone. Only can see them if you're not looking."

This puzzled the boy. "How can you see 'em if you're not even looking?"

"Hush," she said. "Eat your porridge."

Snowlight. The word has stayed with him.

And brought more back memories of Gramma Ida.

She had been such a presence in Roland's first years. Hobbled by arthritis—"the rheumatiz" she called it—she spent most of her days in a rocking chair by the kitchen cookstove, but somehow seemed to direct the operation of the farm. The "boss" his father called her. But she was more than that; she was the keeper of the family history.

She was a believer in spirits, in ghosts, in the invisible presence of the dead.

"When folks are born and die in a house, they don't never leave," she said more than once to the boy.

Her chair is still there, by the stove. Roland sits in it often enough, but sometimes, when he first comes into the kitchen, it's as if somebody is already sitting in it, and he sits in one of the metal chairs by the kitchen table, and other times he'd swear it moves all by itself, knows it's the loose floorboards, but still . . .

There's nothing moving outside. The snow, the heavens, are fixed, immobile, but the light off the snow coming through the windows seems to waver and shimmer, and when he looks in the shadowed corners of the kitchen he can see how you might come to believe in spirits.

Roland lights the lantern, takes kindling from the woodbox, starts the fire.

A JANUARY MORNING, Roland fifteen years old, his father three years gone. His mother had been up for two hours. The kitchen was warm, yellow-bright, oatmeal bubbling on the stove, coffee boiling. Steam filled the air. Condensation ran down the flat, opaque windows, black with the darkness of winter morning. Roland slouched at the table, sleepy-eyed, his hair a jumbled mess. Eliza stirred the oatmeal, looking more like her mother every day. A cold blast of air announced James and Daniel in from milking. They stomped their feet, clapped and rubbed cold hands.

Kitchen smells—scalded coffee, damp clothes, kerosene—and barn smells—fresh milk, manure, hay—mingle in a thick odor that, if you were a stranger, maybe a pack peddler come to show the woman of the house some wares, would turn you back at the door, but when you were used to it, smelled of home.

The family was seated for breakfast. Abitha said grace. James and Daniel were quiet for a moment then loud, talking fast, red-faced from the cold. Roland still with sleep in his eyes.

"Cows are good, Ma. Two more full cans in the milk house," Daniel said.

"Well, bring the milk in, put it in the buttery," their mother said. "It's Monday. Time to churn. How's the new girl doing?"

"You mean Maggie?" James looked at Daniel, Daniel winked at Roland, and the boys could hardly keep from laughing.

"That's not nice," Eliza said.

"You shouldn't name a cow after your sister," Abitha said.

"Does kinda look like her," James said.

Their mother looked at him, shook her head.

"We're going up to the woods today," James said. "Time to start cutting."

"I'm going too." Roland looked up from his oatmeal.

"Look who's awake," James said. "Tomorrow's your turn to get up, start the fire."

"No, Rollie. You have school," his mother said.

"They need my help, Marvin's gone."

"He's been gone for years," James said. "Can't understand why he wants to work in a factory instead of here on the farm, like a real man."

"Jimmy!" Whenever their mother called him Jimmy, it meant she wasn't kidding. "You like that hot coffee you're drinking?"

"Yes'm."

"That coffee was bought with money Marvin earned. Don't go talking him down. We each need to do what we're good at if we're going to make it."

James looked down at the table. He was a big strong man of twenty-three, but when his mother spoke to him that way, he became like the blond-haired boy he'd once been.

"Rollie," Daniel said. "Want to help me with the horses?"

The two jumped up, grabbed their coats, headed for the barn, happy to escape the tense kitchen.

It had been an easy winter, as winters go, only about a foot of fresh snow on top of the solid crust from a recent thaw. The dray pulled nice and easy as the three Tuttle boys headed up the hill toward the woodlot. The mountain watched as they drove the horses through a wide gate, up the rolling pasture, through another gate into the woods. The sky above the white frosted summit was pockmarked, like the underside of a sheet of hammered lead. Roland watched the cloud ceiling flow in from the west, watched it lower and wrap around the mountain, watched it flow away to the east in waves of gray.

"Snow coming," he said.

"Don't get in the way," James said.

It felt somehow wrong to come up here and disturb the silence of these woods in winter, James and Daniel yakking the way they did. You never got a moment's peace when those two were around. His mother could barely get them to shut up in church. It got so bad, she stopped bringing them. They were born one right after the other, so much alike folks thought they was twins. Light colored hair, blue eyes, where Roland was dark. Thick of body, heavy of leg, where Roland was lean and light-footed.

James liked being in charge. By rights, it should've been Marvin. James was too impulsive, too headstrong. He'd rush in where more thought might be helpful. But Marvin was living in Windsor. One thing Roland agreed with James on: why would anyone want to spend their working day in a dim, oil-smelled-up factory instead of out here in the clean, sharp air?

Roland sat on a broad stump, big around as a table, in a grove of oaks, and tried to remember when they'd cut that giant back when their father was alive. He watched his brothers attack a big birch not more than fifty feet away with the two-man saw. Roland looked at the tree. It was a fine tree standing by itself with a heavy trunk at least two, maybe two and a half feet, across. It rose straight up, black-spotted white, for a good forty, fifty feet, then forked in a giant Y with two main branches reaching out to a broad canopy.

Lotta wood in that tree, Roland thought.

The saw kept binding, James pushing too hard, impatient as always. Roland, since he could remember, had loved working the woodlot. His father had been different here, more thoughtful, calmer somehow. It was the one place where he seemed to have time for young Roland.

"Tryin' harder don't always get more done," his father used to say. "You got to work slow, think about what you're doing. Get careless, you could get yourself killed."

The snow in the wood was criss-crossed with wandering deer tracks. He could see patches where the deer had dug down into the snow, searching for acorns.

The scritch-scratching of the saw stopped.

"Timber!" James yelled.

James loved to yell timber. Even back when they were young boys working with their father and a hired man or two, James had to be the one to yell timber.

Roland heard a loud creak, then a ripping, tearing sound. They'd cut so the tree would fall away, but the tree must have had another idea, or they must not have cut the notch right, lined it up proper, because it was falling straight toward him.

"Look out!" Daniel shouted.

Roland sat on the stump like he was stuck in place. He heard a cracking and crashing above him as if the sky was breaking up into little pieces.

"Roland!" Daniel shouted and Roland looked up and saw the crown of that tree, white and black against the gray sky, coming down toward him, crashing into the crowns of the oaks, branches breaking and shattering and flying up into the air, and then with a painful moan the birch stopped, hung up on one of the big oaks, and bits of bark and broken branches and chunks of wood rained down all around him.

His brothers ran up, breathless, panicked.

"Jesus H. Christ, Rollie, what the hell you doing?" James said. "Why didn't you run?'

"Didn't need to. I could see it was gonna hang up soon's you started sawing on it. You never were good at lining up where to fell."

"Why didn't you say?"

"Wouldn't of listened if I had."

"If Ma finds out about this, she'll kill me," James said.

"Don't see why she should," Roland said.

Roland stood and the three of them walked away and looked back at the tangled, dangerous mess. The base of the birch was held to its stump by a thin curtain of wood like it didn't want to let go, the rest leaned away almost horizontal to where the birch's fork was interlocked with a single large branch of the oak.

"What're we gonna' do now?" Daniel said.

"It's a widow-maker for sure," James said.

"Since none of us are married," Roland said, paused "don't think there's any widows likely to be involved."

James looked at Daniel. Daniel looked at James. And then they both looked at Roland and all three collapsed into the snow, laughing.

"You are one piece of work," James said to Roland.

"You see that branch?" Roland pointed. "It's what's holding the whole thing up. Somebody's got to climb up, cut it off."

And Roland did and the big birch was there lying on the snow-covered ground where it was supposed to be. The three brothers sat on the bole of the tree, drank tea from their father's old glass jug which they'd kept wrapped in a thick blanket. The tea was warm and sweet.

"Good thing Pa didn't see that," Daniel said. "He would've been real sore."

"Made us sleep in the barn," James said.

"For a week," Daniel said.

"Two weeks," Roland said.

"No supper," Daniel said.

"No breakfast neither," James said.

It started to snow, soft at first, big flakes drifting around them, dusting their hats, settling on their shoulders, then harder, piling up on the dray, melting on the backs of the horses, deepening the quiet, until everything was silence.

ROLAND CUTS HIS FIREWOOD by hand, always has, always will. Can't stand the grating noise of the new-fangled power saws, the nasty buzzing, the howling, the smell of oil, gasoline. No, he's always done things by hand, the way a man should, and is going to keep on doing them by hand.

He starts on next year's firewood in January when the ground is frozen hard.

Roland brings his two horses, Sam and Joe, out from the paddock, their winter coats all shaggy and thick. Hitches them up to the logging dray.

So many memories working these woods with his father and brothers, cutting the logs for next winter's firewood. Fueled up on hot tea and fried oatcakes and salt pork, they would wrap themselves in layers of hand-knit sweaters and scarves, top it with a canvas barn coat, and step out into a morning so cold it made your nose burn, your boots squeak on the hard-packed surface of the snow.

The cold, how could you forget the cold? Twenty, thirty below.

Your eyes watered, tears froze on your cheeks into little balls of ice, and your breath turned to ice crystals that stuck to the front of your coat.

Roland leads his horses up through the snow-covered fields, the dog—Brown Dog he's started to call her; turns out, you don't name something, it names itself—following in the ruts made by the sled's runners, her fur crusted with lumps of snow and ice. Hard to believe this strong walking beast is the same dog that came staggering up his driveway. They pass through an open fence gate into the park-like woods, the oaks, maples, occasional larch, hackberry, spaced as if they had been laid out and planted by man. The Tuttle men before him tended these trees like a garden, and now Roland does the same, choosing each year the right trees to cut.

He walks the forest in knee deep snow, in thin silver sunlight. Long shadows of the trees stripe the snow. He feels the snow against his legs, the cold through his canvas gaiters, tastes the clean, wood-scented air. He turns to the south, feels on his face the faint warmth of the January sun sneaking in through a gap between two tall oaks. He stops at a tree, studies it for awhile, moves on. Which one to cut? Whose time is it? He decides on a red oak, its broad crown so high above him it seems to touch the sky.

The horses stamp their feet, their breath plumes in the frigid air, crystals of frost form on their muzzles.

He lines up where he wants it to fall. There is an open lane between two maples. He walks around the bole of the tree, analyzing, thinking. "Look for the right place to cut," his father always said. "Before you start, cut a wedge on the side where you want it to fall, then come in from the other side, a little high, on a downward angle, and she'll drop where you want her, easy as that."

Roland prefers the axe, though some thought it easier to use the saw. He likes the feel of the helve in his hands, the weight of the head as it arcs through the air and cuts into the flesh of the tree, the sound it makes, a solid chunk of a noise in the cold air.

He swings; the axe bites.

First the downfall side, Roland opens up a wide cut like a strained smile in the tree's trunk—though he doubts the tree is real happy about it—then attacks the upside. The chunks of green oak flying up into the air release a bitter, acrid smell. "Piss oak," his father called it. He starts to sweat despite the bitter cold, stops, peels off a sweater, goes back to work.

There's a moment before a tree falls when, to Roland, everything seems to stop and the world to hold its breath. When you've cut in far enough on the upside so that a thin line of wood holds the massive tree and the tree stands there not moving, like that tree's saying I ain't gonna fall, nosir, but then it moves a little and starts to lean so slow you hardly notice it at first. This is the moment when you know if the tree is going to fall where you want it to, or if there is a twist in the grain somewhere deep in the middle of the trunk that you couldn't see, and the damn thing is going to spin and twist and head right for you, and you'll have to run for your life. When you've cut right, the tree will fall where you planned.

A final blow from Roland's axe, and the oak leans away, then stops for a moment—but resistance to the pull of the earth is futile—and the tree falls through the canopy of the forest with a great rending of the air, gathering speed, ripping branches from the neighboring maples, and the silence of the winter forest is broken by a great crash and the earth shakes and the felled tree bounces up on its branches and then settles, quiet, still, waiting.

Brown Dog, who's learned to stay well away when Roland's felling, runs up, jumping and leaping through the deep snow, barking and snarling at the fallen tree.

Felling's the easy part, now the real work begins: limbing, stacking the slash, cutting the bole of the tree to length to be hauled down to the house on the dray. Roland remembers cutting with the two-man crosscut saw, his father saying, "Pull, don't push, gentle the saw through the wood."

Though his older brothers were much stronger than he, it was Roland who had the knack, his father had said, the feel, to ride the saw until the man and the boy and the saw were a single being, drawing the saw back and forth, smooth, like breathing, sawdust accumulating in equal conical piles on both sides of the log. Sometimes you had to knock a wedge into the top of the cut to prevent the saw blade from binding, but mostly, if you picked the right spot, you could cut all the way through and the log would fall away, ready for hauling.

Today, though, Roland is on his own, and he stands and looks at the giant he's felled, and knows it will be the work of days to get this one cut up and hauled back to the house. The one-man bucksaw doesn't cut like a two-man. It'll bind if you push too hard, but if you're patient, and Roland is nothing if not patient, she'll cut.

BACK AT THE HOUSE, the fatigue of a good day's work settles in his bones. He opens the wood stove, puts in a few sticks of kindling, two smaller logs, stands with the door open, and watches the kindling burn, flames licking and dancing around the logs. Maple takes a while to catch, but gives good heat once it's going. He sits close to the open fire, trying to warm up, Brown Dog curled at his feet. His hands and feet

throb with the returning blood flow. He only dragged down
two logs, and will have to go back up tomorrow—probably
the next few days—to finish. There'll be the cutting to stove
length, splitting, stacking. Keeping warm during a winter
like this is a full-time job.

There's a crash in the middle of the night. The whole
house shakes and Roland lies there knowing what it is but
not wanting to know. When he comes down the steep stairs
from the loft in the morning, the door from the woodshed
to the kitchen is wide open and snow has drifted across the
kitchen floor. He wades through the snow in his stocking
feet and peers into the woodshed. It's open to the sky, and
most of his winter's wood is buried under slabs and shards
of the collapsed roof and piles of snow. The collapse had
blown the door into the kitchen open. This last storm was
one snowfall too many.

He pulls his boots on over his wet socks and opens the
front door. Snow has drifted up against the door, must be
three, four feet deep. He crawls over the snowbank and
steps out into a blizzard, windblown snow so thick he can't
see the barn. It stings his eyes, freezes on his beard. He
wallows through the snow to the barn, returns with his
shovel. He clears out the kitchen as best he can. There's
enough dry wood in the woodbox to get the stove going—at
least he had the sense to fill it last night. The remaining
snow melts, flooding the kitchen floor. Brown Dog paces,
whining, looking for a dry spot. Roland heats water, sits
with a cup of weak coffee.

He curses himself for his laziness. Didn't used to put things
off. Should of shoveled that roof weeks ago.

All that day, Roland Tuttle is out in the blizzard shoveling, digging, clearing away the debris. The wood of the collapsed roof crumbles in his hands. He pulls firewood out of the debris until his back aches and his legs tremble with fatigue. His hands are numb with cold, his beard caked with ice and snow, and his eyes are near frozen shut. He piles the rescued firewood in a mound outside the kitchen door. The wood is crusted with snow. He doesn't bother covering it. Back and forth he goes into the woodshed, now little more than four rickety walls, coming out with an armload of firewood.

As the afternoon wears on the snow lessens, and then with a last few spits, stops. The storm is over. Shreds of wind-torn cloud blow away to the east, and the rim of the mountain glows faint orange against a scrubbed blue sky. The first stars appear on the eastern horizon. The temperature drops. Roland shivers in his sweat-soaked clothes.

He brings wood into the kitchen, stacks the splits in a tower near the woodstove to dry and stands in front of the stove, his clothes steaming. The smells of wet wool and drying wood fill the room. He'll re-stack the rest of it tomorrow, cover it with sheets of metal roofing off the old sugar house, but for now, time to rest. The kitchen begins to warm.

He looks around this familiar space, at the battered pans hanging from nails, the crockery on a long wooden shelf, the metal sign with its big yellow chick.

These same things have rested in their same places on those same shelves on that same wall for as long as Roland has been alive, but exhaustion has brought to him a strange clarity, and these familiar things seem somehow different, as if they are glowing, quivering.

SNOW IS UP TO THE windows and the storms keep coming, and in between the storms, the temperature drops to twenty, thirty below every night. It snowed another six, eight inches last night, but has cleared off by afternoon, the sky a pale, watery blue. The sun lingers above the southern horizon casting long shadows across the surface of the snow. As Roland trudges the narrow pat—more like a deep trench in the snow than a path—from the house toward the barn, the sun sets behind the mountain and the temperature drops. The cold are worries at his clothes, makes his eyes water, his forehead ache.

—Jesus, it is going to be a cold one, he says to the dog.

He feels it already, the air sucking the warmth, the life, out of him.

It's no warmer inside the barn. The cows stand patiently, necks in their yokes in the milking parlor. They look up, big brown eyes watery, muzzles covered in frost. Plumes of cow-breath swirl in the air. The wood surfaces of the barn—planked walls, posts, feed trough—are coated with hoarfrost.

The dish of milk he put out for the cats is frozen solid.

It is dark by the time he slogs back toward the house, staggering with the weight of the ten-gallon milk can. He'll have to keep it inside, it'd freeze hard in the unheated milk room. He's put fresh silage in the feed trough, laid hay in the stalls. Nothing else he can do, the cows are going to have to keep themselves warm. He's wearing three sweaters and the canvas coverall that was his father's but he can feel the cold trying to worm its way into him. It's hard to breathe. The air is bitter, thin. It's like you can't grab hold of it to pull it into your lungs. Ice crystals swirl in the light from his lantern as if the air itself is freezing.

The stars seem closer, brighter. He stops on the front porch and watches the moon rise up from behind the New Hampshire hills.

"Full moon always brings the worst cold," his father used to say.

Roland steps inside, stomps the snow off his boots, leaving big clumps on the floor. There is ice on the inside of the kitchen windows, the fire is almost out, water he left in a bowl in the sink has feathers of ice on the surface. He fills the firebox, leaves the door open to get it going, and stands in front of the open fire. He builds up the fire, leaves the air vent wide open, and waits while the kitchen warms.

When it's like this—the house snowed in, the cold everywhere—he can't help but think of Edmund and his family, how they lived in this space for years, can't help but wonder how they managed, and how Lucius and Patience and their four children, including the first Roland, still lived crowded into this single structure years later.

It must've been special, Roland thought, when, after years of being crammed in together, they moved into that big house with its parlor, dining room, upstairs bedrooms, and a furnace in the basement. Must have seemed grand.

Roland sits in the rocking chair warming his feet by the stove. He feels a sense of history reversing itself. This family of his, his ancestors, had moved forward, cleared land, built the big house, a new barn, outbuildings. Now, fields return to scrub—he cultivates less than half what they once did—the forest seems to creep down the mountainside toward the barn, and he has moved backward into the original house with its crooked, slanting floor and windows seized shut by the shifting of the stone foundation.

It is long since dark outside. January days so short you could miss them if you don't get going in the morning. He lights the kerosene lamp on the kitchen table, settles back, feels the heat of the stove sink into his bones.

He sits in Ida May's chair and remembers her story of Edmund and Susannah, and feels a slash of guilt that he has somehow allowed the woodshed that was their first shelter to fall to ruin. If, as his grandmother believed, Edmund was still here somewhere, what would he think? It's tolerable here, close to the fire, but on a night like this—the cold so sharp you can hear trees out in the woods crack and split—if you get near the windows, the thin walls, you can see your breath right here in the kitchen.

How had Edmund and Susannah survived?

Edmund Tuttle first knew he was dead when he couldn't feel the heat from the woodstove. He stands in a dark corner of the kitchen and looks at the old man half-asleep in the rocking chair. Surely, he isn't the only Tuttle?

Edmund drifts from the kitchen into the big house and looks at the table set for dinner and wonders where everyone is, wonders why he is here, in this house.

He walks outside. Wind has scoured the snow in the upper meadow to a hard scalloped crust, dusted with an inch or so of light powder. As he walks, his feet leave no marks in the snow. He can't feel the cold, but he remembers too well, that first winter, how the cold was like an invading force, constantly probing, sneaking in through the chinks and cracks in the walls of the hastily built cabin, how it worried at their clothing, finding its way in through the layers, and how it assaulted their very souls.

Susannah suffered the worst, and for the rest of his life, no matter how hard he worked and strived to make a good life for her here, he felt a burden of guilt that he, in his rashful youth, had put her through that long, cold, dark winter.

And when their first child, little Amelia, died even as she entered the world?

He strides up the hill to the meadow and the little copse of trees. The dark stars and thin, pale moon paint the sculpted snow with light and shadow.

In the grove, he looks for the graves. They are covered with bare winter vines. The snowy ground is littered with stones tossed here from the fields. The headstones have fallen over. He can see a corner of one—dark Vermont graystone poking up through the wrack and rubble—a shard of another.

To be forgotten like this brings a sadness to him that he thought he was done with. Had it all been for naught?

ROLAND TUTTLE HUDDLES in bed under a pile of blankets, the dog pressed up against his backside, both of them trying to keep warm. He listens to the north wind blowing across the fields in the dark, keening around the corners of the barn. A tree branch screeches against the metal roof of the house, a sound like a baby crying.

The world's getting colder, seems to him. It's gonna freeze up solid, and me and those poor cows and those damn fool chickens that lack the sense to go in at night, with it. He hears coyotes in the distance, yapping and barking and laughing. How the hell do they keep warm on a night like this?

February

SNOW DRIFTS OUT OF A FROTHY SKY. Day after day, a few more inches. Roads narrow as snowbanks grow. Travel is difficult. Folks stay home. There is a collision in the village where Main Street crosses the Post Road caused by high snowbanks blocking the drivers' view. No one is injured. Notices are posted at the Town Hall and Bowker's Store for the February 17 special town meeting. The river is jammed with large blocks of ice. The roof on Peterson's barn collapses. Deer huddle under hemlock trees. Some will starve before the winter is over.

~

AT THE FARM, SNOW IS PILED up past the windows, the light in the kitchen a filtered white that makes it hard to see the edges of things even in the middle of the day. The cold has eased, though, and Roland finds himself going outside in just a sweater. Snow blankets the farmyard. He walks the deep, narrow path out to the barn, feeds the cows, and lets them out into the feedlot. They don't go far, they've stomped out an area no more than twenty feet to a side. They stand, huddled together, noses in the hay and corn fodder he spreads every day.

There'll be ice under that hay, until the middle of summer.

He walks back to the house, the dog on his heels. Brown Dog stops, squats, does her business in the middle of the path. Same thing every day. Where else is she gonna go?

Roland waits until it freezes up hard, then tosses the turds off to the side with a shovel, but worries that he'll forget, the next snow will cover it up, and he'll track it into the house and the kitchen'll end up smelling like dog turd for the rest of the winter. Sometimes, he thinks, farming is nothing more than dealing with animal crap, shoveling out the barn, raking out the chicken coop, piling up the manure, spreading it on the fields.

Roland takes a seat on the porch and squints at the sun, a little higher in the southern sky, feels a bit of warmth on his face. There's not so much pressing down on him in deep winter, no planting, mowing, haying, harvesting. There's still work to be done—feeding, milking, keeping the fire going— but there's also time to watch the sun, the sky, the direction of the clouds as they drift across overhead, the wind in the trees. His life is marked by these things, how the sun rises a little more to the east, arcs a little higher in the southern sky, sets further up the mountain's ridge. He can feel his life, this place of his, tilting a little more to the warmth of that sun, coming back from the frozen depths of January.

The slow passage of time in the dead of winter leaves room for memory. When Roland was young, there was time to play, to build snow-forts in the yard, to skate in hand-me-down skates on the town pond the village men shoveled clear after every snowfall, to slide down the hill from the upper pasture on makeshift sleds.

It came to be known in the annals of Tuttle lore as the Last Great Toboggan Ride.

They were all in Lambert's General Store in Claremont, the boys—James, Marvin, Daniel and Roland—standing around while their father haggled with Walter Lambert over the price of a new, ready-made, axe handle. James, at fourteen, could not ever be doing nothing. He took down the latest issue of "The American Boy".

"Look at this," he whispered to Marvin. Held the magazine open. Roland, six years old, bounced on his toes trying to see what they were looking at. "Says here we can make our own toboggan." Nothing was too much for James. Always had been prone to big ideas.

They tried to keep the project a secret from their parents, but that was pretty much impossible.

"What do you think, Pa?" James said.

"Long as you keep up with your chores."

First they needed wood: long strips of ash to bend for the runners, maple for the cross-pieces. Marvin who had apprenticed at the Amsden Sawmill the summer before took the one-horse sled over the mountain one fine February day and came back with ten long pieces of ash, and a nice straight maple board.

"Said in the magazine you got to steam the wood so's you can bend it," James said.

"Think I don't know that?" Marvin said. "You forgetting I worked at the mill? I know about wood."

Things could have broke down right there. Marvin, being the oldest at sixteen, didn't appreciate James telling him what to do. James didn't mean to be bossy—once he got an idea, he got carried away. Roland watched as the two, Marvin and James, figured out how to work together, and soon they had a fire burning right there in the yard and a regular manufactory going. Daniel fetched wood for the fire, while James tended the boiling cauldron of water and Marvin held the ash over the steam, and then the two of them, Marvin and James, bent the thin strip of ash around a ten-gallon milk can and tied it tight with rope to hold the bend until it set.

And Roland? He tried to help, but mostly he watched.

The first day, they had all ten pieces bent, stacked in the barn. That evening, James was so excited he couldn't sit still at dinner, couldn't stop talking about how great it was going to be, their very own toboggan.

The next day, after morning chores, Marvin cut six pieces of maple to length with a handsaw. Then James and he laid the bent ash runners out on the workbench. James and Daniel wrestled the pieces into place as best they could—the front curves didn't exactly line up the way they had in the drawing in the magazine—and Marvin nailed the cross-pieces to the ash runners with eight-penny nails.

"What can I do?" Roland said.

"Stay out of the way," Marvin said.

They flipped the thing over, Marvin clinched the nails down flat. They strung rope along the sides to hold onto, and then, there it was: a toboggan, big enough for all six kids.

They dragged the toboggan up to the first pasture fence.

"Reckon we need a test run," James said.

It was a good little hill, but with five of them—Margaret, already working on being a lady, wanted nothing to do with the whole idea—sitting on it, the thing barely moved. It had been a warm, sunny, late-winter day, the temperature for the first time in months above freezing, the snow was soft, and they kept getting bogged down. That night a cold front came through and the snow firmed up. The town came by first thing in the morning and rolled Mountain Road flat and smooth.

This was their chance; conditions were perfect.

"Rollie," James said. "Think you could find Ma's furniture polish?"

They polished the bottom of the toboggan, using almost all of Abitha's furniture wax.

"Ma's gonna be sore," Daniel said.

It was the five of them, the boys and Eliza. Eliza was game for anything.

They hiked up the road, pulling the long sled to where the Tuttle land ended, turned around, pointed the toboggan down the steep hill.

"This is gonna be great!" James said.

Roland sat up front, Eliza behind him, her arms wrapped around his waist. Daniel, James and Marvin pushed to get it going, ran alongside, then jumped in and they were off, flying down the curving hill. They hit a rise, were almost airborne, Eliza laughing and screaming in Roland's ear.

They were going so fast wind whipped their faces. Snow crystals flew around them.

Maybe it was the weight of all five of them, maybe it was that the ash runners got tired of being bent up like that in front. Whatever it was, two of the boards sprang loose and snapped back to straight and dug in to the firm snow, and the front of the toboggan burrowed in behind, and the whole thing flipped up and over sending all five of them tumbling into the air.

They landed in a pile of Tuttles, Roland on the bottom, face pushed into the snow, Eliza on top of him, and Daniel on top of her, and James and Marvin on top of him. There was a moment when nobody knew what to do. Were they hurt?

Daniel came up sputtering and pulled Roland up out of the crater they'd made. Eliza was all covered in snow and looked like she was about to cry, but she was okay, and James looked at Marvin like he was going to be mad—like it was Marvin's fault, like maybe he should've used more nails—then they were both laughing, and then all five of them, piled up there in the snow, snow in their hair, snow down their clothes, were laughing so hard their sides hurt.

They caught their breath, looked up, saw their father standing by the side of the road, arms crossed.

The toboggan lay there all split into pieces.

Roland said, "It'll make good kindling."

There was a scary silence.

Albert looked down at them, a scowl on his face, but then he couldn't hold it, and he cracked up and started laughing and slapping his leg and shaking his head, and then they were all laughing again, rolling in the snow, and their father walked off still laughing.

ROLAND'S SITTING IN HIS mother's rocking chair on the porch, the winter sun full on his face, smiling at the memory. A cloud breaks loose from the cloud-cap that seems to have settled permanently on the summit of Mount Ascutney and drifts across in front of the sun, and the January cold that's been hiding in the shadows hits him. Roland's breath billows out, rolling and swirling. Then the sun returns, pushes the cold back into the shade.

Eddie Wilson comes rattling up the driveway on his big green John Deere tractor. He's got a plow fixed to the front and is wearing a red plaid hat with big fleecy earflaps sticking out like bird wings. He shuts the tractor down and wades up through the snow and leans against a porch column.

—Nice hat, Roland says.

Wilson looks down the valley. They can't see the road work

but both know it had reached five or six miles away before
winter shut it down.

—Finally got some quiet around here, Eddie says.

—'Til you showed up.

Eddie can't see Roland smile through his beard.

—Thought you might want plowing out, Eddie says.

—That'd be alright. Roland looks down at the dog lying on
her side in the pale winter sun. Brown Dog here'd appreciate
it. Roland reaches down, scratches the dog's ears. Brown Dog
rolls onto her back, looks at Eddie.

—Guess you better give her a rub, Roland says.

—How come you never named her? Eddie says as he rubs
her belly.

—Named her Brown Dog.

—Well . . . Eddie shakes his head. She is brown. I'll give
you that.

—How's your Pa?

—Not doin' too good.

—Sorry to hear that. And Annabelle?

—Ma's gettin' old.

—Happens . . .

—What's it like? Eddie says.

—What?

—Bein' old.

—Like bein' young, except it ain't.

Eddie looks at Roland like he has no idea what the man said.

Roland watches Eddie crank up the tractor and push the
snow around until there's a nice flat open yard and piles of
snow next to the barn most of the way up to the eaves. Then,
with a wave, Eddie heads down the drive back toward his
farm, his hat flapping in the wind like a chicken too dumb

to know it can't fly, looking so silly Roland laughs, outright laughs, for the first time in weeks.

Homer Wiggins drives up not long after Eddie finished plowing the dooryard. Roland hears the car, comes out of the kitchen.

—Margaret called me, Wiggins says.

—You don't say.

—Told me to tell you that her husband is coming down tomorrow to pick you up, that you're coming to Sunday dinner whether you like it or not, and that she won't take no for an answer.

THE FRONT PORCH OF THE big house faces south. Standing here like this—the February sun warm on your face, reflecting off the house, warming the air around you—you could start to think winter is about done and spring is right around the corner, but Roland knows, you believe that, you're a darn fool.

Didn't wait long, there he is, Mr. William Fairbanks, in a long blue and white car pulling in to the plowed dooryard, scattering Roland's few chickens off in a panic.

—Nice car, Roland says as he slips into the front seat.

—Yes sir, picked her up a few days ago. The Pontiac Bonneville is one fine automobile.

—Got a good day for it, Roland says.

—What?

—Drivin'.

Roland and William Fairbanks never have got along. The only thing they have in common is Margaret, and Roland isn't sure that counts. Since Margaret got hitched, Roland has felt that Mr. William Fairbanks of the famous Fairbanks family looked down on him, and that since he—Mr. William

Fairbanks—has such an important position in his uncle's company, Roland—a poor dirt farmer in his, Mr. William Fairbanks's, eyes—is barely worth talking to.

That's fine with Roland, and once they have exhausted the subject of the new car and what a fine day it is for driving, they ride in silence all the way to St. Johnsbury.

Roland's got nothing personal against Fairbanks. He's good to Margaret, as far as Roland knows, and his sister was surely good to him, Roland, when he was growing up. They've got nothing to talk about, and when they do talk, Fairbanks, it seems to Roland, always ends up telling him what to do. Maybe it's being a businessman like he is, you end up thinking you can tell everybody what to do.

They pull into the driveway of a white house on Elm Street in St. Johnsbury. It's got green shutters and a green roof and a front porch with nice turned columns running the full width of the house. Margaret is already out on the porch, looking anxious, like she was worried what might have happened, the two of them stuck in a car together for over an hour.

Roland and William get out of the car. William walks into the house past Margaret without saying a word, and Roland stands there, tall, stretching his back like he just woke up from a long sleep.

—Roland, Margaret says. It's so good to see you.

—House looks nice, Roland says. Pretty.

They stand in the front hall. The house is quiet.

—Where are the kids? Roland says.

—The kids, Margaret says, are all grown up, Roland, you know that! Rebecca's got children of her own, Will Jr. is down in the city trying to make his fortune, and Joanne is

married and living in Burlington. They've been out of the
house years now.

Roland sniffs the air. Smells good, he says.

—It's nothing special, Margaret says. Roast chicken, potatoes, vegetables.

—Still, smells like Ma's cooking, like Sunday dinner.

—You could go wait in the den with William. You'd be
more comfortable. He's got the radio on.

—I'm fine right here.

Roland watches Margaret bustle around her kitchen, thinking how she looks like their mother, how she moves like
Abitha did, cooks the same way. She got old, Roland thinks.
We're all getting old. He feels the warmth of the radiator
in the corner, the warmth from the oven that's been on
for an hour, feels a different warmth, one inside, watching
Margaret, his older sister, who took care of him those first
years when she was still a young girl herself. She's wearing
an apron, faded blue with little white checks, their mother's
apron, which Roland recognizes from all those years ago.

Margaret takes the apron off.

—Let me show you the house.

There's new wallpaper in the dining room, new furniture
in the sitting room. Roland can see how proud she is of that
house. They stop at the door to a bedroom.

—This where Ma stayed? Roland says.

—We made it real nice for her, don't you think?

There's a bed with a white and blue quilted bedspread, and
cream-colored wallpaper with vertical lines of little flowers:
posies and small roses.

—You recognize the wallpaper? We had to look all over to
find something that matched the paper in the parlor at the

farm. Remember when she got that wallpaper? How happy she was? How much she loved those little flowers all in rows?

Roland looks at the room.

—You could come live here, Margaret says. I'd fix it up special for you, change anything you want.

He turns away and walks back down toward the kitchen.

They sit down to dinner, the three of them, in that warm kitchen. They eat. No one speaks. As the scrape of cutlery on the plates seems to get louder, the silence becomes more awkward. William eats like it's a job to do. He's finished while Roland is still working on his seconds.

William leans back in his chair.

—So, Roland, he says. What are you going to do?

—About what? Roland says between mouthfuls of mashed potatoes.

Margaret gives William a look that says, if William bothered to take notice, we talked about this, leave the man be.

—The farm, of course, William says.

—Well . . . Roland says, then starts in on how he's got plans for the spring, gonna fix up the woodshed, repair the piggery. William getting more and more impatient as Roland goes on and on about how he's thinking of planting more oats the coming year, less corn, and how he's gonna need to get the herd freshened, start up a couple of the heifers.

—You're going to have to do something, William says. You know that. You should sell, they're offering good money. I heard eighteen thousand.

—Don't remember.

—You could buy yourself a nice little place, relax, not have to work so hard.

There is a long silence. The remains of dinner cool in front of them.

—So happens, Roland says. I like to work.

He reaches out, spears another piece of chicken with his fork. Chews it slowly.

—And speaking of work, I need to get back to it.

They stand on the front porch, Roland and Margaret, William sitting in the car, motor running. A gray scud comes across the sky. Margaret holds Roland at arm's length, looks at him.

—You got a good life here, Roland says. I'm glad for you.

He walks to the car, doesn't turn around, doesn't look back.

THE TOWN HALL MEETING room is packed, overheated, filled with the smell of bodies that worked hard all day and for whom a bath is, at best, a once a week affair. Roland leans against the back wall and waits, sees Eddie Wilson sitting a few rows in toward the front, recognizes him by the bald spot on the back of his head. His wife—Roland can't remember her name—sits next to Eddie on the aisle, and next to her he sees Mackie Wilson in a wheelchair. He looks for Annabelle, but she's not there.

In the front of the meeting hall there's a raised platform that served as the stage for the elementary school's annual Christmas play, and where, during the annual town meeting, Bob Garfield, the town moderator, would stand and try to corral the independent-minded (some say stubborn) citizens of Wethersfield into approving a town and school budget. There is a long table on the stage, a big silver microphone at its center, and behind it Roland can see Garfield; Sheriff

Wiggins; Bill Smith, head of the Select Board; and two men from away. Roland recognizes Mr. John Coburn. Next to Coburn is a gray-haired man wearing a dark blue suit and a red tie knotted up tight and thick-framed eyeglasses, looking to Roland as out of place as a pig in a chicken coop.

Garfield stands, taps at the microphone, blows into it, taps it again. There is a rustling of chairs, coughs, but the general hubbub of folks who haven't seen each other in days or weeks doesn't stop. That's why half of them are there, a chance to catch up with neighbors and friends from the other side of the valley.

Roland looks at the other men—Bill Wilson from up the road, Atkinson from over in Brownsville, Murphy from Springfield— leaning against the back wall with arms crossed, dressed in dirty overalls, faded flannel shirts, their faces worn and creased from years of hard work in the sun. The village men are seated towards the front with the women—Ames, the local lawyer, Hanson who runs a small store in Bolton, Herman Bowker. Roland doesn't see his brother, Otis.

Eddie Wilson turns around in his seat, looks toward the back of the room, catches Roland's eye, nods as if they share a secret.

Garfield taps on the mike again, harder, pulls it closer. There is a loud screech of feedback that gets everyone's attention.

—Folks . . . if we could get started. Quiet down now.

More rustling of chairs, coughs, then general quiet.

—You all know why we're here, so let's get started. I want to introduce our special guests. Mr. Bob MacDonald has come all the way here from Washington DC, our nation's capital. Garfield gestures to the man in the blue suit.

We all know it's the goddamn capital, Roland thinks.

Garfield always has been a pompous idiot. At the mention of Washington there is a general guffaw, a few boos, a smattering of feeble applause. The federal government is not real popular with a lot of folks in these parts.

—And, Mr. John Coburn, the Right of Way Agent for southern Vermont.

Mr. MacDonald from Washington, DC starts talking, but Roland has already stopped paying close attention. McDonald mentions President Dwight D. Eisenhower, which brings forth a round of applause—he is, after all, the man who won the war almost single-handed—but, Roland wonders, what the hell does Eisenhower have to do with town meeting?

MacDonald drones on, talking about great things happening in our nation's capital, about the historic Highway Bill that was passed back in 1956, but he is already losing the audience.

Roland is thinking about the other times he'd come to this hall for town meeting, the times he'd stood like this against the back wall, never saying a word while the selectmen and the town folks argued and talked and voted on things that Roland didn't much care about.

Mr. John Coburn stands—seems to Roland that he keeps turning up—starts talking, explaining how he'd be meeting with each of them when the time came. Roland figures since they'd already met maybe his time had come and gone. Coburn is wearing the same khaki pants, but now with a jacket and tie, as if he's trying to look important, but not too important, like he's still one of them, the farmers, but a little bit better, a little more serious. Coburn says how he looks forward to talking with them soon. Sits down.

Garfield stands up, asks if there are any questions.

Big mistake; everyone starts talking at once.

Garfield implores folks to speak one at a time as Roland slips out the door into the entrance foyer with its dark narrow wainscoting and double doors, one on each side.

It was a shock, it was, Mackie Wilson in a wheelchair, all hunched over. Eddie'd said he wasn't doing well, but seeing him like that . . . and Mackie only a couple of years older than Roland. There's a lesson there, somewhere—a big man brought down to a wheelchair like that—but Roland's not sure what that lesson is.

He listens to the babble of voices on the other side of the wall. The photos he'd seen last fall are still there, faded, and running along underneath them are square sheets of grid-marked paper tacked up, one overlapping the next, spanning the entire width of the wall. He steps closer, recognizes a map, picks out the twisting, turning river. To his mind the river ought to be blue, but it's not—it's two lines with white space in between. At the far left end of the map is the town of Windsor with its square blocks and straight roads. He looks for Wethersfield village, finds it, looks for the mountain, but it's not marked, blank white paper where it should be, and then he sees a wide band marked by two heavy black lines with cross-hatching in between, running the entire length of the map. It misses the village and runs close to the river in places, but curves away in others.

There's markings all along the thing, letters, numbers that mean nothing to him.

He looks back and forth from the aerial photos to the plan, trying to connect the two, but the photos have faded and it's hard to see how things line up. He's seen plans displayed by the town before—new schoolhouse, town garage—always paid them no mind, figured they had nothing to do with him, but something about this long map with its cryptic markings bothers him.

This deep disquiet lingers as he walks back up the hill toward the farm in the February dark. Stars pulse and jitter in the sky, come closer. Snow crunches underfoot. The distant cry of a screech owl. A deep winter night like so many others but different somehow, blacker. There's something unsettled in the air. A cutting wind hits him as he walks slowly up Mountain Road between fresh snowbanks up to his shoulder, but as he goes higher the wind stops and he walks up into warmer air. He stands, sniffing the air like a hound on a scent, feels the wind return but gentle this time and from the south. Wisps of cloud feather the stars.

These things he knows, these signs he can read. There's a thaw coming.

Thaw in February isn't unusual, most times it doesn't last, sets up the snow and moves on and lets things return to the way they should be, cold and white, frozen tight and quiet, but if the warmth sticks around and a front comes in and it rains, like it did back in nineteen and twenty-nine? Roland looks down at the road's surface, macadam seamed by a web of ice-filled cracks glinting silver in starlight, remembers when it was dirt, remembers when that flood—the Great Flood they called it—swept away Mountain Road, when it wiped out most of the state's roads and made travel all but impossible for weeks, and he remembers when the state re-built Mountain Road, paving it for the first time, remembers the noise of those trucks, the smell of the bubbling, steaming tar.

VISITING TIME, FOLKS CALLED IT. Back before the roads were paved, late winter—when the weather stayed cold and the snow stopped falling long enough for the roads to be rolled flat and smooth—was a time when travel was relatively easy. Once things started thawing the roads would be deep in mud and nigh to impassable for weeks. Visiting time, when farm work was less pressing. Once spring showed up, there'd be no time for hobnobbing and gossiping.

When Roland was a boy, the Tuttle family used to visit the Wilson place in winter. There'd be other families—seemed like the Wilson farm was the center of things, the place where folks naturally congregated—the Hutchins family from up by Nelson's Corner, once in a while the Atkinsons all the way down from Brownsville.

Albert would hitch up the double-runner sled, the Tuttle kids would pile in back under thick wool blankets, Abitha up front next to her husband. There was a quietness to it, a silvery glistening smoothness to riding in a sled on the hard-packed snow, cold wind all around, snow crystals kicked up by the horses into the bright winter sun flowing over them.

The last time they visited as a family, Roland was eleven. His father pulled the sled up next to the Hutchins's sled, their two Morgans munching away on piles of hay put down on the snow, slim and elegant next to the Tuttle's stocky, scruffy draft horses. The Tuttle clan jumped down from the sled, stamping their feet, clapping their frozen hands.

The Wilsons had a big two-story center hall colonial. The furnace would be stoked, and there'd be a fire in the kitchen cookstove, and logs in the living room fireplace crackling away. There was hot cider and homemade doughnuts as if Mrs. Wilson had somehow known everybody was coming.

Marvin followed his father and, working hard on being grown-up, hovered around the men as they stood in the living room. Margaret and Eliza—already in their minds grown women—followed their mother to the kitchen, where Elizabeth Wilson and Lydia Hutchins were cooking and gossiping. Daniel and James went looking for the Wilson boys, Mackie, George, Jimmy, and the two Hutchins boys, Peter and Thomas, leaving Roland, years younger than even the youngest of that rowdy bunch, standing alone.

Roland watched the men acknowledge each other with the barest of nods, watched how they stood around, quiet at first, hands in their pockets, shuffling their feet, then talked about farming, when sugaring might start, griped about the price of milk, butter. He saw how the women gathered close, touched each other's hands, leaned together. He listened to the women talk about children and who was gonna marry who, and who was ill but got better, and how Cornie Bowker's mother took sick and died, and how Linda, Cornie's wife, saw her through.

Roland waited until Annabelle Hutchins, the youngest of the whole lot, came looking for him. He saw Annabelle in school most every day where boys sat on the right side of the one-room schoolhouse, girls on the left. She'd look over at him, smile. He'd look away quick, embarrassed somehow to even know one of the girls, but here, at the Wilson's, the two of them being so much younger than all the other kids, they became friends of a sort, though Roland knew his brothers would tease him non-stop on the way home, going on about how he was sweet on her and all.

Annabelle would talk to him like what he thought mattered. She was the smartest kid at school. There were books in the

Wilson house, and sometimes she would read to him from one of her books. Roland didn't pay much attention to the story, seemed silly to him if he thought about it, but he liked sitting beside her on the floor, liked the sound of her voice.

His mother came upon them one time.

"You like to read?" she said to Annabelle. She kneeled down.

"Oh, yes, Mrs. Tuttle," Annabelle said.

"May I see your book?"

Annabelle handed her the book.

"The Bobsey Twins," his mother said.

"Yes, ma'am. It's brand new," Annabelle said.

Roland's mother held the book. Annabelle watched her read a few pages. Abitha turned the pages back to where Annabelle had been reading, returned the book to her hands. "It seems to be a wonderful story. I would have loved it when I was your age . . ."

She drifted off, his mother, kneeling there, and Roland and Annabelle didn't know what to do.

"When I was your age, I read all the time . . . what do you think, Roland?"

His mother had taught him his letters and numbers early on, taught him to write his name, but when he got to school the reading lessons were difficult. He knew A from B alright, but when he was made to read aloud from his primer, the letters wouldn't stay where they were supposed to, and he would stumble over the words. The other kids learned, but Roland didn't. The other kids laughed at him, but not Annabelle.

His fourth year, a new teacher came to the school. Miss Prudence Abernathy was of the firm opinion that children were basically savages that needed strict rules and a firm hand if they were to have any chance of growing up to be good Christians, and she came to believe that Roland was challenging her authority, deliberately making her look bad. She would yell at him, make him stand in the corner when he fumbled his words and mumbled his reading.

His mother waited for an answer.

"It's alright," Roland said finally. He looked away, like he'd been caught doing something he wasn't supposed to.

ABITHA KEPT HER SMALL collection of books on a high shelf in the living room. Roland paid them little mind, those books up there on that shelf well out of reach. He gave little thought to books in general. Matter of fact, the only time he had much to do with a book at all was with Annabelle or at school.

He did know that when, come evening, his mother sat in her special chair near the fireplace in the living room she was not to be bothered, not unless the whole house was falling down, so he'd learned to leave her be when she buried her face in a book, and go play someplace else, maybe with the wooden horse and cart James had carved for him.

Eliza and Margaret read some, but the men in the family didn't have much use for it. Some evenings, his mother would take down her Bible and read to the family and they would sit quiet, respectful, even his father.

"You want to read with me, Rollie?" his mother said one day.

She took down a book from her special shelf, handed it to him. He felt the rough red cover, looked at the words set in gold, recognized the word "family", but the rest? No. How could his mother not know? Just because he sat with that girl listening to her didn't mean he liked to read, didn't mean that he even could.

"Let's give it a try," his mother said.

They sat on the couch, holding the book between them.

"It's called 'The Swiss Family Robinson'." She pointed out the words on the cover. "It was one of my favorites when I was growing up."

She read, then coaxed him to start. When he stumbled, she told him the word, but it didn't do any good. He started to squirm and she got impatient. His father came in, stood, towering over them, looking down.

"You're wasting your time," he said. "If the boy don't want to read, he don't want to read. Reading's no use for a farming man, anyhow. Waste of time, you ask me."

"Don't you listen to him, Rollie," she said after his father walked away.

Roland looked at the book in his mother's hands. "How do books get made?" he said.

"People make them," his mother said. "They take their stories and they write them down so they won't ever be forgot."

"Like Gramma Ida?" Roland said. "Is she going to write a book?"

"She sure as shoot could," Abitha said. "Sure could, except she doesn't know how. That's why you should read, Rollie, learn to write. Maybe someday you'll have a story you want folks to remember."

March

SOME YEARS THE SNOW is all but gone and the fields open and muddy, and crocuses and tulips poke their heads up in the sunny spots on the south side of things. This year snow is piled up to windowsills and barnyards are a frozen mess of snow and crust and mud. A convoy of trucks, some pulling trailers carrying earth-moving equipment, is seen coming up from the south on the Post Road. The sound of big engines grinding to life is heard by residents of South Wethersfield. In a cave under boulders high on the mountain's slope the bear stirs.

∿

THE WINDOW IN THE BEDROOM where Roland sleeps is low, down around knee height, because the ceiling slants down beneath the roof. The ell is only a story and a half. He can't see the sky, not unless he lies down on his back on the floor and presses his head against the baseboard, and that would be a darn fool thing to do. He figures it was because the folks who built the place, his great-great-grandparents, couldn't afford to build a real two-story house, but then, maybe that's the way they liked it.

Can't see the sky from his bedroom, never have, never will.

He leans over, looks down through the window toward the ground. What a miserable day. Two feet of snow and the rain pouring down. All he can see is soggy, collapsing snow banks and the dark, wet trunks of the trees in the yard. Tattered pieces of plastic flap against the glass from when he'd covered the outside of the drafty window years ago.

What a goddamn mess. The mud in the dooryard will be wicked.

He sees dark shapes against the snow.

The turkeys are back. Like strange, hunched old men in dark cloaks on spindly legs they wander among the black columns of the trees. It's been a hard winter, even for them, and these big toms—dark and lumpy and shiny in the rain— come back every evening about this time for the handfuls of corn Roland scatters on the snow at the forest's edge. There is something magic about these wild turkeys, spooky. He watches until it grows dark and their black shapes melt back into the forest where they will look for a tree to roost in. He hopes they find shelter from the rain.

The window is black. He can hear the rain turning to sleet, rattling against the glass, clattering on the metal roof of the house. He listens for a while, then sheds his dirty overalls and stands in the gray-white saggy long-johns he wears most of the year. He walks to the small bathroom slowly, crooked, leaning to his left, favoring his bad shoulder, hurt—must be fifteen, twenty years ago—when he was plowing the big hill in the upper field and the plow caught on a rock and twisted and that fool horse of his kept pulling and his sleeve snagged in a crack in the old wood handle of the sidehill plow and the thing damn near pulled his arm off. His shoulder aches more than usual in damp weather, and his knee creaks and cracks, and the joints in his hands ache. He could go on with the list, but what good would it do?

He looks in the brownish mirror and sees an old man looking back: gaunt, cracked and worn, dark bags under his eyes. Raggedy gray beard down to his chest. He is—what?—sixty-three, four?

March. Damn weather can't make up its mind. Is it winter? Is it spring? Hadn't it been sixty degrees yesterday? Hadn't he sweated as he tossed the hay down to his cows? And hadn't he stopped work and sat on the discarded old table in the dooryard, sat and rested and looked up at the sun and felt the warmth on his face and felt good? Just for that moment? Mostly he felt beat up, and the only thing was to keep moving, do his chores, do 'em one at a time the way he'd been taught, the way he'd always done since he was a boy. Do his chores, and if he does them all, does them hard and full, maybe he'll be tired enough at night to sleep, to not worry.

Like tonight—so tired.

He stands over the cracked porcelain chamber pot. It takes too long to piss, only comes in spurts, so long sometimes his legs start to tire.

He calls Brown Dog and lies down on the narrow bed, pats the covers beside him. The dog jumps up and flops down, her back warm against him.

March can be a dark, dreary, morose month. A fickle, teasing, miserable month. But, spring will come, the snow will melt, the tulips his mother planted before she left to live up north with his sister will come up—even after all these years, they will come up—and the sun will warm the soggy earth and loosen his old bones and things will grow, and babies—chicks, kittens, puppies, calves, lambs—will be born and the season will turn and the farm will come to life and he will feel better. Always has, always will. Piglets. Maybe he'll get a couple of piglets this year. Raise them up on slops, then get Magnusson to come down from Windsor and slaughter them, split the proceeds, and put away some bacon and smoked ham for the winter.

Animals are different from each other, his father used to say. Cows stand there looking at you with their big eyes without a care in the world. A horse, she waits to see what you want from her, then goes along. Dogs, they look at you like you're the center of the world, but pigs, well, they look at you like they know you're up to something, like they know what you got in mind for them. They say a pig knows when it's slaughtering day before you even get started.

But it sure'd be nice to have some bacon, ribs too, put by before next winter—not like this past winter.

Yep, that's what I'll do.

The bed creaks as Brown Dog shifts and whimpers in her sleep, her legs twitching like she was running after some varmint. Roland has always wondered what dogs dream about. Bacon, probably, like him.

He presses against the warmth of the dog and falls asleep.

OVERNIGHT, THE RAIN STOPS, the sky clears, and the temperature drops. The world has frozen hard when Roland steps out of the house the next morning. There is a crust on the snow strong enough to hold his weight. He can see the prints from last night's visit by the flock of turkeys, deep, three pronged holes frozen into the snow.

Everything is encased in ice. Long, jagged icicles hang down from the eaves of the house. The path to the barn is slick and treacherous. The cows won't leave the barn. It's a damn nuisance, but Roland knows that it will pass, that the one thing he can count on is that things will change, and soon enough, not even a week after the rains, a procession of warm, sunny days and clear cold nights follow each other and the night and the day are equal and the snow sets up hard and the red-headed woodpecker hammers and clatters away along the edge of the forest.

Roland remembers what Gramma Ida used to say every year, that when you heard that red-headed woodpecker, you knew spring was coming and the trees were going to wake up and the sap start to flow and you better be ready, get your roads broke out, get your taps, your buckets ready, the smokestack set up, cause when it ran, it ran.

THE FARM WAS, IN A WAY, two worlds. The men's world: the barn and the fields. The women's: the house and the kitchen. Everyone crossed over that boundary now and then, the women brought refreshment out to the men working in the barn, and the men helped in the kitchen when it was canning season, but sugaring the family did as one, and for Roland as a young boy, sugaring season was the best time of year.

The sun would rise a little higher in the south each day, the snow would start to set up, south-facing snowbanks would melt and re-freeze into strange feathery blue-white shapes reaching out toward the sun. Their father would assign the tasks. Marvin and James would clean out the sugarhouse, scrub the boiling vat, make sure there was enough dry firewood stacked and ready to go. Albert would take Daniel and Roland and they would lay out and clean the taps, the buckets. Load it all up on the sled. Lift the collection tub up on the back of the sled, tie it down with rope. The sugarhouse was up the hill from the barn, on the edge of the maple grove.

It was too far for Gramma Ida to walk so James and Daniel would help her up onto the sled and she'd ride wrapped up in a wool blanket, like a queen on her carriage.

She'd set herself in the corner of the closed-in side of the sugarhouse, wrapped in her blanket, kept warm by the roaring fire, and talk about how Grandfather Roland ran the sugaring operation when he was alive.

"Before you was born, Boy," she'd say to Roland, not that Roland needed reminding of that fact.

It was the one time Albert would talk about his father, Roland the Elder, as Abitha had taken to calling him. He was—according to Albert—a tyrant when it came to bringing in the sap and boiling it down. It had to be done just so. Tuttles have the best sugarbush in the valley, Roland the Elder would proclaim proudly to anyone who would listen. Run the best sugaring operation around.

"And right he was," Gramma Ida said, then fixed her son, Albert, with that look she had that meant you better listen up. "Don't you say nothing bad about your father. He was a fine man, severe for certain, but a fine man.

"You remember that time, Albert? You was eleven, wouldn't listen to your father, thought you knew it all, didn't shore up the vat the way he told you to, and the thing tipped over and spilled that bubbling mess all over the floor of the sugarhouse and the rest of us could barely lift our feet it was so sticky."

Roland had a hard time believing his father, this big, strong, serious man, had ever been a boy, had ever been young, could have ever done anything that careless.

Roland's father would counter with the time his younger brother Eric and sister Charity built the fire so hot they almost burned the sugarhouse down, or the time the youngest of the brood, Peggy, when she was about three or four, got into a bucket of finished syrup and got herself stuck to herself. All these stories were told with laughter and a sparkle in his father's eye that young Roland didn't see any other time.

Sugaring brought the family together. If the mud wasn't too deep, the roads too bad, Albert's sister Peggy would bring her kids down from Windsor. It was the only time Roland saw his cousins. His father didn't have much to do with his own brothers and sister. For most of the year, it was as if they didn't exist. It was the sweetness of sugaring that brought them together.

There was work, but there'd be snowball fights and laughter and eating the boiled syrup right off the snow. Even Marvin, serious as he was, joined in the fun.

SUGARING WAS A CELEBRATION of the end of winter, of family, but after Albert died it became merely another set of chores they had to do to keep the farm going, to keep the family alive. James and Roland would go out to the barn when the sun had carved the snow into strange shapes and the warm days and cold nights had set the sap to running. Some years it was March, some April. They'd dig through the farm machines and miscellaneous implements that had been stored in front of the sugaring gear over the past year and get out the tin buckets, the taps, the drill, line everything up, check it all, make sure they were good to go.

James and Daniel and Roland would get the big metal tub

up onto the double-runner sled, hitch up the horses and start up the track to the maple grove. They'd tap the trees, making the holes two, maybe three inches deep like their father had taught them, hammer in the taps, hang the buckets. Without their father, the joy, the fun was gone, but the work remained.

Abitha and Eliza would start the fire in the sugarhouse, and soon they'd have sap boiling away and the thick, sweet smell would fill the air. The women tended the fire. Marvin and his kids, Megan and Molly, would come over from Claremont, and the girls would run around while the sap boiled. They'd carry sticks of wood for the fire when called to, but mostly they would play in the snow, make a fort, throw snowballs at each other.

When the sap started to thicken, his mother would take the long-handled ladle, scoop a bit out, and pour it onto the snow. It'd freeze up and the kids would eat it right off the snow. It was the sweetest thing ever.

It was good, all four of the Tuttle boys together like that, lifting that tub up, driving the sled up into the sugarbush, carrying the buckets, filling the big metal vat. Those were some good memories, working with his three older brothers, feeling strong, an equal . . . thinking they would always be together like that, working the farm, making it better, growing the place.

On a good year, when the days were warm and the nights clear and cold, the boiling could go on for days, they'd boil the sap all the way down to sugar cake. Keep a bit of it for the kitchen, to sweeten things, but mostly take it to the village, sell it to the charter-houses down in Boston. Lord knows, they needed the money.

"I'M GOING TO BE LEAVING SOON," Gramma Ida said to no one in particular. She was sitting in her chair by the stove in the kitchen. It was the first year she had not come up to the sugarhouse.

Roland was at the kitchen sink, washing his hands. They'd been sugaring all morning, and no matter how much he scrubbed his hands in the cold water he couldn't get the last of the sticky sap off.

"You got to use hot water," Gramma Ida said. "Any fool knows that."

Roland kept scrubbing.

Nobody was ever sure exactly how old Gramma Ida was. Abitha thought she was seventy-five, maybe seventy-six, but Ida May claimed she was ninety-two which everyone knew was impossible. She'd outlived her husband, the elder Roland, by a good fifteen years, outlived her son, Albert, by three, and it seemed to Roland that she would live forever. She'd begun announcing her imminent departure regularly—especially come late winter, when she hadn't been outside in weeks, the cold being too hard on her arthritis. No one paid much attention anymore.

Roland had turned fifteen in November, and that winter he started growing so fast his bones hurt and he bumped into things. It was like he didn't know where his feet were. James started calling him Mr. Stumblebum, and everyone picked up on it—he didn't mind; it was kind of strange, not minding the teasing—everyone except Gramma Ida who looked at him with a wistful expression and shook her head slowly and smiled.

"You hear me, young man?"

"What?" Roland looked up from the sink.

"I'm going to be leaving soon."

"Where you going?"

"Oh, don't you worry about that, you'll know soon enough."

When Ida May didn't come down for breakfast the next morning, they all assumed she was sleeping in, she did that sometimes, and let her be. Let her get her rest. Around mid-morning when the rocking chair next to the cookstove was still empty—they'd all been so busy in the sugarbush, that nobody'd noticed—Abitha sent Eliza up to check on her.

Roland was in the barn cleaning the sap buckets when Eliza came running out across the dooryard, tears streaming down her face.

"Gramma's gone!" she cried. "Gramma's gone . . ."

Eliza was older, but mostly Roland felt like her big brother. She rushed up to him as he stepped out into the sunlight and grabbed him and held him and pressed her face against his chest. He didn't know what to do with his hands—Tuttles didn't hug, they barely touched—but he finally wrapped his arms around her and let her cry. He had no idea how long they were there like that, leaning against each other. Eliza stopped crying. Roland held her at arm's length.

"She told me she was fixin' to go," Roland said. "She told me . . . just yesterday. Didn't seem real upset about it."

They walked back to the house together, through the kitchen, past the empty chair—looking at it, Roland thought it was moving—into the big house, up the stairs to her room. She was lying on her back in her white nightdress, white sheet pulled part-way up. Abitha sat by her, gently stroking her hand.

"Oh, Ida May," she said. "You dear, sweet woman. You can rest. You'll see your Roland again."

Eliza went to her mother, put her arm around her shoulders. Roland stood in the doorway.

"God bless her," his mother said. "God bless her . . ."

His grandmother had a peaceful look on her face. She looked younger somehow, happy.

Maybe, Roland thought, maybe dyin' ain't so bad. Maybe, like she said, it's only going somewheres else. To Roland, his Gramma Ida had been someone who was always there, in the kitchen, in her chair, by the stove, someone who would always be there. And, then he thought, who'll tell the stories? Who'll remember? It came to him what his grandmother had said the last time she was up at the sugarhouse, sitting in her corner, telling folks what do, telling her stories, the sweet steam from the boiling sap all around her.

"I don't mind dying," she'd said. She talked about dying a lot. "Nope, don't really mind dying, but I surely will miss sugaring."

ROLAND WORKED THE SUGARBUSH for a few years after he was alone on the farm. He'd hitch up the sled—the horses stamping their feet, restless—lever the metal vat up onto the sled with a pair of long wooden poles, and lead the team up the track that circled through the sugarbush, stop, walk the narrow path worn into the snow to the tree, take the tin bucket off the tap, walk slowly back to the sled, empty the bucket, return it to the tap, then walk to the next tree.

The level of sap in the big vat barely rose with each bucket. Sugaring alone in the muffled quiet of the maples—the snow honeycombed and sculpted by the sun, the shadows of the bare tree boles stretched out across the snow, the March smell of the waking trees—Roland would drift off, even as he worked, into a trance-like state where the present and the past swirled in and around each other.

Roland tapped trees and gathered the sap, but it was too much work to boil by himself, so when the vat was full, he'd drive the sled up to Wilson's and let Mackie and his boys boil it down. Times had changed and they mostly did syrup—not sugar cake—to sell in the grocery stores, the markets, for folks to put on their pancakes. They'd measure out what he brought and when the boiling was done he'd take a couple of jugs back to the farm for himself, and once the rest was sold, get a few dollars to help him through the year.

Finally, it didn't seem worth it at all, and the tin buckets and the taps and the big metal vat lay discarded somewhere in the dark corners of the barn, and the sugarhouse stood abandoned, holes in the roof, getting ready to fall to the ground. So, when March comes and that red-headed woodpecker his grandmother always talked about gets going, he finds himself caught between seasons.

A WARM MARCH DAY, he sits on the porch, feels the sun on his face, the rough boards of the porch underneath him, hears the drips of snow melting, the cows in the feedlot snuffling.

Light's different in March. The snow, blue-white, glows as if lit from within..

When did it start? That's what Roland can't figure out. When did things start shrinking, pulling back? Times like this he would search his memories for what had started things. Was there one thing that caused everything? Was it something he'd done? Roland was a man who liked things to have a cause, a reason for happening. He never could figure it out, but it all seemed to go back to a fight in the snow, to sugaring.

IT WAS THE LAST TIME they sugared together: him, his mother, Eliza, James, and Daniel. That year he, Roland, was seventeen. James seemed distant, and Daniel kept glaring at him, and suddenly, those two who were the closest of brothers, of friends, were at each other, rolling in the snow, pushing and shoving. A whole bucket of sap spilled out onto the snow. His mother broke up the fight.

The brothers got up, brushed the snow off, stood staring at each other.

"We agreed!" Daniel shouted. "We'd go together."

"Never did agree to nothing. Somebody has got to stay here," James said. "Work the farm. You know that."

"What's this about?" Their mother looked back and forth from one brother to the other.

"James gone and joined the Army," Daniel said.

"You might have said something to me, young man." Their mother was furious. The madder she was, the quieter her words became. "You can't do this. We're barely keeping up as it is."

"It's too late, Ma. I signed the papers."

"Well, you go and un-sign them."

"Don't think the Army lets you do that, and besides, I heard down at the store they're gonna start conscription, that's the word old man Bowker used. Means they're gonna make you join up. This way, I'll be ahead of the game, and Bowker said they'll only take one from a farm family for now."

"What about you?" She looked at Daniel. "You want to go and leave us here?"

Daniel looked down at his feet in the snow. "Nah, James is right, I got to stay."

"I won't be gone long, Ma. Whole thing'll be over before winter."

"Let's get back to work," was all she said.

Later, standing in the doorway between the house and the kitchen, Roland watched his mother as she sat alone at the kitchen table. She had not lit the lamps and she was there in shadow, leaning over, elbows resting on the table, head in her hands. He could see her shoulders moving, he could hear small sounds like those a keet makes. He watched, stayed silent, felt himself an intruder, turned away.

AFTER MILKING, ROLAND returns to the house in the last light of day. The yard, thick with mud, sucks and pulls at his feet.

The kitchen is gray-dark and cold. He crosses the room, leaving clumps of mud on the floor, re-kindles the fire, leaves the air vent wide open to get it going, then sits by the stove in the big rubber boots that were once his father's, in the chair where Gramma Ida once sat and where his mother rested when she got old and tired, and where he now rests.

He looks at the kitchen, empty save Brown Dog who sprawls on the rumpled blankets by the stove. It's mostly okay for Roland, this quiet, the chance to rest his bones, let his thoughts settle. He hears the crackle of the fire, water dripping off the roof. Outside, snowbanks collapse in on themselves, water runs across the dooryard, flows down the ditches beside Mountain Road, downhill toward the river. Seems to him the whole world is rushing to get away from this place. But, not him. He can't imagine being anywhere else save this farm.

Thinking about things, making plans, looking ahead, is a comfort. He feels the fire warm on his face. The place ain't perfect, God knows. Got its problems. The herd for one. Not getting the milk I used to, only filled two ten-gallon cans tonight. The girls are slowing down. Might be time to get them freshened. Maybe the six heifers too, get them started. Have to get the vet up here. And see to gettin' that piglet. Maybe Wilsons got one to sell. Have to fix up the piggery, that's for sure.

He drifts off, then wakes with a start to the dog barking. The stove is red-hot, sides glowing, humming and vibrating like it's about to take off.

He forgot to close down the vent.

Roland jumps up, clamps it shut, and watches until the fire calms, then collapses back into the chair.

— Damn fool, he says to himself. You damn fool! Then to the dog, you saved us there girl, yes you did.

There's a great crash outside; a slab of snow has slid off the roof, landing with a whomp, shaking the house to its foundation. Brown Dog jumps up, runs around the kitchen, barking this way, then that.

— You tell 'em, Roland says and laughs and marvels again that this dog came to live with him.

Brown Dog quiets, comes over, sits by his side. Roland reaches down, tugs at the dog's ears, strokes her head, rubs her sides—her fur, matted and rough when she straggled her way up the driveway, is now smooth and soft—then leaves his hand resting on the dog's head and they sit there and feel the warmth from the stove while the world outside turns dark and more snow slides off the roof and the sound of water falling and rushing and flowing is all around them.

SUSANNAH TUTTLE FIRST KNEW SHE WAS DEAD when she saw that her chair was not where it had always been, in the bedroom that Edmund had built above the kitchen. He had worked so hard on that room. She remembered.

Spring came. The snows melted, and she and Edmund had come out of their hovel one morning squinting in the bright sunlight, had stretched their arms toward the soft sky, and had looked around as if surprised that they had survived.

But little Amelia had not.

And all that spring she, Susannah, had mourned the loss of her daughter, dead before she had the time to live, and sat in that rocking chair going back and forth, back and forth. It wasn't fair, she knew now, to have left all that work for Edmund.

He built the house for her, but still she had mourned until baby Lucius looked at her with those pale blue eyes.

It is downstairs now, her chair.

Later, she thinks, I'll go down later—when the man has gone to bed—and sit again. Sit where I sat for all that summer, rocking, unable to rise, unable to eat, unable to live.

But, I got up from that chair, and we had children who lived. Lucius is here somewhere. And they had children and those children had children and things went on, and maybe it was all worth it.

But, she knows, there are no children here.

Who will carry on?

April

*T*HERE IS A FORMATION OF GEESE OVERHEAD, pointing, like the tip of an arrow, north. Their cries echo off the mountain. The days are longer than the nights. The bear rummages in widow Stockton's backyard; she has not brought in her bird feeders. The last of the ice is gone and the river flows brown and thick. Snow hides on the north side of things. Three men in dark suits and white shirts and ties are seen driving into the village in a tan automobile with government license plates. Another convoy of trucks arrives from the south.

~

A DAY COMES, usually in April, but not always—sometimes you have to wait until May—when the snow has finally melted, and the sun is high and almost hot on your face, and you squint up at the pale blue sky like you've never seen it before, and the first flowers poke their heads up out of the wet ground, and the thick aroma of mud and earth fills the air.

Such a day fills Roland with hope, with the knowledge that the flowers will return, grass will turn green, trees will leaf out, crops will grow. Other folks celebrate the New Year on January 1, but for Roland, and for farmers all up and down the north country, this day is truly the start of the new year. "Survival day" his father called it, the day you knew that you'd made it through another winter. A day when his mother would open the windows, air out the house, hang bedding on the laundry line in the sun, and his father would set the boys to work cleaning the barn.

His father would walk the property alone, hands clasped behind his back, a serious look on his face, checking the pasture fences, surveying the place to see what damage winter had wrought.

A ritual Roland continues.

He heads to the upper pasture, Brown Dog at his heels, his boots slipping in the muddy ground. After the bitter cold, dry November he'd been worried that the frost would be too deep, the soil too dry, but the snows that started in December had set things right. The ground is too wet to plow and is still frozen in places underneath the mud, but all in all, the fields look ready for spring. The fence has survived but a couple of posts need replacing, and the pasture gate latch has rusted almost clean through.

ROLAND WALKS UP THE HILL to the pasture gate carrying a small coil of fence wire and a pair of wire cutters. He cuts away the old wire hinges, sets the gate aside, takes the new wire and is beginning to fashion a replacement hinge when Brown Dog starts barking like a lunatic. The gate is in a gentle hollow in the hillside and Roland can't see the farmyard from where he's working.

He stops, thinks it's Wiggins coming by to bother him again, turns to go back to work, but Brown Dog knows Wiggins, wouldn't go this crazy about his old friend the sheriff, so Roland puts down the pliers, leaves the wire hanging half done, and walks up to the crest of the hill to see what's got the dog all riled up.

There's one of those orange trucks with the fancy emblem on the side parked on Mountain Road, and two men wearing orange vests carrying poles are tromping out into the lower meadow. Roland has a mind to go down there and tell them to get the hell off his land, but then remembers what he had all but forgotten: that Coburn fellow telling him how a surveyor was going to be coming by and how they'd try to stay out of his hair and to pay them no mind.

He watches the men. One stands holding a tall pole, the other walks away pulling some kind of cord behind him, stops, fiddles around, then the one with the pole walks up to the other man, and they do the whole rigmarole over again, and then again, and again. They work their way down the overgrown meadow one length of that cord at a time, until they disappear into the pine forest that lies south of the farm.

There's something mesmerizing about the whole process, like when he was a kid watching one of those long, green caterpillars that only had feet at each end of its skinny body, and moved by bending up, bringing its ends together, then stretching out, and doing the same thing over and over and over.

The sun has moved in the sky and Roland realizes he's been standing there, wasting time, and goes back to fixing the gate. It's a vague evening sky, gauzy gray and pink, when he gets back down to the farmyard. The girls are waiting for milking, but he follows Brown Dog down to the road to see what those fellows got up to.

There's two lines a couple of hundred feet apart cut through the tall weeds and brush, and every sixty feet or so there is a thin stake, maybe three feet tall, with a small red flag attached, a whole line of them stretching all the way down the meadow to the pine forest. Roland hesitates, looks back over his shoulder like there might be somebody watching him from up on the hill, or one of those government planes flying low over the farm the way they did last fall, then bends down and pulls the stake up, looks at the pennant. E-8 is written on both sides in thick black.

E-8? He knows he's seen that before, but can't place exactly where. He walks all the way to the pines, pulling up each stake, some of them with that E-8 business, others blank. He comes back on the other line, pulls all those up too. It's almost dark by the time he gets back to the barn; the cows are mad at him for sure. He takes the bundle of stakes, throws them in the back of the barn behind all the broken rakes and wagon parts and plow handles, and goes to do what he should have been doing all along—taking care of his herd.

ROLAND TENDS, HE DOESN'T BUILD, so though all the animals—horses, cows, chickens, dogs—have always been well cared for, the buildings—milk-house, sugarhouse, woodshed, the south end of the barn—are beginning to fall down around him. He is good with harness awl and coarse thread, can mend a broken sled runner, can keep a plow working fine, fix a fence gate, but buildings are another matter. His brother James was a builder—Marvin too. They would've known how to re-build the woodshed, but measuring, fitting, the straight lines, the need for plumb, for square, leave Roland baffled and he's never sure how to begin.

He looks at the wreckage of the woodshed. Least he can do is clean up the mess. He clears the debris from the collapsed roof and makes two piles: one, wood so rotten it crumbles in his hands, the other, cedar shakes, pieces of pine board, he sets aside to use as kindling. He stops. Looks at the hand-split shakes, wonders whose hands made them. As he clears out the last of the collapsed roof, he uncovers the remnants of a soot-blackened brick fireplace and chimney in the corner.

He'd heard Gramma Ida tell how his great-great-grand-parents, Edmund and Susannah, had lived for more than a year in this woodshed with its dirt floor and single small window. He looks around the shed, now four crooked walls open to the sky, with new eyes, sees rough-sawn shelves on one wall, shards of pottery.

Looking at the farm's buildings is like looking into the past. The big barn with its milking parlor and hayloft, a small, older barn with room for a couple of cows, a horse, some farm implements. A piggery off the back of the barn, the roof of which collapsed many years ago. The sheepfold off to the side now filled with piles of lumber, rolls of fence wire.

A couple of barn cats are lolling in the sun in front of the sheepfold. There's a big black-and-white that Roland doesn't think he's ever seen before. Certainly could be, because he has no idea how many cats live in these buildings. He never feeds them other than leaving a tin dish of milk out after milking. Doesn't need to; they have plenty to eat what with all the rats and mice that scurry around the place. The rodents eat spilled grain—the cats eat the rodents. Nothing eats the cats unless one of them is fool enough to prowl the woods at night and get caught by a fisher. The way those half-wild cats look at him when he's working in the barn, Roland figures they'd eat him if they got the chance.

Roland bends over to enter the sheepfold, crouches, looks at a jumbled pile of lumber trying to figure what would work to fix the woodshed. It's a long, low building, with walls of thick, vertical slabs of pine, in one of which, as a boy hiding from his brothers in a game of hide and seek, he'd found, carved, the initials LT and a date: 1842.

HE'D ASKED GRAMMA IDA ABOUT those initials and she'd told him the story of Lucius Tuttle, born to Susannah and Edmund in the spring of 1822.

When Lucius turned sixteen, he took work as a hired hand at the Jarvis place in Wethersfield Bow, south of the village, learning the sheep business from Mr. William Jarvis, former US Consul to Portugal and importer and breeder of the finest Merino sheep in all of Vermont.

Though Edmund Tuttle had dreamed of a small dairy farm, grazing cows, fields with rows of corn and oats, he listened when his son, after two years of working the Jarvis farm, talked about the price of wool, and when William Jarvis, who'd taken a liking to the hard-working Lucius, offered to set Edmund up in the sheep business, he agreed. Within a few years, the hills of the Tuttle land, like those of so many Vermont farms, were dotted with hundreds of sheep.

"Lucius talked his father into the sheep business, built that sheepfold," Gramma Ida said. "Lucius was pushy, had all kinds of big ideas."

She rocked back and forth for a bit.

"Years later, when my Roland was working the place along with his father Lucius, I heard folks talking in the village about how wool prices was going to drop after the Civil War, tried to warn 'em. Did they listen to me? No they did not."

She fixed her gaze on Roland as if it was somehow his fault, though he was only eight.

"Lucius. Not sure he ever took a cotton to me. Don't think he approved much of his son marrying me. He was their second child, you know, and right from the get-go, everyone said he was special.

"Susannah told me how, after losing her first while they was living in that one-room shack, she didn't think she could carry-on, even after Edmund got a house built for her . . . not the big house, mind you, just this kitchen I'm sittin' in and the room upstairs."

Roland thought to point out that Susannah had been dead for almost one hundred years, but a sharp look from his grandmother caused him to think twice.

Gramma Ida rocked back and forth in her chair.

"Susannah told me all about it. It was that baby, that Lucius, done brought her back to life."

ROLAND'S NOT SURE HE remembers where those initials are, thinks it's the back left corner. He goes to look for them, see if they're still there, but the place is so jumbled full of farm discards—broken rakes, busted wagon wheels, tangles of fence wire, the sickle mower that was too rusted to work right, and things Roland can't remember the purpose of—that he gives up not twenty feet in, turns around and stumbles outside, straightens his aching back.

The big maple next to the house is leafing out, its crown a pale green cloud. The tall oak is behind, its branches dotted with buds. From this angle, he can see the house all spread out, can see how it's three houses, one getting built on to the other, each bigger than the one before.

The thing about Ida May Tuttle and her stories was that she told them with such conviction, such certainty, that to Roland as a boy they had to be true, and though he is now a grown man of sixty-four years, there is a part of him that is still that boy, that still believes all of it—her stories, her ghosts, her conversations with people long dead—to be true.

IDA MAY TUTTLE FIRST KNEW SHE WAS DEAD when she could stand up straight. She'd been bent over so long, worn down by a hard life, that it was like the whole world shifted and she could finally see around her instead of the floor in front of her feet.

Spring. She stands by the open window. She can hear robin babies in the nest outside keetching and clamoring for food, mama robin and poppa robin coming and going, keeping up as best they can. She can hear chickens chattering and scratching in the yard, cows snuffling in the barn. Voices in the kitchen.

So much life.

Everything seems new, like when she was a little girl growing up and spring made her heart leap for joy and she would lie in bed and listen to the birds waking up, her father out in the yard, her mother cooking in the kitchen.

Oh, to be young in spring . . .

She turns away from the window, sees a faint, grayish figure lying in the bed in a white nightgown on white sheets. A breeze comes in the window, a thin white curtain flutters across her face, wraps itself around her with a gentle caress. She brushes away the gauzy cloth, looks out the window. The barnyard is empty, the barn looks deserted. She turns back to the room, her room, the familiar pine bureau, dresses hanging from pegs, her favorite apron.

When she looks at the bed it is empty. The figure is gone. Of course! It is time to be up, get dressed, get to work. How can she have slept so late? She hears the sounds of work outside. The men in the fields, Abitha in her garden.

Lord knows that woman works hard enough for two.

But, hasn't she, Ida May, worked enough in her life? Isn't she entitled to a little rest?

She sits back down on the bed, hears her son Albert's heavy footsteps in the hall. It weren't right for a son to die ahead of his mother. Not right at all. She will be glad to see him again.

JAMES, THE MIDDLE OF Roland's three older brothers, had always been James, never Jim, never Jimmy. Their mother could get away with calling him Jimmy, but when she did, it meant she was sore at him, and James knew better than to say anything. Anybody else, they'd get a serious pounding if they called him Jimmy. He was always like that, "stubborn as a fence post" their father used to say.

It was April 1917 when James left. Abitha stood on the porch slowly shaking her head. Eliza gave James a hug then turned away. Marvin had come over from Claremont to see him off. He put his hand on James's shoulder. "You're a damn fool," he said. "Don't have to go, you know. There's exceptions for farm work." When James didn't speak, Marvin walked up onto the porch and stood there, slouched, scuffling his feet.

Daniel was nowhere to be seen.

James stood there in his uniform, kit bag over his shoulder. Roland hitched up the wagon.

"I'll drive him," he said.

It was clear no one else was going to.

"You comin' Ma?"

She came down off the porch. Walked over to James. Put her hands on his shoulders.

"You better take care of yourself, you hear?" She looked away. "Off you go," she said, then turned to Roland. "And you get yourself back here. There's chores waiting."

James tossed his duffel bag into the back of the wagon, hopped up alongside Roland, and they set off. Didn't have far to go. It was no more than seven miles to the train station in Windsor.

"Why're you going?" Roland finally asked.

"My country needs me."

The horse plodded along, the reins slack in Roland's hand. The river to their right was high and muddy from spring rains. Roland felt no impulse to urge the horse faster. Maybe if they went slow enough James would miss his train and wouldn't go, would stay where he belonged, on the farm. A silence rode with them, came between them, prevented them from saying what they felt.

"We need you," Roland said.

"You'll manage fine 'til I get back. You and Daniel. Maybe Marvin'll come back and help."

"Marvin doesn't want nothing to do with farming."

The train was waiting when they got to the station. Young men were lined up in their stiff new uniforms to get their picture taken by George Swallow, who owned Swallow's Photography on Main Street in Windsor. Most of the uniforms were too big for these skinny Vermont farm boys. There was a small crowd of families and local people to see the boys off. Roland felt bad that he was the only one there for James.

"You scared?"

James looked at the train, coal smoke billowing out of the engine's stack, steam hissing from the drive pistons. The whistle screamed and James blanched as if he suddenly realized, as if it finally hit him, what he was about to do: get on a train and head to some Army base somewhere, and then get on a boat and go all the way across the Atlantic to fight in a war that he knew nothing about, when he had never been farther from that farm on the side of the mountain than Springfield, Vermont.

"I'm fine," James said. He walked over and got in line for a photograph. "Give the photo to Ma. Tell her I'll write."

Roland went back a few days later to pick up the photo. Mr. Swallow put it in a nice frame, wrapped it up good, and when Roland brought it back to the house and gave it to his mother, she put it up on the mantelpiece in the living room and stood there looking at it for a long time.

"Lord, how I hate to see him go," she said, turned to Roland. "Don't be getting any bright ideas, young man."

"Don't worry, Ma. I ain't going anywhere."

His mother changed after James left, or maybe she'd been changing all along and it was gradual and Roland hadn't noticed. She didn't smile as much, ran the house and the farm with grim determination. Roland found her one time, James gone a few weeks, standing in front of the cold fireplace, staring at that picture.

"He won't be coming back," she said.

"Course he will. He'll be back, I know he will."

"Oh, Rollie," she said, looked at him, sadness in her eyes.

He knew there was something he should say, something to make her know it was going be alright, but he couldn't find the words.

THAT PICTURE'S STILL THERE, far as Roland knows, but it's been so long since he's checked that he can't be sure. The big house is like another world to him; he never goes in there, doesn't heat it, doesn't care for it, but it is still a presence in his life, looming in his dreams, dark and massive. Sometimes, when he's in that dim kitchen he can feel it pull at him, reminding him of what used to be, and he looks at that door with its panels and frame making a cross like the one hanging in church. "That's why it's called a Bible door," his father said to him once. "Your grandpa that you was named after was a religious man, had that door made to remind us all to behave."

Now, that door reminds Roland only of what has been lost.

Probably seized shut, he thinks. Won't even open.

SHERIFF WIGGINS STOPS his car on the side of the road at the base of the farm's driveway, waves to Roland, stands there waiting for him.

—What're you doing parked down here?

—Didn't want to get stuck in the mud, Wiggins says.

More like didn't want to get his shiny shoes dirty, Roland thinks.

—You hear about Annabelle Wilson? She passed last night . . . thought you should know.

—Didn't know she was poorly, Roland says.

—Been weeks now.

—The boys didn't say nothin' last time I saw 'em.

—They wouldn't, would they? Wiggins says.

Roland watches the sheriff drive off, walks to the barn, takes Sam out of her stall, hitches her to the wagon. Goes into the kitchen, climbs the steep stairs. All the clothes he owns hang from a long pegboard in the dim hall. He looks at the three pairs of overalls, one more worn than the next, his four long-sleeve shirts, all the same, once white, now dingy gray. Realizes he hasn't done a wash in a long time.

How was he supposed to know? Know she was sick, fading, when nobody could be bothered to tell him? How was he supposed to know he was going to need something civilized to wear?

—The hell with them, he says out loud without meaning to.

He climbs up onto the wagon's seat in the clothes he's been wearing all day, clicks his tongue at the horse. The wagon rattles down the rutted drive.

Vehicles are parked up and down both sides of the road by the Wilson farm. There's red ones, blue ones, green ones. There's pickup trucks, sedans, slat-walled farm trucks. Some of them are old, dented, beat-up, others are new, their bulging chrome bumpers shining in the bright spring sun. Roland guides Sam around two big black sedans and a black Cadillac hearse that fill the Wilsons' dooryard. He drives out onto the lawn, drops the reins on the ground, and leaves the horse there, head down, grazing on the fresh green grass. Walks to the front door where Bill Wilson stands greeting the well-wishers.

—Roland, Bill says, a hint of surprise in his voice.

—You boys shoulda told me she was sick, Roland says in a tight voice he doesn't recognize.

He walks into the house as Bill mumbles an apology. The big living room is crowded, the furniture pushed back against the walls. Men, some in suits and skinny ties, others in plaid shirts and overalls, are bunched in tight groups on the right. Women, in dresses of faded colors decorated with flowers or rows of small dots, sit along the opposite wall. There's an opening down the middle, like the aisle at church, that pulls him into the room, as if the whole damn floor slopes down toward the far wall, toward a gaudy display of flowers, toward a coffin of wide-board pine with brass handles, toward where Annabelle Hutchins Wilson lies in that half-open coffin. Roland looks at her there surrounded by puffed-up satin pillows and flounces in pale pinks and blues. She's smaller than he remembers. They've made her up, rouged her cheeks, lipsticked her mouth, but they couldn't hide the pale gray of her face. Done up her hair in a brittle gray old lady's hair-do.

Ain't right, he thinks, barely stops himself from saying out loud. It ain't right. Woman never wore a bit of that stuff in her life. That's not the way she wore her hair. That's not the way she'd want to be remembered.

He steps back, looks around, sees Mackie Wilson. He was a big man once, bigger even than Roland's father, big with a broad red face and a loud booming voice. Now, he sits propped up in the corner, smaller somehow, hunched over, his face shrunken, looking lost, like he doesn't know what's going on around him. Roland wonders for a moment if that's the way his father would have looked, would have ended up, had he lived to be old, then remembers that Mackie is not but a few years older than he, himself, is.

He feels something clench in his chest, catch in his throat, and hinges forward with an inaudible gasp, then straightens back up, turns and walks out without saying a word. Folks watch him go. He feels them looking at him, at his dirty overalls, muddy boots.

As WINTER LOOSENS its grip on the land, something unlocks in his heart. Redwings, hidden in the tangled forsythia bushes next to the house, warble to each other. Robins, returned from the south, scratch for worms in the muddy grass. The barn swallows squabble by the open haymow. In the morning early, he sits on the porch before beginning the day's work. The raucous birdsong brings back memories of other mornings, other days, walking with Annabelle Hutchins.

Annabelle.

Roland, seventeen, out of school three years, had taken to meeting her as class let out. He would head down Mountain Road, be there as the doors swung open, and walk her home, going out of his way to spend that time with her. Him walking, looking down at his feet, scuffing up the dirt and sand on the road's edge; her chatting away, going on about the birds, pointing them out, naming them: jays, redwing blackbirds, a pileated woodpecker. It was good to be with her, to be walking, to have something to do, to not have to talk too much.

For Roland, the fact that he took off from the farm, from his chores, to meet her, to walk with her on a fine spring day, going in the same direction, seeing the same things, feeling the same sun warm on the backs of their necks, hearing the same birds, listening to the same sounds of life awakening after the long winter, was enough to say what needed saying better than any words he might come up with.

But.

Yes . . . But.

That was all he could say when she told him she was fixing to marry Mackie Wilson when school was done.

He had feelings—people thought he didn't—but of course he did. He just didn't go around showing them, talking about them.

Didn't understand then, still doesn't today.

He looks at his hands, cracked, crooked, worn and calloused. Hard-working hands. Hard-worked hands. Realizes that he never once held that girl's hand, never once touched her golden hair.

May

*E*VERY DAY THERE ARE TRUCKS going north and south on
the Post Road. The selectmen have another special meeting
planned. The village smells of diesel and fresh-cut grass.
The river is high, over its banks by Wethersfield Bow. The
maples in the village are leafed out, but trees high on the
mountain are bare. The flower beds planted by the Women's
Auxiliary on the village green are in full bloom, ready for
Memorial Day, but the special service for the new World
War I Memorial has been postponed.

≈

*T*HE SWALLOW PAIR THAT nests every year in the barn
wall has returned, coming and going through the knot-hole
in the wide pine siding, re-building their nest. Roland can
hear them in the wall, chattering, when he enters the barn
to begin his day's work.

It's broke. No doubt about it. The big steel blade—some
called it the plowsward, his father had always called it the
coulter—is loose, no way is the plow going to cut a straight
furrow. It must have been loose when he put the thing away
last fall. Why didn't he fix it over the winter? Had he plumb
forgot? Now here he is with a broken plow and plowing to be
done. He drags the plow closer to the open door of the barn
into the light of the warm, almost sultry morning. He grips
the handles, polished to a smooth golden brown by the sweat
of his hands, his brothers' hands, his father's hands, and the

touch of that fine-grained ash sets off sparks of memory in his mind, like he was transported back through his entire life. How many hours has he walked behind this plow? Hours that added up to days, to weeks, months, years maybe. It seems he's lived a whole life holding onto these handles.

The beam of the plow is a dense hunk of oak, four by six inches, heavy as steel, the grain on it rough and striated from the sun. One of the two bolts that run through that hardwood beam to hold the coulter in place has rusted clean through. He knocks it back through the hole. The coulter dangles from a single bolt. He finds a monkey wrench, clamps it down on the other bolt, but the damn thing won't budge. He pushes at the wrench handle with his foot, stomps hard on it, but the nut is rusted fast. He finds an old can of 3-in-1 Oil, squirts it all around the frozen nut, grabs a five-pound sledge and whales away at the wrench handle.

Still nothing moves.

Half an hour later, his face running with sweat, his back aching, his arms throbbing, about to give up, he gives the wrench handle one last ferocious whack with the sledge and the nut breaks clean off, and the coulter clatters to the barn floor.

He picks up the heavy, knife-like plate of steel. It's rusted but solid. He takes it over to the workbench, cleans it off with a wire brush until it shines, grinds the cutting edge smooth— sharp but not too sharp or it'll chip and break when it hits a stone, and if there is one thing his fields are good at putting up, it's stones.

Now, how to get the thing back together?

He rummages around on the workbench, pulls out wooden boxes of nuts and bolts, nails and spikes, harness parts, buckles and sliders, and all kinds of what-not, but finds no bolts the right size. He walks back to where, in the shadows, is all manner of stored farm implements. He steps around a double-runner sled with a busted runner, and wades into the tangled pile of broken and discarded tools and machinery. He pulls out and tosses aside old scythes, hand planters, cultivators, a rusty two-man crosscut saw, a busted wheel-barrow. He looks hard at the wheelbarrow, but the handle bolts aren't the right size.

Here are things he'd stored and meant to fix, here are things his father had abandoned, and in the back, the original one-way plow his grandfather had started out with. He looks at it in the dim light, no use, the hardware is all wrong.

His FATHER HAD PUT AWAY that old thing away when Roland was what? Nine, ten?

"That's Grandpa Roland's plow," his father said. "Cast iron."

Roland had touched the handles, stout oak beams that his small hands reached barely half-way around. That might've been the first time he felt a connection to, a sense of the man he was named after.

"But, it's a one-way plow," his father said. "Look at this," he said, proud. Pointed to the brand new sidehill plow —the one Roland was now trying to fix—that Strickland & Co. had dropped off.

"Some folks call it a swivel plow," his father said. "It'll save us a ton of work. No more plowing around the field, leaving all them headlands unplowed. You push this latch with your foot—" There was a loud clang of metal and the plow jumped like a startled horse as the plowshare and mouldboard flipped to the other side and Roland leaped back as if he'd been stung.

His father laughed. "Yessir, you got to keep up with the times. You swap the thing over, and you can plow right back along the first furrow, do the whole field back and forth."

HIS FATHER'S PLOW IS BROKEN and Roland doesn't have the parts to fix it. He'll have to go all the way to Claremont, to Lambert's Hardware Store, and see if Lambert has a couple of bolts that will do the trick.

The farms around him —Riveredge Farm, Fairacre Farm, Ascutney View, bigger places with fancy names and fine river valley soil—all use tractors. Eddie Wilson keeps telling him, "You got to get yourself a tractor. Nobody plows with horses no more." But Roland likes walking behind his team on a fine day in May, guiding the plow, feeling the blade cut the soil, the smells of fresh-turned earth and horse sweat, the gentle creaking of the leather harness.

He picks up the rusted bolt and slips it into the pocket of his overalls.

IT IS INDEED A FINE May day, a fine day for plowing, but also a fine day to be walking down the road toward Claremont, waving to folks as they pass in their fancy automobiles. The sky above Roland is that soft, clear blue that you get only in May, but the horizon to the south is smudged with brown haze and dust from the road construction. There is a faint tinge of exhaust in the air.

It's a good six miles to Claremont, but he doesn't mind walking, and anyway, he almost never has to walk the whole way, someone will stop, tell him to hop on in, and chew his ear off all the way into town. He crosses the bridge over the Connecticut River. This first part of New Hampshire is flat river plain, left behind by the river centuries ago, and the plowed fields smell of fresh dirt and manure. Past the fields, the road rises gradually, following the Sugar River upstream toward Claremont. He stops, looks back. The bulk of Mount Ascutney fills half the sky. Looks bigger from here, somehow. He tries to see where the farm sits at the toe of the mountain, but can't pick it out.

Roland remembers the story about Ascutney Gramma Ida told him when he was a boy.

How the name meant three summits, and looking back at the mountain, he can see those three lumps. He remembers hiking up there as a boy, looking for those three boulders that were once three Indian braves, but never finding them. It's strange, he thinks, how you can see something clear as all get out from a distance, but can't from close-up.

The toot of a car horn pulls him from his reverie.

—What are you doing standin' in the road?

He turns to see his brother, Marvin, leaning out the window of his shiny red Chevy. Roland barely recognizes him. Marvin's gotten old since last time he saw him.

Marvin pulls over to the side of the road.

—What's doing? Marvin says as Roland climbs into the front seat. The car smells clean. That's the only way Roland can think of it, clean. Not like soap, but sharp, crisp.

—New car?

—Nope, got it cleaned over at the dealership. They still do it for me. Wax it and everything. No charge. You got to take care of things. Where you headed?

—Hardware store.

—What for?

—Need a couple of bolts for the plow.

Roland looks out the back window of the Chevy, the mountain still fills the horizon. They pass under the railway trestle
and into the outskirts of town. There are small, rundown
houses along the road. Roland swivels back and forth, looks
out the windows, tries to remember what had been there
when the family rode into town in a horse-drawn wagon.

Things have not been good between Roland and his
brother for years. This saddens him. He doesn't understand
his brother's attitude. Hadn't he once come to the farm
every November and brought Roland back to his house in
Claremont for Thanksgiving with his family? Hadn't he
and his wife, Bridget, brought the kids up to visit the farm
almost every summer? Those were good memories: the house
all lit up, kids running around underfoot, the kitchen table
piled high with food.

They drive past a small house, a one-story cape, a few feet
from the edge of the pavement, all boarded up.

—Wasn't that Macauley's store? Roland says.

—Hasn't been for years, Marvin says.

—Remember when we used to get penny candy there?
Always loved that candy . . .

But then came that last summer Marvin and his family
had visited the farm. Marvin's oldest daughter, Megan, was
working on being a surly and unpleasant teenager, and Roland
had caught her in the barn sneaking a cigarette and had a
fit. The girl could have burned the whole place down. It
seemed like Marvin never forgave Roland for yelling at his
kid. Stopped visiting. Just like that.

Here they were sitting side-by-side in the car, nothing
to talk about.

—You still working at the garage? Roland says.

—Nope. Retired. Takin' it easy.

They drive over the dam on the Sugar River into downtown, past tall, empty mill buildings, their windows all boarded up, the brick dark and streaked with age. Claremont had once been a prosperous town, but when the mills started closing, the whole place went downhill. There are empty storefronts on both sides of the road, but Lambert and Sons Hardware is still in business.

—They're gonna' close down, Marvin says.

—What?

—Lambert's. That new Aubuchon on the edge of town is taking all the business.

Marvin stops in front of the store. See ya, he says.

Roland sits for a moment. The store takes up most of an entire block. Lawn mowers, wheelbarrows, garbage cans, a rack with shovels, rakes, line the sidewalk in front of the building. He turns to his brother.

—You still mad at me? Roland says.

—Mad at you? Marvin shakes his head. Never was . . . Bridget died, he says finally. A year ago, Roland. A year. I never heard from you. Didn't see you at the funeral.

Marvin sits with both hands on the wheel looking straight ahead as if they were still cruising down the highway. Roland holds the bolt in his pocket, turns it around and around in his hand. He thinks about the bolt, how he needs two of them, hopes Lambert has the right size.

—Bridget? Roland says. Didn't know...

Roland watches his brother drive off. He turns toward the hardware store, pulls the rusted bolt from his pocket, looks at it. He hasn't been in town for months; things seem different, can't say exactly how, just different. He is still digesting what his brother said.

Inside the store, Roland sees empty shelves. Never used to be empty shelves. Thomas Lambert is the grandson, his grandfather, Walter, founded the business back when it was Lambert's General Store and sold about everything a person could possibly need, from farm implements to housewares to boots to clothing.

Roland still remembers the big sign that was behind the counter: If We Don't Have It, You Don't Need It.

—Roland Tuttle, Lambert says from behind the counter. Haven't seen you in ages.

Lambert's short, stocky, going to fat, with thinning hair and a pallid complexion, dark circles under his eyes. Roland hands him the bolt.

—Need two, Roland says.

Lambert examines the rusty thing as if it was a fine piece of jewelry, turns it in his hands, fingers the battered head.

—Looks like it put up a good fight, he says. Strickland sidehill plow? You still using that old thing?

—Still works.

—Don't get much farm business anymore, it's all gone out to the big John Deere place east of town, but let me look out back. I think I got something that'll do you.

The bell on the front door tinkles, a couple comes in, the man wearing a tie, the woman carrying a shiny red handbag. The woman looks at Roland standing by the counter in his baggy, dirty overalls, floppy straw hat, mud on his boots. Roland sees the look on her face before she turns away, the way she wrinkles her nose like he smells bad, and he suddenly feels out of place in a place he has been coming to since his father carried him on his hip.

Lambert returns. Sees the couple.

—Be right with you folks, he says, then turns to Roland, hands him two shiny new bolts with nuts and washers. These should work, he says. Grease 'em good before you put them in, that way they won't rust up.

Roland fumbles in his pocket, pulls out a small wad of crumpled bills.

—Don't worry about it, Lambert says.

Roland puts two dollars on the counter, walks out the door.

That's the trouble, Roland thinks, things that should change, don't; things that shouldn't, do.

OUTSIDE THE HARDWARE STORE, lost in thought, Roland is trying to understand how Lambert's could be closing, how things could go away that had always seemed like they would be forever, when a blue Ford pickup pulls over, stops.

—Hey old man, whatcha doing? Eddie Wilson leans out the passenger window. His brother Bill's driving.

—Heading home.

—Hop in. Eddie slides over on the front seat. We'll give you a lift.

Roland squeezes in. Eddie pushes over against his brother.

—Jesus, Eddie, give me enough room to shift, Bill says.

Bill's wearing a green John Deere hat pulled down low. He spits tobacco out the window. Says, how's your season, Roland?

—Fixin' to plow tomorrow. What're you boys up to?

—Been out to the John Deere place, Eddie says. Looking at tractors.

—And buying groceries, Bill says. That new Market Basket opened up? Sure is something.

—Right sorry about your Ma, Roland says.

Both Wilsons look straight ahead, don't say anything. Roland wishes he hadn't opened his big mouth.

The three men, quiet men, men more used to work than talk—especially squeezed together on the front seat, trying to ignore that their hips are touching—ride in silence all the way to Roland's front drive. Bill pulls in, skids to a stop.

THEY'RE SITTING ON THE PORCH, talking about plowing, seed, when to fertilize. Eddie's pulled a six-pack of beer out of the groceries he bought.

Marvin drives up, looks at Roland.

—I was thinking to give you a ride home, guess you didn't need it, Marvin says.

—Come on up, says Eddie. Have a beer.

—Got a new dog? Marvin says to Roland.

—That's Brown Dog, Eddie says.

—I can see that, says Marvin.

—That's his name, says Eddie. Ain't that right, Roland?

Roland is sitting on the top step of the porch. The dog lies next to him, head on her out-stretched paws. He pulls the dog closer, scratches her behind the ears. She sighs, leans against him.

—All I know is that is one ugly mutt, Marvin says.

Eddie hands Marvin a dark green bottle, glistening with condensation. Marvin takes out a pocket knife, pops it open.

Holds it away, examines it like he's looking for some hidden message.

—New truck? Marvin says.

—Ford's one fine vehicle, Bill says. I'll tell you that. You used to work at Preston's Garage, didn't you?

—Thirty-five years, Marvin says. Always been a Chevy man.

They start arguing. Marvin always did love to argue. Going on about how he's worked on so many trucks. Ought to know what he's talking about. Marvin and Eddie going back and forth about which truck is best. They're starting to get worked up when Roland says.

—Always preferred mine with four legs.

Bill laughs so hard he spits beer all over his boots, and they go back to talking about the weather, how it's fixing to be a dry summer according to the almanac.

Marvin looks at Bill, says, When're you going to get hitched, start a family?

—Eddie's family's enough for me, Bill says. Those kids'll run you ragged.

—Ain't that the truth, Eddie says.

Homer Wiggins, seeing all the vehicles, pulls his car over to the side of the road, walks up.

—We're having a party, Eddie says. Come on up, grab yourself a beer.

—Last time I saw you boys drinking, I had to haul you in and get your father to come take you home.

—Hell, Sheriff, that was twenty years ago, Bill says. Come on, sit a spell, have a beer. We won't tell no one.

—What the hell, why not.

Wiggins sits and soon everyone's talking so fast Roland can't keep up. He's used to silence, and now all these voices. He looks across to the barn, wonders when the herd will start down the hill. Thinks about what he needs to do. The haymow door is wide open, and he sees something moving around inside. A shadow.

ALBERT TUTTLE FIRST KNEW HE WAS DEAD when he couldn't smell the odors of the barn, not the manure, not the spilled milk, the hay, the silage turning sour. Those smells had been with him all his life and now they were gone.

He walks across the carriage bay and stands in shadow inside the open door of the haymow. He looks past the bright, tawny dirt of the dooryard to the men sitting on the porch drinking beer, feels a thirst he knows too well.

Roland sits in Abitha's chair, but of course, she wouldn't mind. Wouldn't mind at all.

The boy has tried, he knows that, but still . . .

The cows look good, though, and Albert realizes he missed their smell, their big, brown eyes, most as much as anything, the feel of their hard, bony hips through the thick coat, the way they chewed slow, like it took a lot of thought to chew grass, and the way they came down the hill every day in the late afternoon, their bells clanking softly in summer's sweet evening air.

They didn't tell you that you could die and still miss things, that you could die and still feel regret for the things you'd done and the things you hadn't. They didn't tell you that.

He watches the men on the porch. Thinks about going out into the sun to be with them, but steps back deeper into the shadows. Wiggins he knows, and there's Marvin. Never did think he'd see Marvin back at the farm. He wonders who the other men are, and hopes that they are kind to his boy, Roland, and that Roland is kind to this place, and that everything will be alright in the end.

THE MEN ARE TALKING; Roland's attention is on the barn. If it's those coons, he's going to have to get up, do something about it, but he'd hear the clanking and clattering if they were getting after the bins, and when Eddie Wilson finally takes a breath, he hears only silence in the barn, but he still can't shake the feeling something's there.

—Eddie doesn't believe me, Bill says. But this highway's going to be good for this place. We'll be able to get things to market faster. And look at all the jobs building the thing.

The brothers go back and forth, picking up in the middle of where they left off the last time they argued about the coming highway.

—I drove it, Marvin says.

The men all look at him.

—What? Eddie says.

—The highway. Me and Harvey Preston from the garage drove down south to the border. They got seven miles finished from Massachusetts to Brattleboro, opened it up so folks can drive it, see the future. Had to wait in line. It is something, alright. Smooth, wide, like nothing I ever seen. Cruising along like that, you feel like you're flying.

—What do you think, Sheriff? Bill says.

—Gonna be a tough year, I'll tell you that, Wiggins says. Israel Hutchins says all the signs are there for a wicked drought, says the animals know what's coming, birds having fewer chicks, ants building smaller hills.

—Bah, Hutchins is crazy, Eddie says. Claims the animals talk to him.

—The man's never wrong about the weather, Bill says. It's downright uncanny.

A quiet settles down over the men as evening comes on. Peepers start up down by the pond. The calls of tree frogs ricochet along the edge of the forest. The liquid music of a warbler. Roland looks at the cold bottle in his hands as if he doesn't know how it got there. Takes a sip. Remembers the first time he tasted beer.

JAMES WAS OFF TO THE WAR, Marvin had moved to Claremont to work at one of the area's first car dealerships. That left him and Daniel. Roland was seventeen. Didn't seem possible to him that the two of them could manage. James had always been the leader and Daniel the quiet follower, but with James gone, Daniel had come into his own, and Roland came to realize he hadn't known Daniel, obscured the way he'd been by James's big personality.

Daniel was a planner, didn't charge ahead, thought about it first, then set the two of them working the right way. After only a few weeks, Roland began to see that things were getting done, the cows well fed, milked on time, the barn clean, the milking parlor spotless, with less work than before. Didn't seem possible, but Daniel had a way of thinking things through. Daniel had a plan for everything.

They finished plowing the lower field.

"We'll sow tomorrow," Daniel said as they rested in the shade of a big maple. "Then we'll plow the middle acres, sow that, then move on to the upper. That way things'll be staggered out, not come to harvest all at once."

Roland nodded. Made sense, but it weren't how they'd done before.

"Town ball tonight, Roland," Daniel said. "You should come. We're playing Windsor. Gonna be a tough one. You should try out for the team. You got a good arm. Remember that time James talked you into throwing at the hive? That was a helluva throw."

Roland remembered alright, but what he most remembered was the trouble that followed. He was maybe seven or eight, tagging along behind his older brothers while they repaired the spring house. They wouldn't let him help, and having nothing to do he started throwing stones, bouncing them off a big maple about fifteen feet away.

James stopped his work.

"Bet you can't hit that oak," he said, pointing at a tree another twenty feet off.

Roland looked, took aim, nailed it with the first throw.

Then the two of them got on him, daring him—nobody thinking he could throw that far—and he reared back, whipped his skinny arm forward, and hit that hive right square, and that black swarm rose up out of the hive and James and Daniel took off leaving him behind and he ran, those bees right on him, all the way down to the house into the kitchen breathing so hard he thought he would fall right over and his mother worrying he was gonna faint. Those bees never did come back, they flew off, swarmed up in a tree on the edge of the woods.

"James sure was a troublemaker," Daniel said.

"What do you think he's doing?" Roland said.

"Ma got a letter," Daniel said. "He was still at some camp in Maryland. Training. Getting ready to ship out."

They walked down Mountain Road together, turned north on the Post Road, Daniel pounding his fist into his glove over and over.

"Vermont's got a professional league now," Daniel said. "Four teams. Fellows get paid. Boy, I'd like that. Imagine. Getting paid real money to play ball."

Seemed like everybody was there, boys, men, all standing around waiting for something. The Windsor men had uniforms, these baggy white outfits that looked downright silly to Roland. The Wethersfield men were all in their farm clothes, sleeves rolled up, work boots laced up tight. Turned out what they were waiting for was Daniel Tuttle. Daniel raced out into the field, yelling and joking with the fellows from the village. Roland stood off to the side, trying to stay out of the way.

"You gonna play?" Mackie Wilson appeared next to him.

"No, sir."

"Sir?" Mackie said. "Who you calling sir? How old are you, Roland?"

"Seventeen."

"Hell, I ain't that much older than you. Mackie's the name. Don't you be sir'n me." He slapped Roland on the back, laughed, "Come on. We need another body. Only got eleven in the field."

"I don't have a glove."

"You got hands, don't you?"

Roland found himself standing out in right field with no clear idea of what was happening, of the point of it all. He'd hear the crack of the bat, then watch as the guy ran around the bases with everyone throwing the ball at him and missing. He'd make it back to where he started, then another man would step up, smack the ball, and start running. Fortunately, the ball never came Roland's way and he found himself looking at the ground, wondering about the soil, and what would be good to plant here if they didn't waste the land on all this foolishness.

And then it happened. He looked up, the ball was coming right at him. It bounced twice, found its way into his hands like the ball had been looking for him. Roland stood there. The ball was lumpy, lighter than he'd expected. Guys were yelling. *Throw it! Plug him!* It was like James egging him on all over again, so Roland reared back, slung his arm forward, and nailed Big Jim Tolliver from Windsor right square in the back. Tolliver sprawled face-first in the dirt and got up looking mighty sore, and Roland was getting ready to run when Daniel ran up laughing.

"You plugged him good, Rollie!"

The Wethersfield men gathered around him, pushing and shoving like little boys.

"Never saw Tolliver get soaked that good," Mackie said.

Wethersfield lost, 37 to 14, but the men were happy sitting under the shade trees as evening strolled across the sky, still talking about Big Jim Tolliver getting plugged so hard he landed flat on his face.

Tolliver came over, looked at Roland. "Good throw, kid. Wait'll l I get a crack at you . . ."

Cornelius Bowker, everybody called him Cornie, came up with a tin bucket full of ice and a big glass jug filled with a brown liquid. "Have a taste, Roland," he said. "Made it myself"—he winked—"Don't tell no one."

"Nah," Roland said.

"Rollie don't drink," Daniel said.

"Hell," Mackie Wilson said. "One won't hurt you."

Roland took the jug. It was wonderfully cold and wet in his hand. He held it to his sweaty forehead for a moment, then took a drink. Made a face, all puckered up.

"You'll get used to it," Cornie said.

It was a warm spring evening and Roland was thirsty. He took a big swallow, then another.

"Save some for the rest of us," Mackie said.

Roland felt a warmth spread through him and he was glad to be there with those men—farmers, store owners, townsmen—and Daniel.

SITTING HERE ON HIS PORCH, it's like that ballgame happened yesterday. It's funny, he thinks, how things come back to him from so long ago, how the company of these men—the Wilsons, Marvin, the sheriff—and the taste of beer, can send him back. Roland drifts in and out of the conversation as the men argue about the weather until he realizes they're talking about him.

—I got a big empty house, lots of room, Marvin says. Bridget is gone, the girls are off on their own.

—He can come live with us, Eddie says. We can always use another hand on the farm.

Roland's not sure how he feels about all this attention. All of a sudden, everyone's got to worrying about what Roland Tuttle's gonna do. Not sure why it's their concern. But, secretly, he feels a comfort he wouldn't put words to, sitting here, everyone gathered around him on the family's porch, talking like old friends, drinking beer the way men do.

THE NEXT MORNING ROLAND is alone. There's empty bottles lying around. He picks them up, carries them to the barn, tosses them into a pile of junk, gets back to fixing the plow. The bolts fit perfectly.

Lambert always did know his stuff.

Roland goes to put the plow in the back of the haywagon so he can get it up to the fields without dragging the thing all that way. Can't lift it. Too heavy. He stands there, looking at the plow lying on the hard-packed dirt. Tries again, almost drops it on his foot.

Used to be able to hoist it up no problem.

—Don't think it got any heavier, he says to Brown Dog.

He takes it apart, loads it piece-by-piece, hitches the horses up to the haywagon, drives them up to the first field, unloads the plow, puts it all back together.

—Not the most efficient operation in the world.

Brown Dog looks at him, her head tilted to the side like she understands every word.

Once he has the team hitched up and starts cutting the soil in long furrows across the gentle hillside, and the horses are moving together ahead of him, and he starts sweating, and he gets to the end of the furrow and looks back at the long curving lines of plowed earth, he forgets the frustration. It's hard work, but Roland loves to plow, loves the smell of the freshly turned earth, the way the furrows line up across the field, the way they follow the hillside, curving with its contours, the way he can see the shape of it, the land.

He stops about half-done with the field, bends down, takes up a handful of soil. There's a dryness to it that ain't right for May. He sifts it through his fingers. Picks up a large clod. It crumbles in his hands. He looks to the south; a yellow dust cloud hangs over the river valley. Even here, up on the hill, he can hear the noise of the machines. He looks at the dust cloud, then down at the plowed earth. Remembers what Sheriff Wiggins said the other day about Hutchins's predictions. He knows there can be no connection between the work on the highway and the weather, but still . . .

Later, two fields done. He'll sow tomorrow.

May has always been a time of promise, of the crops to come, but today he feels a seed of doubt, of worry. He walks back down the hill toward the farmyard. Even the green of the pasture seems to him somehow muted. The cows lift their heads, watch him pass, go back to grazing. In the farmyard, a warm breeze lifts the leaves of the maples.

June

*H*IGH ON MOUNT ASCUTNEY leaves unfurl, the mountain-sides are pale green dotted with the near black of pine, spruce, and hemlock. The river is low and runs slow and dark. The nights are warm. The dry weather continues. Hayfields wait for first cut. Surveyors are seen again on Mountain Road carrying transits and tall orange poles. Yellow earth-movers, some as big as a small house, are parked in a field south of the village on the Post Road next to a large, black fuel tank. Men come and go from two office trailers. The sound of engines stuttering to life disturbs the morning.

~

*S*CYTHING HAY ON THE UPPER FIELD, Roland stops, looks south to where the Connecticut River curves around Fall Mountain on the New Hampshire side. He can see the water, shining hard and metallic in the hot sun. He remembers, as a boy, sitting on its banks in back of the old schoolhouse in Wethersfield, hiding behind the thick bushes that lined the river when he was supposed to be in that school.

The schoolhouse was a one-story building of flaking white paint and faded red brick. There were two doors in the gable end facing the road. Boys entered on the right, girls on the left. Through the door, you first came to a wood-paneled coat room, with pegs for jackets, and a raised wood plank for boots underneath, cubbies for lunch sacks. Then another set of doors, boys right, girls left, into the large classroom

with its rows of worn wooden desks and benches on either
side of a central aisle. Four large windows lined each side
wall. Roland's desk was toward the back, the next to last row,
under the fourth window. He would sit there, looking out
the window at the bright blue sky, a white cloud would drift
by and his mind would go with it, the teacher would call on
him and he wouldn't know the answer.

The winter after Roland's father died was long and dreary.
When spring finally came, he couldn't stand being in
school. He'd head out from the house—same as always—
walk down the hill alone, then north on the Post Road,
and on those warm heady days of spring when the sky
was a softer blue and the clouds seemed to drift slower,
he would check to see that no one was looking and duck
into the hedge that lined the road, skulk along a cornfield
that was part of Riverview Farm to a path that threaded
its way through a band of underbrush, then scramble down
a steep dirt embankment to a shale ledge that jutted out
a dozen or so feet above the river. He would perch there
in his secret place and spend the day watching the water
slide endlessly by, coming from places he'd never been,
going to places he'd never go. He was waiting, waiting
until he was old enough to quit school and work on the
farm with the rest of the family.

Now, EVEN FROM THIS DISTANCE, after all these years, Roland
can see the same current, the river still flowing, still passing
him by, and he still sometimes feels that yearning he'd felt
as a boy when he'd skipped school and watched that dark
water all day, a yearning for which he doesn't have words.

The river flows. He works.

Hot, dry weeks have his hayfields ready for first cut. Spring and summer are a time of unrelenting work: plowing, sowing, planting, cutting, tending, harvesting. Roland was raised to believe in work, work as the reason for being born, for living, and to believe that if he works the farm, puts his whole self into it, day in, day out—rises to tend the cows every day, plants when he should plant, cuts when he should cut—everything else will take care of itself. Despite this faith, there are times when a worry creeps into his mind, when every task seems pointless, when he feels he can't keep up, and he will sit on the porch and look at his hands and wonder. But then he'll hear his mother's voice, talking to him the way she did after the two of them were alone on the farm, telling him that when God put you in a place, well then, you got to make the best of it.

Abitha Dixon Tuttle was a believer. That she'd spent much of her life married to a man who had less than no use for religion or God, and that her father, the Right Reverend Benjamin Dixon's religion had been harsh and unforgiving, had not lessened her faith. She attended church every Sunday, read from the Bible in the evenings. That she had been unable to impart that belief to any of her children was the one great regret in her life, and that she had been able to keep that faith through all that happened was her great comfort.

THE WAR WAS ALL OVER THE front pages of the Claremont Daily Eagle and the Windsor Telegram, but life and work at the farm continued as it had before. James had sent letters from Fort Meade in Maryland where he was training, but after he shipped out to Europe almost a year to the day after he'd climbed aboard that train in Windsor, there had been

no news until a telegram was delivered to the Tuttle farm
the morning of Friday, June 14, 1918.

Marvin came over from Claremont. He pulled into the
farmyard in a car borrowed from Preston Chevrolet where
he worked, and chickens went flying in all directions. He
hadn't been to the farm in a couple of years. Roland, now
eighteen, was sitting in the parlor with his mother and Eliza.

Roland handed Marvin a flimsy piece of yellow paper. He'd
read it, Roland had, over and over, and no matter how many
times he read it, it still said the same thing.

"We deeply regret to inform you . . ." it began. I bet you
do, Roland thought, I bet you goddamn do, but it don't make
a bit of difference, whoever the hell you are, Mr. Adjutant
General, how deeply you regret it—James is dead and gone.

Marvin put the telegram on the dining table and Abitha
and Roland looked at it, like if they stared hard enough it
would shrivel up into dust and blow away and it would be
like the damn thing had never come.

"Whatever shall we do?" Abitha said.

"Where's Daniel?" Marvin said.

"Out in the barn," Roland said. "He's real cut up."

Eliza was sitting in Abitha's big chair, curled up like she
was trying to hide.

"Will they send him back?" Abitha said. "So we can have
a proper service? Put him next to his Pa?"

None of them had an answer.

"Whatever shall we do?" his mother said, then looked long
and hard at Marvin. Roland knew what she was thinking.
She was not a sentimental woman. A few minutes of grief
was all she would allow herself.

"You got to come help us, Marvin. We're your family."

"I can't, Ma. I've got a family of my own, two baby girls."

"Well, bring 'em on over. We got plenty of room."

"I've got a good job, Bridget's a town woman, Ma. She's not cut out for farm life."

She turned away from Marvin.

"Woman's too fine for us, that's what it is, too fancy to work on a farm," she said to Roland.

"She's a good woman and a good mother to your two granddaughters. Don't you start in on her. Maybe you should sell, come live in Claremont."

Roland saw the hard look on his mother's face, that look she got when she'd made up her mind about something, and there weren't no chance of persuading her otherwise.

"I'll send more money," Marvin said. "You can get a hired man."

"We'll make do," she said. "The four of us can handle it."

Roland caught up to Marvin as he was getting into his car.

"Poor James," Roland said.

In a life whose work is marked by the seasons, June was, for Abitha Tuttle, devoted to the garden, and the garden was for her a refuge, and June of this hot, dry spring brings to Roland Tuttle thoughts and memories of his mother.

She kept her seeds in a basket on a shelf in the kitchen. Some evenings, she'd sit at the kitchen table and take out the packets and sort them on the kitchen table and talk quietly to herself, planning what to plant, where, when.

June, when her garden was tilled and laid out and the early things—lettuce, peas, kale—were in the ground, and the tomato plants were poking their heads up, and the rhubarb patch was tinged with purple, was her favorite time of year.

Roland's father would be out in the field with the older boys, haying, working the potato field, fixing fences. She would stand on the porch, wiping her hands on her apron after washing up from the morning meal, look out to her garden.

"Rollie," she'd say. "Grab the basket, we got planting to do."

Roland would run to the kitchen, take that basket down off the shelf—he could reach it if he stood up on his toes—and carry it out to his mother on the front porch, carry it like it was the most precious thing in the world.

Abitha's kitchen garden was off to the side when you stepped out the front door. It was long and narrow, bordered by a slat-wood fence. Gramma Ida worked in the garden alongside Abitha until she got too old. Then, on days when the air was warm and gentle, one of the older boys, usually Daniel, would move her chair out to the porch and Ida May would sit and rock and, as she put it, supervise.

"We're late this year," Gramma Ida said.

Roland was seven.

"Lord, after that winter, everything's late," Abitha said.

His mother handed him the spade-fork. "Go on," she said. "Fluff up that patch over there, we're going to put the carrots in."

Not sure how much good he did, that fork was near as big as he, but she was patient with him in the garden in a way she never was anywhere else. She would talk, to herself mostly, but somehow Roland felt included, like she was talking to him.

"We'll do the carrots first, then if we get to it afore lunch, we'll start on the pumpkins."

She showed Roland how to put the seed in. "Make sure the dirt's good and loose. Dig your hands in, get 'em dirty. Poke the seeds in, maybe an inch apart."

She'd show him the rhubarb, with its purple-red stalks, the asparagus starting to bolt, going to seed. Show him the day lilies, the bee balm, the feverfew she'd planted around the edge of the vegetables.

"Are they not the prettiest things?" she'd say. "Good for all kinds of ailments, too."

He'd look up and see her smile.

In the house, Abitha worked with grim determination—mouth set, eyes hard and flat—but in the garden a light came to her face, and it was the time when young Roland felt closest to her. Mostly, he felt tolerated. Looking back he can see that she had been tired, worn down, her mothering all used up. He had been one child too many. But that didn't stop him loving her.

YEARS LATER, ROLAND AND HIS mother were alone on the farm. The seasons passed, each revolving into the next, a constant flow of work: Roland milking twice each day, plowing, sowing, harvesting, felling, splitting, stacking; his mother churning, keeping the house, planting her garden, cooking, tending the stove. Roland was milking thirty cows, his mother making butter. They had the chickens, the garden.

Long, long days, each one after the other, each with its prescribed tasks. They worked and lived and each spring, with the coming of the sun and the warming of the earth, they would be filled with hope for the bounty to come, and Abitha would take down her seed basket and sort the packets on the table as she had the year before and the year before that, back as far as Roland could remember.

But then had come a spring when she sat staring at the seed packets spread out on the kitchen table as if she had never seen them before, and that spring she didn't plant, and as summer approached she spent her time sitting at the table gazing off into nothingness, and the weeds, wild and thick, took over the garden plot.

Roland came out of the barn into the hot June sun, and was shocked to see his mother laboring in the garden, bent over, digging ferociously at the weeds, talking to herself, berating herself that she'd let things go.

She stopped, stood, looked at the sun high overhead, and keeled over into the rhubarb patch.

He picked her up, carried her into the house—she was so thin, he could feel her bones through her gingham dress and apron—got her comfortable on the couch in the parlor, went into the kitchen and stood there looking at the telephone on the wall. He'd never liked using the thing, didn't like that woman's voice asking who he wanted to call when he didn't want to call anyone.

His mother used it, called Marvin in Claremont once in a while, called all the way up to St. Johnsbury to Margaret, but he'd never liked talking on the thing, the way the voice on the other end sounded tinny and strange.

He took down the earpiece, turned the crank.

Sheriff Wiggins arrived before the ambulance.

"She's worn out," Wiggins said.

He kneeled next to the couch where she lay staring at the ceiling, her breath coming in shallow, quick little gasps.

"We'll get her over to Cottage Hospital."

Roland stood in the dooryard as the ambulance backed out of the driveway onto Mountain Road and drove away. He was standing in that same place three years later when Sheriff Homer Wiggins drove up the driveway and got out of his car and walked up to Roland and told him that Margaret had called, and that he was downright sorry to have to tell him that his mother had passed away in her sleep.

She wasn't coming back. He had known that day in the hospital when Margaret took her north to rest that she would not return, but had not let himself know that he knew.

The kitchen was empty, her churn was there on the floor, waiting. It will keep on waiting. Her nature books were there on the kitchen table. They will keep on waiting.

Fifteen years they had worked that farm.

Fifteen years, just the two of them.

There was a hole in his life.

Roland took the churn, carried it into the buttery, pushed it back against the wall under the wide shelves where they used to store the big wheels of cheese that Ida May and Abitha and Margaret and Eliza produced back when the kitchen was in full swing. He went back into the kitchen, picked up the three nature books from the table where she kept them, didn't know what to do with them.

He stood there, rooted in place, then carried the books into the pantry, then came back out, put them back on the table. One fell open to a picture of a black and yellow butterfly. It pained him to look at that picture, knowing that it had been her favorite, knowing how many times she had sat there with that book open looking at that picture, touching it with her finger as if she could feel the texture of the butterfly's wings there on the paper of that book. He left the books there, lowered himself slowly into the chair by the cookstove.

He sat there rocking gently back and forth. There was a stone, a heavy round gray Vermont fieldstone, where his heart should be.

Sam, this one a tall black and brown beast, stood in front of him, the dog's head almost level with Roland's. The dog looked at the man like he, the dog, had something to say.

"What're we gonna do, Sam? What're we gonna do?"

He heard the cows coming down the hill, their bells clanking softly in the gentle evening air.

"Cows are gonna need milking," Roland said.

The light in the kitchen was dim, the kerosene lamp in the middle of the table, dark. The woodstove cooled, ticking and clicking as the metal contracted. The chair rocked back and forth, forth and back. He heard the cows pushing against the gate into the feedlot, getting restless, snorting, lowing. Still, he sat. Rocking. Back and forth, forth and back. They didn't know, the cows, that the world had changed while they were at pasture. How could they? Their complaints grew louder. He felt them pull at his heart.

"I guess . . . I got to go milk," he said.

He left that book there, open, and walked out to the barn.

THE GARDEN HAS BEEN neglected for years, and when Roland looks out from the front porch at that overgrown rectangle and the rotting, fallen-down fence surrounding it, he feels a sense of regret as if he is somehow letting his mother, now long gone, down, as if he has failed to honor her memory. He tried at first, but it became too much, what with the milking and haying and all. The rhubarb patch still comes up every spring with its purple stalks and poisonous leaves, and the asparagus grows so wild that by early summer it is almost as tall as he with stalks near as thick as a small tree.

Sometimes at night he hears rustling outside and comes out onto the front porch and sees, in the moonlight, a shadowy figure in the garden, bent over, digging in the dirt, and tries to remember her face, that rare smile, remember as a boy working with her and Gramma Ida, remember the feel of the warm dirt in his hands, the smell of the tomato plants in summer, their fuzzy branches hanging low with the weight of the ripening red fruit.

In the morning, the abandoned garden is as it always is, thick with undisturbed weeds, thick with memory.

THEY STOOD ONE TIME, Roland and Abitha, at the edge of the lower south meadow. It had not been mowed in years. He'd been meaning to get to it. They'd been alone together on the farm for five years.

"Look at this, Ma," Roland said. "Land going to waste."

"Rollie, we got enough land to cultivate."

They walked out into the meadow, weaving through clumps of weeds almost head-high to his mother. A thin cloud of white blossoms hovered above the ground.

"That's Wild Aster," his mother said. "Folks call it flea bane."

The meadow was dotted with wildflowers, small bushes, tall clumps of golden flowers.

"Look at that goldenrod. There's Black Eyed Susan's, Queen Ann's Lace." She pointed to some tall plants with chalky, hairy leaves.

"Milkweed," she said. "Butterflies love it."

A gold and black butterfly fluttered in the air between them.

"That's a monarch," she said. "They go away come winter. Nobody knows where."

To Roland all the things she'd showed him had been only weeds growing where a crop should be planted.

"This land isn't wasted," she said. "It's fine the way it is."

He tried to see what she saw, but he was still a young man, caught up in a young man's concerns. Letting this land go wild, not grazing it or cultivating it, seemed to him a criticism, the land saying he wasn't man enough to do his work.

"Some things," she said, "you can't do nothing about. The weather for one. You got to stick to what you can do something about. You do your work, the rest of it will take care of itself."

Uphill, toward the woods, there was a large gray boulder sticking up out of the meadow, one side flat, almost like a bench facing down the meadow toward the river. Roland, thinking his mother would head back to the house, to her chores, walked up to it, sat on that rock bench, and looked out over the meadow. He couldn't see the water; it was obscured by the tall weeds and bushes.

His mother followed him. She stood, leaning against the rock, looking where he was looking.

"How old are you now, Rollie?"

A strange question, thought Roland, considering he was certain she knew how old he was.

"Twenty-three."

"Twenty-three," she said in quiet, far-away voice. "The time I was twenty-three, I had three children. Imagine that."

There was a long silence as they watched the flowers and bushes of the meadow rustle and twitch in the early summer breeze.

"You should find yourself a wife, Rollie."

How? Roland thought. How do you find yourself a wife? Where do they keep them, these wives waiting to be found? He thought of Annabelle. He thought of her often, married to

Macklin Wilson, with babies of her own, or so he'd heard—
even though he was trying not to listen—down at the store.

She reached out to him, but saw him shrink the way he
did, as if he didn't like being touched.

"I was my parents' only child," she said. "Grew up alone
in a big empty house. Families are meant to be big, to grow
and sprawl, and spread out into the world." And then, as if
she sensed Roland's discomfort, she stopped. "It's okay, son.
You need to do what you need to do, to live the life you want
to live. We'll be fine here, we will. You'll see . . ."

EVENING. ROLAND RESTS on that outcrop of gray Vermont
stone looking down toward the lower pond and the
overgrown meadow and remembers that time with his
mother, remembers the things she'd shown him that he
hadn't been able to see then, and the things she'd told him
that he hadn't ever forgot.

A songbird sings in the trees to his left. The calls of tree
frogs bounce back and forth through the humid air. The pond
is surrounded by tall cattails, a thick growth of swamp maple,
scrub oak, small trash pines. The surface of the water is dark
and patched with green algae. Beyond the pond is a wall of
bulging wild sumac, scrub maples, thin saplings all covered
with tangled vines and creepers so heavy they threaten to
pull the trees down.

Life . . . life everywhere. Birds singing to their mates,
frogs calling. Wild things growing, pushing toward him,
nature taking back what his great-great-grandfather had
wrested from it. He looks back toward his farmyard, the
hard-packed dirt, rusting tools, gray, worn buildings. Vines

grow up the side of the barn. It seems dead compared to the pulsing, grasping chaos of the New England spring. Insects everywhere, rustling, biting, burrowing. Summer is short. Life must waste no time if it means to carry on. Mates must be found, roots must push down.

It's all in such a hurry, but Roland feels no sense of hurry. His life is measured out in the slow, deliberate repetition of daily tasks. What had seemed to him, to the family through the generations, as a steady march forward, seems now merely a holding back of the forces of nature. That's the thing, without work, constant sweat and toil, it would all go back, swallowed up by this green tide.

Farms ain't natural anymore than roads and cars and buildings, he realizes.

It's this great jumble in front of him that's natural. At that moment he decides to go see what he's so far refused to look at, refused to acknowledge. He hears a rustling in the bushes next to him, turns with a start, but sees only Brown Dog coming out of the weeds all covered in mud and green slime from the pond. She rubs up against him, soaking his pant leg, tail wagging.

Happy as a pig in shit, his father would've said.

And, Roland thinks, smelling like one, too.

—Come on girl, he says. Let's take a walk.

They skirt the pond, the edge marked with animal tracks: deer, fox, coyote. Brown Dog takes a quick detour through the shallows, hunting frogs, comes back muddier than ever. They weave their way down the lower meadow on narrow game trails—Brown Dog nose to the ground—skirting the thicker clumps of weeds almost head-high to Roland, then follow one of the lines trimmed by those men back in April.

They come to the property line. The stone wall piled up long ago, when the Tuttles first cleared this land, is covered with vines. Thin maple shoots grow up between the stones, but the dry-stacked wall stands solid, though a few rocks have fallen off, and it's collapsed a bit in a couple of places. Roland turns to look back toward the farm.

The weeds have started to grow in, but he can still see where they'd been, the surveyors, their cut-lines pointing straight at his house.

Roland climbs over one of the low spots in the stone wall, holds up a rusted strand of barbed wire for the dog. They pass into the pine forest, the bare trunks evenly spaced, the forest floor deep in shadow. There's no undergrowth and Roland walks easily among the tall, straight trunks of the trees on a thick, soft mat of pine needles. It's strangely, wrongly quiet—all that to-do around the pond is behind them—un-naturally quiet, like he's entered a dead space where nothing lives, where every living thing has moved out, gone someplace else.

And who can blame them? he thinks, when he steps out of the forest and sees the devastation before him.

There's no transition. One moment he's in the green shade of the pines, the next on the edge of a vast plane of rucked-up earth, big piles of rock shards, mounds and mounds of tree slash, stacks, twenty, thirty feet high, of pine logs. He's hit by the dry smell of sun-baked earth and the sharp tang of dripping pine sap. He looks to the south, and can see the progression of the work. Here, raw piles, uprooted trees, piles of rock, to the south, where they've been at it longer, the earth has been scraped clean, leveled and graded, a wide swath between walls of dark forest.

What kind of road needs something so wide?

It's early evening; work has stopped for the day. The only sound is the hiss of the hot wind in the pines behind him. Giant yellow machines are lined up against the long line of forest to his right, backs to the mountain, facing what they have done. He can't help but think of these machines, the likes of which he's never seen before, as somehow alive. Like they might up and start gnashing and grinding and digging all by themselves. They look greedy to him, those machines, all lined up, ready to go. Greedy, like they want to eat everything, chew it all up, devour it. They look hungry in a way Roland can't understand.

How can a machine be hungry?

He walks over on dirt, sun-baked hard, rutted, nothing growing. There's a dozer big as a house, trucks with tires taller than him. It's all so much bigger than he ever imagined even with all that noise coming up the valley to his house every day. He can't encompass the expanse, the size of it, in his mind.

Brown Dog's out in the middle of it all running around like a crazy person, like she's never seen anything like this either. She stops in front of a bulldozer, spreads her front paws wide on the ground and starts barking and snarling at the thing, ready to take it on.

He walks further south to where fill, sand, and loose gravel has been graded smooth. There are weeds, small, tentative, already growing up through cracks in the surface.

He looks up toward where the mountain broods over this insult at its base, then back to where, beyond the pines, the meadow and the pond go on growing and reproducing and getting on with the business of life.

It's a comfort, when he thinks about it.

Things'll go back to the way they were before, before we-all showed up. Even this mess, if they ever stop working on it, ever stop maintaining it, will be gone some day. It's not the kind of comfort that makes him feel better for himself, for his life, but a comfort nonetheless.

It's something, he realizes, his mother had showed him that time they stood in the overgrown meadow—that out of neglect, or maybe out of simply leaving things alone, can come beauty.

He's had a lot of time in his solitary life to think about these things, and he's come to some conclusions, not conclusions that, if asked, he would put words to, could explain necessarily, but things that he knows, certainties maybe. And one of these conclusions that he's come to is that what's going on today ain't all that important, that he, himself, ain't all that important.

July

*I*N THE VILLAGE, DUST IS EVERYWHERE. Clouds form and grow in the afternoon but bring no rain. A hot wind blows up the valley. A fuel depot had been established on the ball field north of the village, and the Post Road near Wethersfield Bow is closed at night to permit the passage of huge fuel tankers heading north. The ground shakes as they rumble past. Blasting has begun on the northern edge of Mount Ascutney. First, the warning siren, then the dull whomp. Small rocks and debris rain down. Doc Ferguson reports a dramatic rise in lung ailments. Children are kept inside.

~

*T*HE INTERIOR OF THE BARN IS COOL and sweet with the smell of hay despite the hot sun of July outside. Roland stands at his workbench, the curving blade of his scythe clamped in front of him. The upper hayfield waits for him to finish the second cut. He takes a mill bastard file, blows the dust off it, draws it in a smooth motion along the blade. It makes a sound that would set most folks' teeth on edge, but he likes it, that grinding, metallic ring. He can feel the file snagging and catching on burrs and dents in the old blade, draws it again and again along the cutting edge, each pass a smooth motion, effortless, one he's done a thousand times before. He flips the blade over, repeats the process, then takes it out of the vise and holds it up to the light filtering through the gaps in the back wall of the barn. The edge shines clear silver against the dark, tarnished steel of the ridged body of the blade.

He tests it with his thumb, draws a tiny line of blood.

The horse-drawn sickle mower broke down that morning, axle snapped clean through. He could get it welded down at Ed's Automotive in Claremont, but Roland doesn't feel like dealing with the trouble. He's done more than half the field, figures he can finish it by hand.

It's a shame, though. He looks at the broken machine. The thing's been with the farm since long before Roland was born. Great-Grandfather Lucius C. Tuttle bought it new, from McCormick Harvest Machine. Had it shipped on the train all the way from Chicago right into Windsor. Lucius drove the wagon into town with his son, the first Roland, sixteen years old and already taller than his father, sitting beside him to pick up that mower.

Roland the Elder, his mother called him.

"To keep you two Rolands separate," she said. Soon, everybody called him that when they talked about his grandfather: Roland the Elder. Always sounded kinda fancy. Roland looks at the mower, all bent over, folded, the seat tipped off to one side. This isn't just a busted bolt. It's like the whole damn thing is worn out, done run its course.

SHERIFF HOMER T. WIGGINS turns off Mountain Road and pulls into the dooryard.

—Sheriff, Roland says. Been seein' a lot of you lately.

—Hell, Wiggins says. Got nothing else to do. I'm Sheriff Emeritus now. You know that?

—What the heck does that mean?

—Means I'm too old to do the job, but they don't know how to get rid of me.

Roland ponders on that for a bit.

—Besides, Wiggins says into the silence. I like visiting old friends.

—Old is right.

Wiggins waits, waits like he's expecting something more from Roland. He looks at the mower, at the broken axle lying crooked on the ground.

—Don't look too good, Wiggins says.

—You could say that, Roland says, wipes his hands on an oily rag.

They walk around to the south side of the barn, sit in the hot sun on a bench made from a split-in-half log, lean back against the board-and-batten siding of the barn, the wood old and sun-baked, the grain of the wide pine boards dried up into ridges that swirl in strange shades of orange and yellow around big knots a dark brown that is almost purple. Brown Dog lies down next to Wiggins, rests her head against his leg. He reaches down, scratches behind her ear.

—You ever going to mow that field? Wiggins says.

—Nope . . . no reason to, Roland says. Ma loved that meadow the way it is.

A grasshopper lands on Roland's right shoe. He looks at it for a bit, then with a sweep of his hand so quick Wiggins hardly sees it, scoops up the insect, holds his cupped hand up to his ear.

—Listen, he says. Holds his hand out to Wiggins.

A thin coppery sound, like a rusty gate far out across a field swinging in the wind.

—You ever hear such a sweet song? Roland says.

Roland looks at the overgrown meadow, remembers sitting on this bench with his mother years ago, opens his hand, the grasshopper jumps out, disappears into the high grass.

—Been thinking about James, Roland says.

Wiggins stays quiet.

A week past, the village had unveiled a new memorial to the men lost in World War I. The old one, a thin panel of slate put up more than forty years ago, had started to crumble. Folks complained you couldn't even read the names. The new one was supposed to have been done for Memorial Day back in May, but when it wasn't, Mrs. William Frederickson, Chair of the Memorial Committee, decided the Fourth of July would work fine. Pedrini and Sons, the gravestone masons from Springfield, had set a wide slab of granite into the ground in the middle of the north side of the town green with a bronze plaque bolted onto it. The plaque had the Great Seal of the United States of America, the eagle holding arrows in one claw and a bough of peace in the other, and a list of names under that seal. Young men, boys, had their names there, James Tuttle one of them.

—You remember that time at the train station? Roland says. When I dropped him off . . . you think he knew? Knew he might not be coming back?

—I was on that train, Wiggins says. We all thought for certain we were coming home. Turns out it didn't matter what we thought, what we wanted. Didn't matter . . .

—What was it like, the war?

—Long time ago, Roland . . . long, long time ago. Not something I like to talk about.

Roland nods.

—Yep, lotta things not worth talking about.

—Take a ride with me, Wiggins says.

—Where to?

—Got something I want to show you.

It is stifling hot in the car. Wiggins wipes the sweat from his face.

—Jesus, what a year, Wiggins says.

They drive north through the village on the Post Road. Roland cranks down his window, feels the hot wind on his face. Wiggins slows, turns onto an arrow-straight freshly paved street. Roland looks at the sign: Mountain Meadows.

—Didn't this used to be Wilson land?

—Yep, Wiggins says. Sold it a couple of years ago.

They turn onto Hayfield Lane. Every fifty feet or so, there's a driveway and a mailbox and a mobile home. All of them white, some with turquoise trim, others with yellow. Lined up, white boxes, one after the other, almost no space between them. Small squares of lawn in front burned brown by the sun. Most have a car parked in the driveway—one's got a kid's metal swing set, another a push hand-mower sitting on the parched grass.

Wiggins pulls into an empty driveway.

—Want to take a look? They're real nice inside, modern and everything.

—What for? Roland says.

—Thought you might find it interesting.

—Nope.

Wiggins turns in his seat, looks at Roland like he's waiting for something, then shakes his head.

—Okay, then, Wiggins says. Backs out of the driveway.

—How come, Roland says as they pull out onto the Post Road, How come they name things after what ain't there anymore?

THE LOWER HAYFIELD. Roland is still thinking about that sign, about how there weren't any mountains there and about how, after they built all those box-like houses, there wasn't a meadow nor a hayfield. He feels the sun on his back, feels the stiff stalks of hay against his legs, feels in his hand the coarse grain of the wood of the scythe, tastes the dry dust on the back of his throat, the heat of the day already building.

Mid-afternoon, the sun on him like a weight; he's moving slow, the air around him thick, like molasses. His arms are heavy, there is a shooting pain in his lower back. No more than half done, he stops and stands on the hillside leaning on the s-curved handle of the scythe, the pointed, curving blade arcing up out of the cut hay toward the brutal sun. He looks down at the farm, the weathered gray barn, plow shed, chicken coop, spring house arranged around a courtyard of hard-packed earth. A yellow dust cloud traverses the southern horizon.

A car drives into the yard, stirring up plumes of dirt. It's pale blue and white, has long angled fins and sharp stripes of chrome. A woman he doesn't recognize gets out of the driver's side door, walks around to the other side of the car and helps an old woman that he does recognize out of the car.

He picks up the scythe and walks slowly down through the uncut hay to the back fence, leans the tool up against the rusty barbed wire, opens the gate, and walks toward the two women.

—Roland Tuttle, what are you doing? Out in the hot sun like that?

His older sister, Margaret, always had been kind of bossy.

—Haying.

—I can see that, Margaret says.

She fans herself with a folded newspaper.

—Sheriff Wiggins called me.

—That so.

—Said I should check on you, see if you're doing alright.

—Well, now you have. Roland looks at the other woman. There is something familiar about her.

—Uncle Roland, she says. Remember me?

—Don't you remember your niece? his sister says.

—Becky? he says.

They used to visit in the summer when they were little, Margaret's kids, when Roland's mother was still alive, and each time Margaret seemed different, more citified. Nicer clothes, fancier shoes. Roland liked those visits, all those kids running around, playing in the hayloft, splashing in the pond, and back when things were good with Marvin and his family there'd be more cousins than he could count. He'd put them to work, though it was unclear how much work got done.

Becky was the oldest of the bunch, too old for kid's games, and the one time Margaret and William left the kids with Roland for a few days, Becky took over running the house, made sure everyone got fed, cleaned the place, looked after Roland. He would stop at the door on his way in from milking, watch her working in the kitchen, cooking, baking, putting food up like his mother used to do. It was almost as if he had a wife in the house, as if he had a family.

—It's Rebecca, now, she says. Steps forward and hugs him.

—You don't want to do that, I'm filthy.

He stands rigid, doesn't know what to do with his hands. It has been a long time since anyone touched him, much less wrapped her arms around him and held him close.

—I don't care. It's so good to see you.

They sit on the porch, drink cool water from the spring behind the milk house.

Roland takes off his battered straw hat, wipes his forehead with his shirt sleeve.

—It's too hot to be out in the sun like that, Margaret says.

—And wearing that heavy shirt, Rebecca says.

—Probably still has his long-johns on, Margaret says.

—Nope, took 'em off.

—Well, thank God for that, says Margaret.

THEY SIT ON THE PORCH, Rebecca—she was still Becky to him—all grown up with kids of her own. Maybe it's the heat, but a quiet thoughtfulness comes over them.

—I swear, says Roland to Rebecca. You're the spitting image of your Grandma Abitha.

Rebecca turns to her mother.

—How come you never talked about Grandma Abitha when I was growing up?

—You know how your father was, Margaret says. William didn't like me talking about the farm, thought we were better than all that.

—Where was she from? Rebecca says.

—Windsor . . . her father was the minister of that big church on Main Street.

—She was one strong lady, Roland says.

—She had to be, Margaret says.

—Her father, the Reverend Benjamin J. Dixon didn't
approve of his daughter running off to live on a scrappy
old hill farm, didn't approve of us Tuttles, Margaret says to
Rebecca. He was a hard man. I never did understand how a
religious man could be so mean. He cut Abitha off. Wouldn't
even let her own mother come to visit.

Margaret stops, fans herself, looks down at the parched
grass at her feet.

—Mary Cabot Dixon was your great-grandmother's name,
she says to Rebecca. I met her once, at your grandfather's
funeral. Oh my, she was an elegant lady. I think she was from
Boston. And educated; she taught your Grandma Abitha to
read when she was growing up.

Roland feels the heat working on him. It sits, heavy. He
hears cicadas in the trees, their buzzing whine rising and
falling in waves. Margaret keeps talking, maybe to Rebecca,
maybe to herself.

—I remember Momma sitting in that big red chair with
a big book and the happiest look on her face. I was a little
girl. She'd take me up on her lap. Read to me from a story set
way off in England about a orphan boy, on his own. Oliver
Twist was his name. I still remember that story.

She turns to Rebecca.

—Your Grandpa Albert put an end to that. Said it was a
waste of time when there was work to be done. I mean, by
the time Roland came along, she didn't much have time, with
the six of us and the farm and all, now did she?

The shade from the big maple moves slowly across the
dooryard. A few birds peck at bits of grain. The sound of
cowbells comes slowly down the hill. The heat settles over
them, it seems to take too much energy to talk. Rebecca fans

herself with a magazine. Roland tries to picture his mother sitting, resting, reading. She didn't get enough, he thinks, rest. Was it his fault that she didn't get time for herself?

—He could come live with us . . . Rebecca says.

They'd been talking about him.

—Why would I want to do that? Roland says.

Margaret and Rebecca look at him, surprised, as if they'd forgotten he was there.

—You're going to have to do something, his sister says.

Roland looks out across the heat-baked yard; he can hear flies buzzing by the manure pile.

Hell, he thinks, you always got to do something.

—We're going down to the churchyard, Margaret says at last. You should come.

—Have to milk.

—We can wait 'til you're done.

—That's alright. You go on.

Later, Margaret and Rebecca gone away back north, the sun passes behind the mountain but the evening sits hot and humid. The leaves of the oak droop, stunned by the heat.

THERE ARE BARE PATCHES in the upper hayfield, pale dirt, dried hard and cracked. He reaches down, takes a handful of stalks, they crumble in his hand to dust that sifts through his fingers like sand. Roland wonders if it will even be worth harvesting. He walks on, up the rolling hills, sun hard on his back, grass crackling and breaking underfoot, the air so harsh it hurts to breathe. He turns, looks out from under the wide brim of his straw hat. All he sees is brown. The dust cloud hovers south of the farm.

He detours to the side, walks over to the copse of trees.

It has never grown tall, this little group of trees. There's a maple, two oaks, some ash. Ever since Roland was a boy, those trees have been there, in the middle of the meadow. He'd asked his father one time, he must have been seven or eight, why they didn't cut them down. "That's the way it is," was the only answer he got. "We go around 'em. Always have, always will."

Roland remembers Gramma Ida, wonders why no one ever said what he was sure they knew—that Edmund and Susannah Tuttle were buried there—wonders why they let those graves go, then walks on and passes through the upper fence into the wood lot. He doesn't come up here much in summer, usually too busy with things lower down.

He steps into the shade of the woods and it's as if the drought, this hard, miserable season, has not happened. The air is cool, almost damp, and quiet—not the sharp, dead silence of winter, but the soft peaceful quiet of things growing and beasts resting. He wanders among tree trunks, tall straight columns, green with verdant moss. Great arching branches reach out to each other forming a vaulted ceiling high over his head. Breeze quivers in the leaves. Sunlight dapples and ripples on the forest floor like water flowing over rocks on a stream-bed, making even the biggest of the trees seem somehow insubstantial.

Roland has come to think of memory as an unreliable thing. His memories come and they seem like things that happened for sure, but then come memories of things that surely never did. His Gramma Ida had filled his young head with stories so vivid they became like memories. He feels a sense of something out of reach, the memory of a dream perhaps where he stood once in the humble church in the village, under the beamed ceiling staring at a tall wooden crucifix above an ornate altar, but the cross was empty.

He remembers his grandfather, though he knows that's not possible, the first Roland, dying days before he, the second, was born.

But remember him he does.

Perhaps it's that everyone talked about him so much that he was a presence in the family's life long after he was gone. He knows that Great-Grandfather Lucius built the big house, but the family always said that without the energy and drive of his son, the first Roland, it would not have become such a great and fine house, and that in its way the extravagance of that ornate structure reflected the size of that young man's personality, the expanse of his dreams.

Perhaps, Roland thinks, in the naming of him, his parents had hoped to create a link, a connection, between the two Rolands, and somehow ensure the continuation of those dreams, but had created only an expectation, a burden, that he, the second Roland, could never live up to.

He stops at the largest stump, now weathered and half rotted, so big across he can't span it with his long arms. He remembers the taking of that tree, the tallest, straightest oak in all the wood lot, sees himself directing the woodsmen.

That can't be.

It was his great-grandfather did all that, but Roland sees it now as if he'd been there. The sawing going on for hours, the earth shaking when the great tree fell, the team of four huge draft horses dragging the massive logs down to the building site, the carpenters with their axes and adzes and mallets and chisels, hewing and shaping the timbers, the posts, the beams, that will form the frame of that house. The frame going up, men from all over there for the raising. He feels for a moment what his great-grandfather must have felt then—an audacious, unshakeable belief in the future—but cannot now, himself, feel.

He walks down the hill, stops at the spring house. Water flows up from a crack in the rock ledge into a deep pool, water so clear he can see the stones that form the bottom, rounded and shining and polished, but knows that if he reaches deep into the cold water and pulls one of those stones up into the air, that it will dry and turn dull and ordinary. He takes up the long-handled tin pot that has been beside the spring as long as he can remember, dips into the water sending ripples out, drinks a long cold slug of water, watches the ripples bounce back toward the center, and waits until the surface of the water calms and turns clear again.

THE SUN PASSES BEHIND the shoulder of the mountain and the light fades. Cumulus clouds to the south gather and rise up, tinged with pink. The earth-movers are quiet. Roland hears the yelp of a coyote somewhere in the forest, hungry, ready for the night's hunt. Brown Dog lifts her head, pricks her ears, decides it's none of her concern, settles. The cicadas quiet, the crickets come alive. He feels the night coming on. In the overgrown meadow, fireflies wander, disappearing, then reappearing as they dart through and around the tall clumps of weeds.

He realizes he's been waiting for something. Not sure what. Something to happen, something that will change things. Change the direction of things. He's not stupid. He knows what's going on. Just because he doesn't jump up and down at one of those meetings and start yelling, or just because he doesn't go off and hire a bunch of lawyers the way others have, doesn't mean he doesn't know what's happening. Maybe he should've done something.

But what?

What would have made a goddamn bit of difference in the course of things?

He tries to stand, pulls on the porch railing, it starts to give way. He sits again on the front stoop. He hears the cows in the barn, chewing, snorting. Swallows reel and turn, slicing the air with their wings. The sky turns blood-red, like the sun is dying, not setting.

NIGHT. A HOT WIND. THE HOUSE moves and sighs. A restless wind, a south wind that carries the smells of dust, overturned earth, diesel oil, rusting steel. A pair of great horned owls has settled in the forest. In the night there are calls back and forth. Roland, awake, hears the big house move and creak, sounds through the wall next to his bed like footsteps, doors opening, closing, but knows it's the house settling, adjusting to the wind.

JAMES TUTTLE FIRST KNEW HE WAS DEAD when, despite the battle raging around him, he was no longer afraid. Others, thin diaphanous shapes, rose and hovered above the tortured earth littered with bodies, lighted by the sulfurous red-yellow-orange flashes of explosions. Bombs fall, wounded men cry, but in his ears only a ringing silence. Then, a voice, Lieutenant Tompkins, killed weeks before in the first attack.

Go, he says.

But . . .

Go home while you can.

He stands outside the house, the windows are dark, only a weak yellow light in the kitchen window. He walks to the barn. It is too quiet. Where is the rest of the herd? It had taken so long, so many years, to return home. Had he been afraid to come back? Or had it been just the way things were after the war? After all that happened?

Everything is old, worn, the mower with its busted axle, the rusting plow, the barns crooked with dried, cracked siding.

He passes into the house. The dining table is set for dinner but the chairs are empty. Everything is coated with years and years of dust and silence. He drifts up the stairs. Stands at the door to his room. His models, the metal train, the wood haywagon, plow. All there, unchanged. Why does he have to see these things? He lies on the bed, his uniform crusted with dirt, a large red stain on the chest. In the ceiling, the familiar web of spidery cracks. Voices in the hall, whisper-quiet. He feels, then sees a shadow in the doorway, a long flowing nightgown white in the dark. He senses the presence of others, shadows, but can't face them, to know who they are.

ROLAND TOSSES AND TURNS in his bed, the damp sheets cling to his legs. He listens to the restless night. The dry leaves on the oak tree outside his window rustle and whisper. A branch breaks off the big maple, clatters on the metal roof of the barn. The cows snuffle and moan. The fox prowls the farmyard looking for eggs. Brown Dog whimpers in her sleep. In the forest a whip-poor-will calls. Whip-poor-will. Whip-poor-will.

August

*F*OREST FIRES BURN, UNCHECKED, in the north, and a pall of woodsmoke hangs over Wethersfield Village. Windows are closed despite the heat. Talk in the village is of the drought, the struggling crops. The river is low, sluggish, the color of lead. Foxes are seen walking near the village, their mouths open, panting. Crows feed on roadkill. Herman Bowker has been ill, but is better and the store has re-opened. Orange pickup trucks are seen heading back and forth, north and south on the Post Road.

~

*I*T HASN'T RAINED IN WEEKS. Day after day the sun pulses and throbs in the sky, seeming to get larger as the summer's hot, dry days pass. Fields are baked brown, grass crackles and crumbles into powder underfoot.

Sheriff Wiggins pulls in to the dooryard, kicking up a cloud of yellow dust, his car so dirty Roland can barely make out the big emblem on the side.

—Roland

—Sheriff.

Seems to Roland the sheriff has been stopping by a lot lately, like he thinks Roland is up to something.

—Your water holding out? Wells are drying up all over town. Taylor Brothers can't drill fast enough.

—Spring's still running clear and cold.

—I guess you're lucky. Town well's gone dry. They've drilled down four hundred feet and still nothing. You seen the river? Damn near gone. There's fires up north, burning the forest. Washington, Lamoile, Caledonia counties're half up in flames.

Roland doesn't feel lucky. His hay is stunted, his oats so dry they're turning to dust. It's so damn hot at night he can't sleep.

THAT EVENING HE SITS on the front porch. He remembers that porch when it was first built across the entire front of the house, the posts and beams and rails all trimmed with gingerbread and ornate corner braces, the lead paint fresh, so white it was almost blue. The machines are quiet.

He listens as the distant, daytime rattling of cicadas fades and the shimmering of crickets rises up around him.

They sat here, the family, of a summer's evening. His father smoking, drinking from a glistening brown bottle, resting from his day's labor, his mother knitting, his two sisters squabbling in the swing at the far end of the porch.

His father was so proud of that porch, built by the Thomas brothers. "Best damn carpenters in the valley," he would brag.

And his brothers, where were they?

Were they already gone?

No, he thinks, this is a memory when the family was still together. They were in the barn. He remembers the sound of them laughing, teasing, as they finished their chores.

Now, it is him, alone, weary from a hot day scything hay.

In the south great piles of cauliflower clouds reach up to the sky. They've been building up every afternoon for the last few days, threatening to storm, to bring thunder and lightning and rain and break the iron grip of the drought, but the air is so dry the clouds dissipate without producing a single drop. The smell of distant wood-smoke drifts down from the north, the sky is a strange flat white, the sun fuzzy, too yellow.

SUMMER, 1918 IT WAS, Marvin working and living in Claremont, Margaret married, living in St. Johnsbury. James, lost to the war, was a distant memory to Roland. Not seeing him, not knowing what happened made his death seem unreal. Sometimes it seemed to Roland that maybe James had never been real, had been only another Tuttle story.

Eliza worked in the house and kitchen with their mother. Roland and Daniel, who'd turned twenty-five, worked the fields, the barn. Roland had grown. He stood half-a-head taller than Daniel. This came as a surprise to him because he'd always looked up to Daniel. Daniel had a way with people, loved to talk, was a friend to all. Smart too, good with his hands. Roland wanted to be like Daniel. He would watch him, the easy way he talked, the way folks opened up to him.

He wanted to be like Daniel, but he wasn't. Daniel spoke a language that Roland couldn't.

They had worked together, him and Daniel, every day in the months since James left for the war, every day since that telegram came. They made a good team. One day, Roland would guide the sidehill plow, Daniel would follow behind planting seed. The next day they'd switch off and Roland would seed. Or, Daniel would drive the haywagon and Roland would fork the hay up, and the next day they'd trade places. They milked side by side, each on his own three-legged stool, Daniel talking a blue streak about the village, the other farms, the men he knew from playing town ball most evenings. He seemed to know everyone and loved to gossip. Roland would sit and listen without paying much attention, Daniel's voice blending with the rhythmic sound of milk splashing in the metal buckets.

It had been a good year for hay, enough rain, enough sun. They were loading the second cut, Roland driving the team, having a bit of a struggle getting the new horse, Sam, to work with Joe. Daniel walking behind.

They stopped for a break.

"Hey, Rollie," Daniel said. "How many horses we had since you was a kid?"

"I dunno," Roland said. "Four? Five?"

"Five," Daniel said. "And you named every one of 'em either Sam or Joe. Why is that? I mean there are plenty of other good names, you could've named this new one here Frank or Bill . . . or Albert for that matter."

Roland laughed, thinking about naming a horse after their father.

"Don't know . . . makes it easy to remember."

Daniel chuckled, slapped Roland on the shoulder.

"Brother, you are a character."

Roland liked being a brother. Liked it when Daniel called him brother. It was special being somebody's brother, but he didn't feel the same when he thought about his sisters. Maybe it was having a brother that he liked, a brother that you worked with every day. He felt a growing closeness, an ease that he'd never felt with anyone else. He didn't have to talk much. Daniel took care of that. Roland felt that Daniel knew what he was thinking without him having to get the words out.

BACK AT THE BARN, ROLAND unhitched the team, wiped the horses down, watered and fed them while Daniel hung up the harnesses, still going on about the names.

"What're you gonna do if we get a third horse so's we can give one of these two a rest once in a while? We going to have two Joes, two Sams? How's the horse supposed know who I'm talking to?"

"We can't afford three horses . . ."

"And besides, you know Sam here's a girl?"

Roland was trying to think of something to say when Daniel started coughing.

"Jesus, Rollie," he said. "I don't feel so good." He slumped onto the bench inside the barn.

Roland had noticed his brother dragging a bit, working slower than usual, but figured he was just having one of those days. It was cool in the shade of the barn, but sweat poured down Daniel's face.

"I'm sorry," Daniel said. "I got to go inside, get something to drink, take a rest."

"That's okay," Roland said. "I can finish up here."

Daniel didn't come down for supper and the three of them, Roland, Eliza, and Abitha, ate in silence listening to Daniel upstairs, coughing. Roland went up to Daniel's room. He lay on his back in bed under a pile of blankets, racked with chills.

"One minute I'm burning up, the next I'm shivering like the middle of winter." He started coughing, couldn't stop. Finally caught his breath. "Hand me my glove, will you?"

Roland took Daniel's ball glove from the dresser top, handed it to him. Daniel could catch, throw, and hit better than anyone. Everyone said he was the best third baseman in the whole county. Good enough to turn pro, some said, play with those college boys who came up in the summer. They played Town Ball, different rules than Knickerbocker rules like they used down in New York.

Roland only played the one time, would've said it was a silly waste of time if anyone asked, which no one did, but he liked to watch Daniel play, to see the way the men, even the older ones, looked up to him.

Made him, Roland, proud.

Daniel slipped it onto his right hand, pounded it with his left. Roland always forgot Daniel was a lefty.

"I'm supposed to play in Windsor this weekend," he said. "I got to get better."

He coughed, gurgled like he was being strangled.

The next day, Doc Ferguson came down from Windsor. "It's the Spanish Flu," he said. "It's all over town." He held his hands up. "There's not much I can do."

Eliza did her kitchen chores and tended Daniel, going up and down the stairs to make him drink his tea, take the aspirins Doc Ferguson had left. Roland did his best to keep up with the farm work. He would stop, look back at the house, certain he would see Daniel come down the front steps, ready to get to work.

Friday Daniel made it down the stairs for the first time, came into the kitchen carrying his ball glove. He looked terrible, his face pale, splotched with red. He walked crooked, like his side hurt.

"Come on, Rollie. Let's toss the ball around. I need to get ready for the big game."

Roland could throw a stone better than most, hit a squirrel right out of a tree, but he never did see the point of tossing a ball back and forth, and besides, looking at Daniel, he knew there was not a chance Daniel would be playing ball the next day.

Daniel made it to the front porch before he had to sit down. He slumped in their mother's rocker, then bent over and vomited. Nothing came up, but he dry-heaved over and over, bent double holding his stomach, moaning. Daniel was a stocky man, thick and strong, had always carried a little extra around his waist like his father, but Roland could feel his ribs through his shirt as he helped him back up the stairs, back to bed.

The fever hit him hard, and he lay in bed, delirious, raving about the big game and how it was his chance, there'd be scouts there from Burlington, and how he was going to be there, he was okay, he could do it, just needed to rest a bit more. Roland, though saddled by work, spent as much time as he could at Daniel's bedside.

"I'm fearful cold, Rollie." Daniel was shivering and shaking under his blankets.

How could he be cold? Roland thought. It's high August, blazing outside. Roland had watched his father die at the age of twelve, and in that moment he realized he was watching his brother die. Daniel lingered for two days and died late one night while the rest of the family was asleep. Roland couldn't understand it. Daniel was the strongest man he knew. How could he die like that?

The Spanish Influenza epidemic of 1918 reached its peak in late summer. It had started in the cities to the south, but had spread quickly north, coming up on the train with travelers and businessmen, jumping to the men who worked at the Windsor train station, spreading with the traveling pack-peddlers, the milk delivery wagons, spreading at church and in the local stores. Vermont was hit hard, more than forty thousand cases, almost two thousand dead. It was worse in the cities to the north—Montpelier, Burlington—but rural areas did not escape its ravages.

The farm made no allowance for grief: animals had to be fed, cows milked, garden tended. The morning after the hearse from Rupert's Funeral home in Windsor came and took Daniel away, Roland rose before dawn, hitched up the team and drove the haywagon to the upper field. The hay that he and Daniel had cut—was it only five days ago?—lay in rows. Tall, massive clouds piled up to the south. He heard a distant rumble of thunder. Roland threw himself at the work. He forked the hay up into the wagon, first the right row, then the left, moved the team a wagon's length, grabbed the pitchfork, forked the hay up into the wagon. Back and forth, move the wagon, lift up the hay, move the wagon, lift up the hay, doing the work of two men like one possessed, drenched in sweat, lost in the motion, the work, no time to think, to mourn, to feel.

"Roland Tuttle!" His mother stood at the edge of the field. "That's enough, now. You come on in, you hear?"

"I can't, Ma. I gotta get this done."

"It'll wait."

A clap of thunder, closer now.

"No! It won't. It's gonna' rain. I have to get this hay in. Daniel would've had it done by now."

"Come over here, son."

Roland walked over and stood at the fence.

He and his mother had barely spoken, both lost inside their misery, watching each other warily, afraid to see the slightest sign of a cough, a sniffle. They stood that way for a time, the fence in between. His mother looked hollow, like she wasn't all there. Roland was afraid to get close, afraid she would pull him to her, and something would break inside him, and the full force of what had happened to their family would hit him, and he wouldn't be able to bear it. He wouldn't.

"You can't do it all, Rollie. You're just a boy."

"I ain't."

"You done enough. Bring down what you got."

Roland was like a balloon that had lost its air once he stopped moving and the tiredness hit him all at once. He drove the wagon down, parked in the open bay of the barn, climbed down from the seat and stood there, too tired to move. He was all choked up, close to tears. He clenched the feelings tight inside him, locked them up, swore he'd never let them out.

"You go on in the house," his mother said. "I'll take care of the horses, do the milking. I'll write to Deputy Wiggins, tell him we need help getting the hay in. Eliza's got food going in the kitchen. You go in, get something to eat, you hear?"

Two days passed, no one came.

She wrote to Marvin in Claremont, Margaret up in St. Johnsbury. They didn't even come to the funeral. Too afraid to travel. They weren't the only ones. Folks all over the area stayed home. Deputy Sheriff Wiggins would stop down on the road, shout up to see if they were alright, but other than that, they were isolated, alone.

James gone, the telegram there on the mantel in a frame from the photographer's store, and now Daniel. His mother and Eliza worked the kitchen, churned butter like always. Stored it in the spring house until folks and things started moving again and they could sell it. Roland kept up with the farm work as best he could. He woke late one night, Daniel dead no more than five days, to coughing from Eliza's room. He tried not to hear, tried to deny what couldn't be denied.

In two days, she too was gone.

Sweet, kind Eliza, never said a bad word about anybody, never did no one wrong. It ain't right, Roland kept saying to himself, ain't right. Roland worked himself almost to exhaustion but still couldn't sleep. He lay awake at night, afraid to breathe, convinced the air of that house was poisoned and that he would be next.

August turned, weeks passed, the flu died out, the danger was past, and life on the farms and in the village returned to something like normal, but those weeks left their mark on Roland Tuttle. Work was what had saved him, what helped him to forget all that had happened, and Roland came to believe that if he worked hard enough, did each job through, did it right, that somehow, some way, everything else would take care of itself.

But a young man of eighteen can only do so much.

He finished milking one day late in the afternoon, and too tired to walk back to the house, lowered himself onto the half-log bench on the south side of the barn and sat there looking out across Mountain Road to the river valley beyond.

Abitha found him there when he hadn't come to the house for dinner.

"Are you alright?"

"Just tired, Ma."

She sat down next to him. Ran her hand over the rough surface of the bench.

"You remember when your father made this bench?" she said. "Split this log right in half. That log was stubborn, but not as stubborn as my Albert . . ."

She looked up to the sky.

"Took him two days. Waste of time, I thought then, but this bench is still here after all these years and we're sitting on it and I come out here sometimes, to sit, to remember. He was a good man, your father. I know you had your problems with him, but . . ."

Roland shifted on the bench. He was not used to his mother sitting so close, not used to her talking like this.

"They're gone, Ma." He tried to keep his voice under control, felt his throat close up. "Why?"

"Oh, Rollie. There's not always a why."

"What're we going to do? How can we get by?"

"You know I lost two babies before you were born?"

Roland knew, of course he did, but to hear his mother say those words so matter-of-fact? He'd only heard whispers. Some things in the Tuttle house weren't talked about.

"I was lost, then, didn't know if I could go on. Didn't know if I could get out of that chair."

Roland was afraid to move, to break the spell. It was if she was talking to herself as much as to him.

"Ida May, your gramma, came to me, and said something I've never forgotten. Said 'Child, I know you're hurting, but you got five children living downstairs that need you, a farm that needs your work. It's time to get up.' So, I did."

"But—"

"And then she said, 'You carry on, girl, that's what you do, because that's what the good Lord wants you to do.'"

"They're dead," Roland said. "We're the only ones left."

"That's right, son." She turned to look at him. "You and me, and that's why we're going to carry on. We've got each other and a farm that needs our work and animals that need our care. We have to be strong."

Roland saw the lower meadow, the hay tall and pale, saw the pond edged with cat-tails where once he swam with his brothers, heard a Redwing Blackbird sing, watched the silver-gray river flow. He sat hunched forward, his hands gripping his knees, like he was trying to prevent himself from coming apart, the way that log they sat on had split apart when his father drove the wedges deep into its heart.

"A farm ain't nothing but life and death"—Abitha put her hand on his—"flowing through and along and running from one into the other. You know it, Rollie, good as I."

He nodded.

"Why should we be any different?" she said.

THE DUST CLOUD IN THE SOUTH seems to grow and surge. Each day it is closer, advancing like a coming storm front. And the sound, the noise, the grumbling, growling, like some great beast ramping and rending the landscape, gets louder, closer. It is there, past the overgrown meadow with its wildflowers and clumps of Goldenrod and milkweed and Queen Ann's lace as tall as Roland himself, there just beyond the pine forest.

The heat sits on everything, the cows produce little milk, crops dry and wither and the sun beats down every day. Roland walks south through the overgrown meadow, sees the butterflies, more than ever before, gathering, getting ready to leave to wherever they go or maybe getting ready to die and the butterflies he'll see next summer will be all new ones, fresh-born.

A hot, dry wind blows up the valley.

He feels himself swept by an inner wind.

He returns to the farmyard and is standing where he always stands, next to the left-hand pillar of the front porch, as Marvin pulls into the dooryard, his red car coated with dust. Marvin gets out of the car, fanning himself with a folded newspaper, walks up to the porch, stands with one foot on the first step, his face beaded with sweat. He's stooped, has lost weight. Looks old. Roland waits for him to speak.

—How you doing, Rollie? he finally says.

Marvin never did call him Rollie. Why's he starting now?

Roland's too tired to talk. It's like the heat has cooked his brains. He can't think for the noise and the smell of diesel and the heat.

—Hot, Roland finally says.

—It is that. Marvin keeps fanning himself, as if moving the air around is going to help. So, what are you going to do? he says.

—'Bout what?

—You know good and well what. The house, everything.

A train whistle, long and low, echoes up from the valley.

—You hear that? Marvin says.

—'Course I do.

—There's folks coming up from New York, buying old things, furniture, antiques, going to all the towns. Why, Danielson can't get enough of the stuff for his store, says they're offering all kinds of money. What's in that house could make a big difference for us, Roland.

—Then what'm I going to do? Live next to an empty house?

Marvin keeps fanning himself, looks at Roland, shakes his head.

—You're going to have to move, Roland. You know that.

—Don't know nothing of the kind. That man, he said he'd see what he could do.

A machine starts up down on the Post Road. They have to shout to hear each other.

—You believe him, you're plumb simple-minded.

—It's simple-minded to trust someone?

—In this, yes it is.

Exhaust fumes drift across the yard.

—How can you stand it? Marvin says. Come on, I'll take you down to Bowker's, buy you a pop.

They drive down to the store in Marvin's red car. Park alongside the road. Roland watches Marvin step up onto the porch, holding on tight to the railing, moving like the steps are too high for him. Marvin was always a big, stocky man—not big like Otis Bowker there, hunched over in his rocking chair, same as always, wearing the same dirty overalls rolled up at the ankles, no shirt, feet spread wide—and it's like Marvin's shrunk, got skinny, got bent over.

—The brothers Tuttle, Otis says, as I live and breathe.

—Do you? Marvin says.

—What? Otis says.

—Live and breathe, Marvin says.

Otis looks left, then right.

—Last time I checked.

Roland waits on the porch while Marvin goes into the store, the screen door creaks then slams behind him. He comes back out with two bottles beaded with water from the cooler. Hands Roland a Coke.

—Always did prefer Moxie, Roland says to Marvin.

—Herman stopped carryin' it, Marvin says. I guess no one buys it anymore. It's all about Coca Cola now.

Roland takes a drink, the bubbles tickle his nose. He holds the bottle, wet and cold in his hand, takes a longer swallow.

—Not bad, he says.

Herman comes out through the screen door wearing his long white apron, leans on one of the posts holding up the porch, stares off into the distance.

—Closing up, Herman says to no one in particular.

—'Bout time, Otis says. This place ain't cleared a dime in years.

His big dome-shaped head, bald as bald can be, glistens with sweat. An orange pickup drives past, going south.

—Flatlanders, Otis says.

The store faces west, across the Post Road to where the sun hangs in the flat, dusty sky. Herman is wearing a white shirt, sleeves rolled up, dark stains under his arms. Roland steps into the store to get out of the sun, but it's no better inside. The air is hot, stuffy, closed-up. He looks around. The dark wood shelves are almost empty, the tin ceiling is corroded in places, the big cooler wheezes in the corner. He opens the lid. A few bottles drift in the ice-water.

Roland steps back out into the sun.

—Time to head back up, he says.

—Good to see you, Roland, Herman Bowker says. Sticks out his hand to shake. Roland looks at the hand like he doesn't remember what he's supposed to do, then takes it, gives it a quick pump.

—Things are changing around here, Otis Bowker says.

—Things're always changing, Roland says.

THAT EVENING, MARVIN GONE back to Claremont, Roland walks down Mountain Road, takes a left and walks north through the village, stops at the ballfield. A large black fuel tank sits where once he watched Daniel and the village men play ball, where Mackie Wilson had talked him into stepping onto the field of play. The grass of what was the infield is all blackened and dead from spilled fuel.

Ancient history. Different times.

The dank, sweet smell of oil hovers over the field.

He walks on to the First Congregational Church. It's a square block of a brick building with a tall white steeple. His mother went to that church almost every Sunday. She'd made him go when he was young, sat him down next to her, put her hand on his leg to stop him fidgeting. Roland hasn't been inside that church since her funeral.

A heavy damp hangs in the branches of the maples surrounding the graveyard. He comes to a low drystone wall where a rusted wrought iron gate stands open. Once inside the gate, Roland looks at the crypts of the town's four most prominent families: Bowker, Jarvis, Wilson, Garfield. Why folks want to be put to rest in a building, Roland can't understand, the ground seems more than good enough.

These mausoleums—marble buildings once white, now green and mold-stained, with shallow peaked roofs—lined up in a row, remind Roland of the trailer park and those other long white boxes, one after the other. Putting him there, seems to him, wouldn't be much different than putting him here.

Mist swirls among the markers, curls around a tall statue of the winged angel of death and drifts toward the back of the graveyard where the land slopes down toward the river, and settles around more modest graves. There's Tuttles here, a whole section of them going back as far as Lucius H. Tuttle.

Lucius's marker lies on its side in a tangle of weeds.

He comes to a newer gravestone, the area cleared of bracken and sticks. A small clutch of flowers rests against the headstone, dried almost to dust by the heat.

> *Abitha Dixon Tuttle*
> *Born 1868, Died 1938*

THE FUNERAL. MARVIN WAS there with Bridget and their two girls. Margaret and William with their kids, and Roland, alone, a single man with no family. Marvin, his face grim, his arm around Bridget's shoulder. Margaret crying softly, leaning against William.

They had gone back to Marvin's house in Claremont after the burial service. Margaret and Bridget had laid out food on the big table in the dining room, sandwiches, cold cuts of meat and cheese, deviled eggs and potato salad. The kids, teenagers mostly, descended on the food. Marvin did the drinks. There was a bucket of ice, bottles of whiskey, gin, beer. He put ice in a glass, poured a generous portion of whiskey—the ice clinked and crackled as the whiskey hit it—handed it to William Fairbanks. Poured one for himself.

"What'll you have?" Marvin said to Roland.

"Got any soda?" Roland said.

"Check with Bridget in the kitchen, she's got some for the kids."

Roland came back out of the kitchen holding a bottle of Coke, saw Marvin and William sitting in the corner, cradling their drinks, leaning in toward each other, talking quietly. Talking about him, Roland figured, deciding what Roland should do now that Abitha was gone.

In her will, she'd left the farm to Roland.

"What're you going to do?" Marvin had said as they walked away from the graveside.

"Keep farming," Roland said. "What else would I do?"

But, Roland thought, these two serious men, whiskey-drinking men, men with jobs, men who lived in the city, men who thought they knew what he should do better than he knew himself, would not let it rest.

There were chairs lined up on both sides of the room. Roland sat by himself, back against the wall. The cousins sat against the opposite wall, Megan and Molly Tuttle, in their teens, Margaret's William Jr. already in his twenties, a young man, and her girls, Joanne and Rebecca, already young women. Roland looked at them there, good-looking young folk they were, all lined up, and Roland felt an overwhelming sense of time moving on, of things changing, of new generations coming along. This gathering, these people were all that was left of the Tuttles. These folks—fine folks, Roland knew—were his family, but he felt himself somehow separate from them all. He knew there were no farmers in this new generation.

Margaret stood next to him, put her hand on his shoulder.

"How are you doing, Rollie?" she said.

Maybe it was her touch, or her soft voice, or the way she called him Rollie like she used to when he was little and she cared for him like she was his mother . . . maybe it was all of those things. Something broke inside him. He felt as if his chest would explode, and he had to clench himself tight to hold it in, and he thought of those times back on the farm when it was him and his mother and how, through all the tragedies, she never once had shown a moment of weakness, and he knew that he could not, now, let weakness take him.

MARGARET WANTED to bury their mother near St. Johnsbury, but Abitha, not days before she succumbed, had insisted she be taken home, put next to her husband, her children. And here they are: Daniel, Eliza, the two babies, Rachel and Marlene. And here he is, her husband.

> *Albert Robert Tuttle*
> *Born 1862, Died 1912*

Roland's not sure what his father would have thought about being buried in a churchyard.

Next, a small square of granite set in the ground.

> *James Dixon Tuttle*
> *Born 1892, Died 1918*

No one knows where James is. There's nothing here of him.

Roland comes to his grandfather's grave, the marker a slab of Vermont graystone, turned almost black, the edges splitting into thin layers of slate. He looks at the inscription, the carving rough and uneven from the ravages of time.

> *Roland Baker Tuttle*
> *Born 1841, Died 1900*

It's strange, standing here looking at a gravestone with his own name on it. Thinking back, there were times when having that name was a kind of burden, like he had to live up to it, be somebody that maybe he wasn't.

Remember man as you walk by
As you are now, so once was I
The rest of the inscription is covered by dark green moss, but
Roland doesn't need to scrape it away to know what it says.

As I am now, so you must be
Prepare for Death and follow me
Gramma Ida picked it out. She always was hard. Used to
drag young Roland down here, stand in front of the grave,
make him read it out loud.

Roland the Elder.

He has never been sure why his mother called him that.
Like he was some kind of king or something. Figures it
makes him Roland the Younger. Another thing he never
understood was why his parents had named him the way they
did, Roland Edmund Tuttle, names of folks who'd already
lived, who'd already died, why they couldn't have come up
with a new name, a name that would have been all his own.

IN THE VILLAGE SOME HOUSES are dark, but in others curtained
windows are lit by warm electric light. The night is heavy
and dense and strangely quiet. No peepers, no frogs, no dogs
barking. Nothing. It's a silence like the end of a sigh, like
the land's holding its breath. He walks slowly up the hill to
the farm. The stars are blurred by the humidity and a milky
half-moon is creeping out from behind the New Hampshire
hills, casting a strange half-shadow before him, like it wasn't
a whole man walking up that road.

ABITHA DIXON TUTTLE FIRST KNEW SHE WAS DEAD when the
state of her garden did not concern her. The weeds grow up
to her knees, but she knows the weeds don't matter anymore.

She goes into the kitchen and sees how dirty it is, but her stove is still there, and Ida May's rocking chair is still there, and the big metal sign with the bright yellow chick that Eliza loved so much is still there.

In the buttery, her churn sits neglected in the corner, but even that does not concern her.

She walks out into the meadow with its teeming life, its grasshoppers and wildflowers and butterflies. She loves it all so much.

The songbirds of spring are gone.

The butterflies gather around her.

—It's time to go, she says. Time to go.

She watches Roland go down the road, the dog following. Knows where he's going. It gladdens her to see that dog. To know that he is not alone.

He is there, in the graveyard; it is there, her grave; there, her name etched in stone. She kneels in front of the gravestones. They are all there, the ones of her family that she'd lost, lost to her no more. She will see them again, this she knows, just not yet. Not yet.

The mists of the graveyard pass through her and she drifts as the mists of the graveyard drift.

She sees him walking back up the hill. An old man, worn by life, yet, she knows, still strong. Her boy. Her Roland. She'd watched and seen how he'd worked, how he'd tried. No man could have done more, could have done better.

She feels his love—for her, yes—but more for everything, for this place, these hills, the river, the mountain, for the farm and all the animals that live there, that have ever lived there, and this love lifts her and carries her up the hill behind him, up the hill toward home.

The house stands empty, dark and silent, but for her it is filled with the light of lanterns and the voices of those that she has loved and loves still.

OUTSIDE, A BREEZE LIFTS the dry leaves of the maples. The night grows thicker, the stars misty, indistinct, then gone as clouds drift in from the west. Roland hears noises coming from the big house as he lies in bed, like footsteps on the wide-pine floorboards, like a chair scraping across the floor. He hears the big clock ticking in the living room, the old swing churn creaking in the pantry below him, water running in the kitchen sink. Voices in the parlor.

September

*T*HE HEAT WAVE CONTINUES. The days are dry and harsh, the sky a pale, dusty blue; nights are clear and still. Maple leaves, parched by the drought, turn brown and drift to the ground, crumble underfoot. Wild turkeys are seen in fields picking through the dry leavings. The blackberries have not ripened, and the bear is observed close to town eating garbage. Giant earth-movers are parked on the village ball field, waiting. The noise of the work is everywhere in the valley.

~

*R*OLAND STANDS AT THE EDGE of the overgrown south meadow with Mr. John Coburn, Right of Way Agent for southern Vermont. The man came by a couple of times during August, but each time Roland managed to avoid him. Didn't hide, just didn't get found.

Coburn comes off casual-like. He stands loose, relaxed, one hip out, slouching a little, like he's one of the boys. Something about the way he dresses doesn't sit right—khaki pants, pressed at one time but now deliberately rumpled, blue work shirt, light cotton jacket, leather work boots that don't look like they've seen a day's work. It's not that the clothes don't fit; there's something that makes Roland think these are not the clothes the man usually wears, not a costume exactly, but something he's put on for the rural folk, the farmers.

The man's been talking for a good fifteen minutes, explaining how things are, what's going on.

Roland looks south, past the meadow to where a great gash has been hacked out of the pine forest. It's a wide gap that wasn't there the day before. To the left of the opening there's the wall of pines, to the right, the pines, but straight ahead there's . . . well, there's nothing.

—The crew will be working this way in the next week or so, Coburn says.

He speaks in a flat, single-toned voice, like the words he's saying don't belong to him.

This overgrown meadow, so vibrant and teeming with life in spring, thick with fresh growth, redolent with the sounds and smells of critters mating and reproducing and growing, has been burned dry and wilted by the summer's unrelenting heat. The pond is little more than a puddle of green sludge surrounded by dried, cracked mud crusted with countless animal prints. Never in all the years Roland has lived on the farm has the pond dried up like this. Never.

Roland wonders what Mr. John Coburn sees.

The open gap in the pine forest? The tops of those yellow machines visible above the tall weeds and bushes of the meadow?

—Have you spoken with Sheriff Wiggins recently?

—Talk to him all the time.

—You have to look at the big picture. Do you have any idea how big this is? It's not about one small place, one little town, one farm. We're talking forty thousand miles, thousands of men, working all across the country.

Coburn stands looking south, then for the first time, turns and looks at Roland square.

—Sooner or later, you're going to have to face reality.

Reality? Roland has no idea what this man's reality is. What reality has he faced? Has he seen a farm crop fail, like Roland's father had, and wondered how he was going to feed his six children? Has he watched his own father die? His mother work herself to the bone?

Has he watched a cow give birth?

—Why, in Vermont alone we're spending more than two hundred million dollars. Coburn keeps talking. That's a lot of money, Mr. Tuttle.

Does his reality include butterflies and songbirds on a spring morning, fireflies in a summer meadow?

—Are you listening to me? An edge of exasperation, impatience creeps into Coburn's voice.

— I'm listening.

— Like I said, you're going to have to face reality. You have no choice.

—Man's always got a choice, Roland says.

A HOT, AIRLESS NIGHT. The upstairs stifling. Roland goes outside, stands in the middle of the dooryard. Fireflies flit about, sparks drifting in the dark. A dry wind with no promise of rain. Stripes of cloud cross the full moon. He stretches his arms out, reaches wide as if to hold all that is around him, hold it and keep it safe. He turns slowly, spinning, sees shadows—barn, coop, milk house—moving around him. The big house looms dark and mute, moonlight glinting off the leaded windows. Coyotes yammer somewhere in the distance. Dogs in the village answer. Distant thunder all around, flashes of heat lightning. The rumbling and flickering on the horizon like some distant war front.

SHERIFF HOMER WIGGINS pulls into the hard-packed dirt
of the dooryard, skids to a stop, steps out into a cloud of
dry dust. Walks up to the porch, stands there in his khaki
uniform for a minute looking at the old man sitting there
hunched over, knees apart, hands hanging limp like broken
birds between his legs, old dog, brown with gray around its
muzzle, lying next to him.
—Roland.
—Sheriff.
—Fifty years, we known each other, Roland. How many
times I got to ask you to call me Homer?
—Thought you was retiring, Roland says.
—End of the year, Wiggins says.
Wiggins looks around the yard, like he expects to see
something he's not seeing.
—You ready? he says.
—Gettin' there . . . Yep, getting there, Roland says.
—It's the twelfth, you know they're coming whether you're
ready or not.
—You think I don't know that?
—Pastor's got some boxes lying around at if you need 'em.
A long silence ensues. Roland sits, deep in thought, ponder-
ing, perhaps, what to put in those boxes: his mother's figurines
in the old hutch in the dining room, the little Christmas
scenes, the cute animals dressed in human clothes? Her
sewing kit? Notions? His father's beer glasses, pipe, smoking
things? The family photos, the picture of his brother in uniform? That telegram? His own wooden toys from boyhood?
There wasn't that much—not much at all for five generations
of Tuttles. Not much at all. He thinks of his tools in the barn,
harnesses, rakes, hoes, the plow.

How do you fit those things in boxes?

—So he told me last week, Roland says.

Brown Dog comes down off the porch and ambles over to Wiggins. Gives his crotch a good sniff, then sits down and puts her head against the sheriff's knee, looks up at him. Wiggins reaches down, scratches the dog's ear.

—Least this one likes me, Wiggins says.

—I see them, you know, Roland says.

—What?

—The Tuttles came before. Gramma Ida said I would . . . when I was ready . . . and now I see them.

Wiggins stands there, doesn't know what to say. His uniform hangs loose, doesn't fit him right, and Roland wonders if he's been sick, but then he thinks that maybe the uniform doesn't fit because the job doesn't fit anymore.

—These boxes. They dry? Roland says. Not damp or moldy or anything?

—No, they're good.

—Well, bring 'em on up. If I'm not here, put them in the kitchen.

—Not here? Where you gonna be?

—I don't know . . . taking a walk maybe.

Sheriff Homer T. Wiggins looks puzzled, as if the idea of Roland Tuttle taking a walk is the about craziest thing he's ever heard.

But walk he does, all the way to Crystal Falls. It has been many years since he's hiked up that trail, and he feels as if the mountain has become steeper, gravity grown stronger. His knees ache, there's a sharp pain in his right hip, but he has to see it again, one last time.

He sits on the lip of the cliff dangling his legs over the edge as he'd done when he searched for those three young braves turned to stone, as he did that day when he'd run up here to hide from the awful fact of his father's death. He'd sat here, then—the bare November canopy of the forest rolling down away from him—until past dark, until he heard the voices coming up the trail calling to him, calling his name, calling him back.

He returned to that place many times as a boy and as a young man, to stand on the edge of that shale rock table, and look out over the valley and wonder if the Abenaki tribe that he'd learned about in school had used this place as a lookout. From here they could see the advance of the settlers, their fires as they burned slash, their cleared fields. Yes, they could see them coming, but what could they do?

Morning fog fills the river valley, pools against the low hills of New Hampshire, but is starting to dissipate, rising, following the folds in the land, thin tendrils of vapor drifting up the hillsides and disappearing. Roland looks for the buildings of the village, but can't see them through the trees. Looks across the river to the east where the tip of the bell tower on St. Mary's Cathedral in Claremont is visible above the low hills.

Wonders for a moment what Marvin is doing.

Further south down the valley he can see the work, the wide swath of devastation cut through the forest north of Putney, the pale brown stripe dug right through the middle of Wilkerson's fields—pointing straight at him.

He sits. The sun crosses from east to west, and the day turns, and the light angles in through the trees, and the stream flows beside him, and the water drops over the shale edge toward the shadows below, feathering out in the slight breeze that comes up from the valley like cornsilk tossed into the air.

He feels the warmth of the sun on his face and the cool stone beneath his legs.

At moments like this a feeling that there is something important out of reach comes over him. He has never been a religious man, but this feeling that comes to him when he looks up into the endless blue sky and the sun paints the world with this golden light . . . well, maybe that was how the people in the church where his mother took him Sundays so long ago felt when they looked up at the simple wooden cross on the wall and thought of their God.

Maybe it's the sky that stretches out before him, maybe it's being in a place not hemmed in by farm buildings, tasks, chores. Here, he can see to a distance. Here, he can see things more clearly. Here, he can see the history of things. Here, he can see how things change, how time moves along, and how he is only one little part of it all.

For an instant the sun, before disappearing behind the rim of the mountain, catches the falling water and it glows like molten fire. He feels himself lifted up—up in that moment of light, up as the water falls to the shadows below.

THE FARM IS IN SHADE, the evening damp setting in, fog creeping up from the river. He is tired, his legs quiver as he steps up onto the porch to find Brown Dog waiting for him.

—Where were you, old girl?

Brown Dog had always come on his hikes as a boy...but, no, of course, that was a different dog. This dog is old, her muzzle flecked with gray, too old for mountain hikes. She looks up with big brown eyes. Sometimes, to Roland, all the

dogs he's had since he was a boy—the strays, the pups, the
Sams—all blend into one, and it's like he's had this one dog
as a companion his entire life, this one dog that has seen
everything, that knows everything, and who could, if only
able to talk, help him understand it all.

—I know, Roland says. He reaches down and scratches
behind the dog's ears. Hikin' all that way. Damn fool waste
of energy.

He used to run up and down that mountain when he was
a boy; now, as he lowers himself down onto his chair, he is
plumb tired out, but there's things to do. He can hear the
cows snuffling and pushing at the pasture gate waiting to be
let into the barn, waiting to be fed and milked. The fire in
the cookstove is out, the wood box is empty.

He unfolds himself from the chair and walks stiffly down
off the porch and across the packed dirt of his dooryard
toward the barn, the dog at his heels.

THE COWS MILKED AND FED, he sits on the edge of the front
porch, feet on the steps, Brown Dog next to him. Evening
mists drift above the fields. The barn is a dark wall. The last
of summer's fireflies spark here and there. Crickets call back
and forth.

—Don't think I can ever leave this place, he says to the dog.

A weight settles on his shoulders, presses in on his chest.
It is hard to breathe. His heart like a stone.

—Nope, don't think I can.

The dusk comes on. He can see the dark shapes of the
machines parked on the edge of the lower meadow.

Then, it comes to him that it's not him leaving, it's this
place—the farm, the hills, the meadows—that's leaving him.

How can a place leave?

Makes no sense.

It's not like the barn can sprout legs and walk off. Maybe the buildings will vanish and the cows will meander up to the upper meadow and keep on going? It's all leaving and going away forever, and there's nothing he can do about it, and with that realization he feels as if that heavy weight has been lifted from his shoulders.

But, he thinks, if all this is gonna be gone, wiped out, then by God it's gonna be so folks remember, so people will say the Tuttles was here, and when the Tuttles was gone, they were gone with a bang.

BOXES ARE PILED IN THE MIDDLE of the kitchen, some of them plain brown, some bright and colorful with names that mean nothing to Roland. He stands there like a man lost, thinks about supper, but realizes he isn't hungry.

He looks toward the big house, then back at the empty boxes. He goes to the door, turns the handle, pushes.

It doesn't move.

He steps back, looks at the almost-bare panels of dark wood, the cross in the center. Tries again, leans his shoulder into it, and with a grating complaint, the door opens to the big house for the first time in twenty-five years. The door's groans are muffled by the thick layer of dust that covers everything. Roland brushes spider webs from his face, is hit by the pungent, bitter smell of rot and mouse shit and decay. A few flakes of blue paint from the door cling to his clothes.

He goes back and forth to the kitchen carrying the boxes, piles them in the middle of the dining room. Clouds of dust rise up each time he adds one to the pile. He places a kerosene lantern on the table.

Motes, like sparks, dance in the lantern's yellow light.

It's all there, where it was when his mother went north to Margaret's, never to return: place settings on the table, dishes in the sideboard, photos on the mantel, his mother's porcelain figures, all draped in webs filled with clumps of dirt and dead insects and dust. He hears scuffling in the dark corners as mice retreat. Everything is so coated in dust, obscured in webs, that he, himself, feels coated, weighted down by this dust of ages. He rubs his eyes as if he can't be seeing right.

On a shelf held up with curvy braces, he sees his mother's books, counts them. Seven. So faded he can barely see the titles. He takes one down, the cloth cover must've been red at one time. He pries it open with his thumbs. The book resists, like it's all glued together, as if there's something inside doesn't want to come out, then cracks open. The binding protests, dust swirls, and a musty smell of sadness and neglect rises up into the air. He sees where she wrote her name and a date on the inside of the cover:

Abitha Dixon, 1890.

He tries to see his mother as a young girl, but the last months of her time at the farm before the hospital are all he can see, her, hobbled and stiff, trying to do her chores, to run the house like she always had, to cook, to clean, to garden . . . but lost somehow, lost inside her own mind.

He replaces the book, takes another, can make out the title. *Wildflowers of New England.* Holding the book, touching the cover where his mother would have held it, he feels her close, but at the same time wonders if he ever really knew her.

He stops before the carved oaken mantel above the fireplace in the living room. Here are family photos. He lifts one, holding it carefully by the frame, wipes the dust off with his sleeve to reveal an ancient, faded sepia of Roland and Ida May Tuttle in their finest: his grandfather in a thick tweed coat and dark tie, grandmother in a print dress and black knit shawl, wearing a small cloche hat, squinting through small, round eyeglasses.

He looks back at the boxes he has piled in the dining room, then returns the photo to the mantel. He takes down and cleans the others, each in its turn: his mother and father on their wedding day, his mother tall, young, beautiful, his father proud but uncomfortable in his wedding suit; his brother James in his uniform, taken in Windsor the day he boarded the train to New York; a family portrait from a Fourth of July celebration in the village, all nine of them, together. He holds longest a photo of himself taken before his first day of school. He stands barefoot, his hand-me-down clothes too big, head down, shy, unwilling to look at the camera.

Here is that telegram—his mother had it framed—all yellowed and faded and next to it the little circular piece of aluminum with James's name engraved on it that had arrived at the house a couple of months after the telegram. That's all you get, a little bit of metal and a fading piece of paper.

Roland returns the framed telegram to the mantelpiece then turns and looks back across the living room, through the double French doors into the dining room, down the long dining table to the door that leads into the kitchen, through the kitchen all the way to the door to the woodshed. It's like he's looking through the wrong end of a telescope, back through time, back past his time alone on the farm, back past when the family was all together, back past his mother first coming to live here, back past his father being born in this house, back past it all to that one-room cabin that his great-great-grandparents built so long ago.

The big grandfather clock stands in the corner, its hands stopped a bit shy of twelve noon.

Or was it twelve midnight?

Roland climbs the stairs to the second floor. The treads groan at each step, the sound muffled, distant. He stops, looks back as if he is being followed. Remembers how his brothers used to chase him up those stairs.

At each bedroom in turn, he stands at the open door, looking in. Here is his boyhood room, the pictures he'd cut from magazines and pinned to the walls, faded, hanging loose, tattered. His older brothers' rooms. James's models on a shelf —train, haywagon—shrouded in clinging white cobwebs. Daniel's baseball mitt on his dresser. It pains Roland to see that glove yellow with mold. Daniel loved that glove. When he slipped it onto his hand, it became part of him. Roland can see him, lying there those last days, too weak to pound it with his fist. Next to the glove, Daniel's ball. Roland picks it up. It's gone soft and almost crumbles in his hand.

His mother's room. He looks in the closet. Her clothes, faded and yellowed, hang as she left them. He walks into the room Margaret and Eliza shared; there's nothing of Margaret here, she took her things north. A white nightgown hangs from a hook on the wall.

He stands longest in the doorway to a small room in the back of the house.

The birthing room, the dying room.

Ida May died in this room as did her husband Roland before her. Babies were born in this room and died without ever leaving this room. A single bed is set against the wall under the small window. His father, Albert, died in that bed. There is something of him there, a shape.

Roland sees thin wavery forms from the corner of his eyes, like the swirls of mist that drift across the meadow in early morning. He turns to look, they're gone, then turns away and they're back.

On the landing halfway down the stairs is a big oval mirror with an elaborate golden frame, now pitted and tarnished, a gift from his grandfather to his grandmother on their wedding anniversary. The surface of the mirror is thick with opaque dust. Roland takes his sleeve and clears a place in the middle. Looks at himself. Sees an old man staring back at him, beard halfway down his chest, hair thin, sticking up in places. Chalky pale-blue eyes, wide, with a startled look to them. Sees someone standing behind him. Turns. Nobody.

Back in the dining room, he looks at the boxes like he can't understand what they're doing there, how they got there all piled up like that, though he, himself, put them there.

These things don't mean much to him. This house always had been too damn big. It was not for this house that he kept working, it was for what was outside: the fields rolling up toward the mountain, the rock walls, the sugarbush, the woodlot. It was for the way hedgerows, filled with birds and all kinds of living creatures, grew up wild along the stone walls, and the way the lower field blossomed in summer with ragweed and Queen Ann's Lace and all those wildflowers—red, white, purple—that his mother named for him that day, and the butterflies she loved, bright flits of color. And for the cows, with their big trusting eyes, and the bear that he sees on the edge of his fields in the fall.

And the mountain. I could have lived up there, he thinks, built a shack, scavenged . . . but no, he realizes, the farm is where he was meant to be. He can't trace all the events, big and small—deaths, frosts, war, disease, drought, floods— that took his hand and led him to this point. He can't put it together, lay them out in order, grasp how one had led to another. No, he can't make sense of it all, but thinks that by being here, in this room, in this house, at this time, on this farm, that, in its own way, it all makes sense.

But then he thinks, as he looks at the un-lived-in rooms, the abandoned possessions, perhaps the exact opposite is true. He became a farmer and stayed a farmer all these years, not because he had planned to be a farmer, but because he had never planned to be anything else.

Then again, he thinks, he is here, at this moment, because he was meant to be, because he is the one who can do what has to be done.

ROLAND GOES OUTSIDE, stands in the middle of the dooryard. Stars, more stars than he's seen all summer, move close. He walks to the barn, stands at the open door to the haymow, listens to the cows breathing and snuffling in the dark. He herds them out into the feedlot. He closes the door so they can't go back inside.

He ducks under the feedlot fence, stands among the cows, feels them press in against him, breathes in their grassy, milky smell, their breathy warmth. He feels himself one of

them, these calm, accepting, gentle creatures that he has
spent his life among.

They grumble at having been disturbed, settle.

—Don't you worry, he says, but then, when has he ever
known a cow to worry about anything?

He leaves the pasture gate open.

He walks out to the road, looks back at the farm, small
and insignificant against the bulk of the mountain. The big
house is dark, but the kitchen windows glow with the light
from a single kerosene lantern. Crickets shrill in the fields.
Coyotes chatter in the distance. Dogs bark in the village.
The meadow is dark. Fog drifts up from the river valley,
shimmering with the lights of the village.

BACK IN THE HOUSE, ROLAND looks down. Brown Dog is
there, sitting on her haunches, looking up at him.

God, those big goofy eyes.

—What're you doing here? You got to git.

He leads the dog back through the dining room to the
kitchen and out onto the front porch.

—Go on, git!

But he's not halfway across the kitchen before Brown Dog
has pushed open the front door and is there, looking at him.

—You got to stay outside, you hear? Got no business being
in here with what I aim to do.

The look on the dog's face like to break his heart.

—Don't you worry, your old friend the sheriff'll take care
of you.

He puts Brown Dog back outside. Roland never did figure
how that dog learned to open the door. Too smart for her

own good. He takes a hammer, nails the door shut. Goes to the front door of the main house, does the same.

He walks to the kitchen, goes into the pantry, brings out the can of kerosene, returns to the dining room. Pours it over the pile of cardboard.

Vapors fill the room.

He coughs. His eyes water. He realizes he's known for a long time—since he first heard about the road, saw the devastation coming up the valley toward him, heard the cold words of the men who came to measure his place, mark it out for ruin—that this was what he was going to do, but didn't know that he knew.

He goes back into the kitchen, picks up the burning lantern from the table. Shadows gather in the dark corners of the room, move with the flickering light of the kerosene lantern, follow him toward the dining room. He feels them here, all of them. Would they approve of what he is to do? Maybe not, but surely they would understand, surely that.

The house shudders, sighs as Roland Tuttle closes the kitchen door behind him.

$\mathcal{T}$HE FIRST SIREN SOUNDS AT 1:23 AM, September 13, 1964. It is the Wethersfield Volunteer Fire Station, a small, one engine garage on the north side of the village. The blower itself is old, a little rusted. It warbles weakly in the night, calling to the men of the village, echoes off Miller's crag on Mount Ascutney and is answered by the whoop of the Windsor Fire Station, then the long, powerful moan of the Claremont Fire Department across the river in New Hampshire.

By the time the first truck arrives at the Tuttle farm on Mountain Road it is too late. The house is consumed by fire. The flames reach into the autumn sky sending a column of sparks up toward the stars themselves, flames so hot they melt the bubble light on the top of Engine Number 7 out of Claremont.

Homer T. Wiggins, Windsor County Sheriff—soon to be retired—arrives, stands back, the heat from the fire, even at this distance, almost too much to bear. He watches the great spiraling tower of flame dance and twist. The fire has a noise to it, a moaning, screaming rush of air as if the house itself is crying out.

Sparks jump the farmyard and soon the barn is in flames.

Columns of water arc from the pumper engines, rolling clouds of steam swirl around the firemen in their helmets and high boots and heavy jackets, and billow up into the blackness. The sound of cracking and hissing is everywhere, punctuated by crashes as the house collapses. Wiggins stands, a silent witness, as the rambling structure—the ornate Gothic main house with its gingerbread trim, the colonial ell, the attached shed—is reduced to a smoldering hump of black debris. A few charred timbers stand, lonely sentinels.

The smell of damp coals and smoldering wood and burned things fills the air.

Windsor Chief Fire Marshall, Bill Smith, walks up to the sheriff.

"Well?" Wiggins says.

"Too hot, no way to get in there. We'll have to wait until morning."

As all but a skeleton crew pack up and head for home, Sheriff Wiggins stays and watches smoke and steam rise up from the smoldering wreck. There is a crash as a massive oak corner post falls, sending an eruption of sparks up toward the heavens. His eyes water, maybe from the smoke, and the stars swim about in the black dome of the sky.

"Goddamn," is all he can say. "Goddamn."

He spends the night in his cruiser. He watches the first hint of morning fringe the eastern sky. A hot, listless morning. He walks up to the smoldering remains of the house and stands there slowly shaking his head.

How has it come to this?

He feels old, tired.

The branches of the big maple that grows close to the front of the house are blackened and singed. Steam rises from glowing embers. Firemen have been there all night, spraying what remained of the house and the barn and the sheds with water. They lean, exhausted, against the last firetruck on the scene, holding cups of coffee.

Eddie Wilson, his volunteer fireman's pants folded down, suspenders hanging loose, hands Wiggins a styrofoam cup of coffee. Roland's old brown dog appears from nowhere, tail wagging, nudges in between the two men, whimpers, looks up. There's a knowing in the dog's big eyes that hits Wiggins hard.

"Think your kids might like to take care of Brown Dog?"

"I reckon they'd like that," Eddie says. "They'd like that just fine." He reaches down, gently strokes the dog's shaggy head. "What do you think, girl?"

Wiggins is still there when the state fire inspector, Mr. Alistair Cookson, arrives from Montpelier. There is almost nothing left of the house. The wreckage has cooled. Men, black like shadows, sift through mounds of ash. Wiggins watches. He hasn't eaten, feels weak, light-headed. Too old to be standing here seeing this. Too old to be knowing what they will find.

Cookson comes up to him.

"Well?" Wiggins says.

"The whole thing has collapsed on itself," Cookson says. "The fire was set in the dining room. Looks like he was in a bed upstairs, in the back."

Sheriff Homer T. Wiggins turns away, walks to his car. He sees the big yellow machines lined up, ready to go to work, the wide swath of dirt and stones and mud that has been carved through the farm fields.

A diesel engine rumbles to life.